THE JEWEL OF AN EARL'S HEIR

LINDA RAE SANDE

Twisted Teacup
PUBLISHING

ALSO BY LINDA RAE SANDE

The Daughters of the Aristocracy

The Kiss of a Viscount

The Grace of a Duke

The Seduction of an Earl

The Sons of the Aristocracy

Tuesday Nights

The Widowed Countess

My Fair Groom

The Sisters of the Aristocracy

The Story of a Baron

The Passion of a Marquess

The Desire of a Lady

The Brothers of the Aristocracy

The Love of a Rake

The Caress of a Commander

The Epiphany of an Explorer

The Widows of the Aristocracy

The Gossip of an Earl

The Enigma of a Widow

The Secrets of a Viscount

The Widowers of the Aristocracy

The Dream of a Duchess

The Vision of a Viscountess

The Conundrum of a Clerk

The Charity of a Viscount

The Cousins of the Aristocracy

The Promise of a Gentleman

The Pride of a Gentleman

The Holidays of the Aristocracy

The Christmas of a Countess

The Knot of a Knight

The Heirs of the Aristocracy

The Angel of an Astronomer

The Puzzle of a Bastard

The Choice of a Cavalier

The Bargain of a Baroness

The Jewel of an Earl's Heir

The Vixen of a Viscount

Beyond the Aristocracy

The Pleasure of a Pirate

The Making of a Mistress

Stella of Akrotiri

Origins

Deminon

Diana

PROLOGUE

March 27, 1839, Rosemount House dining room, Mayfair

For a reason she knew quite well, dinner was dragging on entirely too long. Deciding it was time for the dessert course, Estelle Jones Tennison, Countess of Everly and known to her friends as Stella, waved at the footman who stood ready at the end of the dining room. He disappeared through a panel in the wall, and she turned her attention back to the conversation that had her son and daughter at odds over something their father had been discussing.

Probably something to do with plants or trees. Something about changing colors being a sign of something important.

Although she was usually interested enough to follow whatever they talked about over the formal meal, Stella found she was distracted this evening.

The encounter with Lord Framingham earlier that afternoon had been so unexpected, so unnerving, she had replayed it in her mind's eye at least a dozen times in an effort to determine if it had really happened or if she had merely imagined it.

Wincing at the thought that she could have conjured such a despicable situation, Stella decided that, yes, *it* had happened.

Lord Framingham had propositioned her at the counter in Floris.

Until that day, the perfumery shop had been her favorite store in Jermyn Street. She and her best friend, Nike Bradley, would marvel over the latest in hair brushes and combs, toothbrushes and shaving tools, and of course, perfumes and colognes. Now it would be forever tainted with the reminder of what the marquess had said to her as his bushy brows waggled and his pudgy ringed finger traced the outline of her jaw.

"I would very much like to tup you over the edge of my library table," he had whispered as his eyes gleamed with delight. "Is there a chance you have finished your last *affaire* and might be amenable to a new one?"

Shocked, not only by what he wished to do to her—and where—Stella wondered how he had the impression she'd ever had an *affaire*. She'd only ever been with her husband, Harold. For over twenty-two years, she had only ever shared a bed with him.

When she recovered somewhat from the scandalous query, Stella shook her head and said, "You must have me confused with a different countess, my lord. I've never engaged in an *affaire* in my entire life."

The marquess furrowed the brows that had been dancing only a moment ago, his expression sobering. "Well, then allow me to be your first," he said, as if he were offering her the world.

Given his girth and the odor that permeated the air around them—definitely not a scent Floris had created in the back room—his world was not one she wanted.

Stella had angled her head to one side and adopted the

most apologetic voice she could manage. "Although I appreciate the offer, my lord, I am afraid I must decline. Everly would be *terribly* jealous should he discover what we'd done, and although he's a horrible shot, he's an excellent swordsman." She leaned in closer, attempting to hold her breath lest the man's body odor cause her to faint, and added, "I should hate for you to lose a particularly... proud part." Her glance down confirmed that beneath his portly middle, his pantaloons were tented where only moments ago they displayed a more rounded silhouette.

Her comment must have hit the mark, for Lord Framingham hissed and immediately moved away. "I trust you'll keep our little tête-à-tête between us?"

Stella exhaled softly. "Of course, my lord. Good day." She dipped a curtsy and took her leave of the shop. Her lady's maid had been forced to practically run after her as she made her way to the Everly town coach.

Stella felt terrible when she had to send Thompson back into the shop to finish ordering her favorite perfume.

If only Nike had been able to join her on this day, she was sure Framingham would have kept his distance. But one of Nike's children had come down with a cold, and she had insisted on remaining home with him. "Despite having a nursemaid, you did the same," Nike reminded her when Stella practically begged her to come along for her weekly foray in Jermyn Street.

Stella had to agree. Had her two children still been the age of Nike's youngest, she would have remained at home as well.

But they were grown now. Old enough to be out on their own. At least Alexander was. At one-and-twenty, he might have looked like a Greek god, but he didn't allow his handsome features and otherwise charmed life to get in the way of his avocation—metallurgy. He was determined to create beautiful things with gold and silver. His choice of colors with respect to gemstones wasn't always pleasing, but his craftsmanship was exquisite.

Helen, about eighteen and anxious for her come-out, was learning everything her father deigned to teach her with respect to botany. Stella wasn't sure if she did so just to earn her father's approval or if she was truly interested in the natural sciences. Either way, if Helen didn't end up married to an aristocrat after her come-out this year, she would probably agree to a marriage with a member of the Royal Society. She had been introduced to nearly every member in the course of her eighteen years.

As for Stella's husband, the few minutes alone in the coach had her reviewing her entire married life in her mind's eye.

Harold Tennison, Earl of Everly, hadn't been particularly amorous after their first few years together. They had since settled into a comfortable routine in Rosemount House in Park Lane—perhaps too comfortable. Harold joined her in her bedchamber most Saturday nights. They spoke of mundane topics for a few moments, and then they made love.

Their sessions were by no means earth-shattering. The bed shook, of course, the headboard sometimes thumping against the wall. Barely mussed, the bed linens were easily put to rights. Harold would thank her profusely for the tumble, sleep for a few minutes, kiss her on the cheek, and then remove himself to his own bedchamber by way of the connecting dressing room.

Given their routine, Stella couldn't exactly claim they were having an *affaire*. But for Lord Framingham to infer that *she* was having an *affaire*... that meant someone's tongue was wagging, either in a Mayfair parlor or in a men's club.

Or perhaps Framingham was merely testing her?

The thought was a relief, but at the very same time it

angered her. How *dare* the marquess infer she was ripe for the plucking? Or poking? Or tupping?

Perhaps her ire had her heated enough, for a waft of her perfume drifted in front of her nose.

The same perfume she had used since she had married Harold.

As the footman set her dessert plate in front of her, she vowed she would have the perfumer create something new for her. Something more sophisticated. Something a bit less floral. More spicy.

Something to wake up her husband.

The thought had her lifting her gaze to discover he was looking at her.

"This dessert is delicious," he announced, as if he hadn't been eating the same dessert every Wednesday night for the past twenty years.

Alex and Helen chimed in with their positive reviews as Stella held her husband's gaze. Rather than say anything in response, she merely arched a brow.

Harold blinked.

When he didn't look away, she slipped her tongue over the lower edge of her lip.

He blinked again.

Not exactly a seductress, Stella angled her head to one side and drew a finger along the edge of her low neckline.

Harold swallowed. "Are you... are you flirting with me?" he asked, his voice a half-octave higher than usual.

Stella blinked as she exhaled. Loudly. "Yes, as a matter of fact," she replied, sounding ever so disappointed.

"Mother!" Helen scolded from her right, her look of shock appropriate for one her age.

"Good for you, Mother," Alex said from her left, his grin magnifying his handsome features.

Stella decided he was now her favorite.

Aiming a lopsided grin in her direction, her husband seemed to grow three inches taller in his chair. Perhaps he was growing in another area as well, for he turned his attention to the footman and said, "I will forgo port on this night."

Stella turned her gaze onto Helen and said, "I'm going to forgo tea this evening. But do stay at the table and have some port with your brother. Continue your conversation on photo sin the sis—"

"Photosynthesis, Mother," Alexander interrupted.

"Whilst I engage your father in a completely different science."

Harold leaned toward his son and murmured, "She's referring to magnetism."

Alexander rolled his eyes. "I rather doubt that's what *she's* thinking, Father."

Helen's eyes widened as she watched first her mother and then her father rise from their chairs and depart from the dining room.

When she and her brother were alone, Helen watched with glee as the footman set a glass of port in front of her and then did the same with Alex. "They're going to make love, aren't they?" she asked in a hoarse whisper.

His attention on the bite of dessert on his fork, Alexander said, "If they remember how."

The comment left Helen with her brows furrowed. She drank the port in one swallow.

CHAPTER 1
A FENCE IS FOILED

he following day, Ewen & Ewen in Ludgate Hill

Margaret Ewen pinched an emerald between her left thumb and forefinger and held it up to the light from a nearby window. She sucked in a breath.

About to recite its qualities, she couldn't when her caller said, "It's perfect, isn't it?"

Dropping the gemstone onto the black velvet that covered the middle of her messy desk, Margaret lifted her gaze to regard her visitor with suspicion. "In a manner of speaking, yes," she admitted. "From where did you get it, Mister...?"

"Smith-Jones," the short man replied as he gave a bow. "Lately of Manchester, but now of London." His attention darted to the news sheet that lay atop several others on her desk. "Follow the gossip, do ya?" he asked as he pointed to the latest issue of *The Tattler*.

"Only for the advertisements," Margaret murmured, as she placed the stone beneath a loupe. She struggled to withhold a sound of appreciation, for it was apparent the emerald was perfect. There were no occlusions, and the gem cutter had done an exceptional job on the facets.

Had she done business with the odd little man who stood before her at some point in the past, Margaret wouldn't have been so suspicious. But she had never seen him before. Anyone bringing her a gemstone for valuation—and only one —meant he could be a thief looking to sell a recent illegally acquired piece from a jewelry heist, or he could merely be a down-on-his-luck aristocrat in need of funds for his next visit to a gaming hell.

Sellers of single gems were rarely legitimate sellers.

As if he sensed her hesitancy, he cleared his throat. "It fell out of this," the man said as he held out a gold band.

Margaret furrowed a brow as she reached for the ornate ring, keeping her withered left arm close to her body as she did so in an effort to hide it. "Rather fortunate the stone was not lost," she commented as she examined the gold filigree around the setting. She thought she recognized the familiar design as one done by a jeweler at Rundell and Bridge, but it could have been the creation of any jeweler in London.

"My mother was wearing it in the coach when we were on our way back here to London," Mr. Smith-Jones explained. "Her sister recently died, so she's seeing to closing her house. Paying her creditors and all."

"Do you wish for it to be reset?" Margaret asked. "One of the prongs appears to be bent quite badly. My father can do the repair, though. It will only take a day or two at most."

Mr. Smith-Jones lowered his head. "My aunt's estate is in need of funds, miss. Is there a chance you would buy the stone and the gold? For a fair price, of course?"

Usually able to discern when someone was lying, Margaret found she couldn't determine if Mr. Smith-Jones was attempting to pull the wool over her eyes or if he was really what he claimed. Although she had reviewed the list of items that had been reported stolen—a list provided by a Bow Street Runner who specialized in solving jewelry thefts—Margaret couldn't remember a mention of an emerald ring.

Before she could give Mr. Smith-Jones an answer, her father appeared in the doorway.

"Ah, Mr. Bridge," she said quickly, a code name she used to let her father know she was suspicious of a gem seller. "Mr. Smith-Jones is wondering if we might buy this perfect emerald and the gold ring it used to decorate," she said as she held up the ring.

Tall and lean, his physique kept trim from fencing, Adam Ewen regarded Mr. Smith-Jones with an assessing glance before he turned his attention to the gold ring his daughter held out to him. He took it and gave it a passing glance. "Looks like John's work," he murmured, confirming Margaret's assessment. "What ever did you use to bend the prong so badly?"

Mr. Smith-Jones gave a quick glance in Adam's direction. "Oh, I didn't, sir. My aunt was merely careless. Hit it on a post—"

"Your aunt? In the coach?" Margaret clarified, her expression suggesting she hadn't heard his earlier claim. She was sure he had said it was his *mother* who was wearing the ring when the damage happened.

"Yes, yes. The post... inside the coach. The one she hung onto when the driver took the turns too quickly," Mr. Smith-Jones claimed, his eyes widening.

"You aunt's name was...?" Adam half-asked as he exchanged a quick glance with Margaret.

"Caroline," Mr. Smith-Jones said quickly. "Uh... *Lady* Caroline."

"Oh, Lady *Framingham*," Adam said with a roll of his eyes.

"Yes! Yes! That's her name," Mr. Smith-Jones affirmed.

When neither Margaret nor Adam made a move, he frowned. "She's my favorite aunt."

"Who seems to have no nephews of record," Adam said with a sigh.

Realizing he'd been caught, Mr. Smith-Jones attempted to leave the office, but Adam stepped into his path and held up a staying hand.

"Mr. Bridge, you really must let me depart. My mother is waiting—"

"Lady Caroline Framingham is alive and well and missing her favorite emerald ring," Adam stated.

Mr. Smith-Jones' eyes rounded. "Well, I... I didn't *take* it," he claimed. "I... I found it. In the gutter. In New Bond Street."

"Oh. Well, then you'll want to tell that to the Bow Street Runner who is waiting for you outside," Adam said as he stepped aside.

Seeing his escape route opened, Mr. Smith-Jones hurried out of Margaret Ewen's office and through the front of the jewelry shop. A Bow Street Runner stood in the doorway, preventing him from making a complete escape.

A small kerfuffle ensued, which resulted in Mr. Smith-Jones on the floor of the shop with his hands tied behind his back.

"What shall we do with the evidence?" Adam asked as he joined the Runner. He held out the ring and the emerald in the palm of his hand.

"Repair it and collect the reward, of course. Lady Framingham will be quite generous," the Runner said before he lifted the thief from the floor and pushed him out the door. "Apparently that was a gift from an *admirer*," he added with an arched brow.

Margaret joined her father and frowned as Mr. Smith-Jones was loaded into a wagon.

"I don't remember a mention of a stolen emerald ring on the list," she said quietly.

"Lady Framingham was too embarrassed to report the crime. Seems she knew her nephew was the culprit," Adam explained. "And I rather doubt it was a gift from Lord Framingham."

Well aware most of their clients purchased jewelry for mistresses and lovers, Margaret understood why the marchioness hadn't reported the crime to the authorities. "So, how did you know to have the Runner here?" she asked.

Her father gave a shake of his head. "I didn't. The Runner has been following Mr. Smith-Jones' every move this morning. Apparently, this is the second of his stops. The Runner explained the situation to me when Smith-Jones was in the office speaking with you."

"Pity," Margaret murmured.

"Why's that?" Adam asked.

"The emerald is perfect. In clarity and fire. The cutting is exceptional—"

"Why, thank you, daughter," Adam remarked. At seeing her wide eyes, he added, "It was one of my earliest creations. Back when I had a steadier hand and sharper tools," he added.

Margaret stared at him in surprise before she gave a huff. She had only ever known her father to be a goldsmith. A silversmith. Never a gem cutter. That had to have been before she was born. "If you cut the gem and made this ring that long ago, then who was it for? And how did Lady Framingham end up with it?"

Adam cleared his throat. "As the Runner said, it was a gift from her admirer." He rolled his eyes. "I'm surprised you're asking me. Aren't you the one who reads the gossip sheets?" he teased.

Inhaling softly, Margaret said, "Only to discover if they

mention us in the articles. And to see the advertisement you arranged." She aimed an arched brow in his direction. "I was rather surprised to see my name with the word 'gemologist' after it," she added.

"That was my idea," Adam claimed happily. "So we might have more women coming to us with jewelry in need of gems."

"Well, it's certainly worked, although I can't imagine we'll make enough off of repairs to pay the debt," she murmured. Her gaze went to the issue of *The Tattler* that had drawn Mr. Smith-Jones' attention. "As for Lady Framingham, she took a lover last year when it became well known her husband had hired a mistress. It's one of the reasons she's become such a regular client of ours," she added in a quiet voice. "For every woman her husband is rumored to have approached with an offer of *carte blanche*, she buys a piece of jewelry and has me send the bill to him."

Adam shrugged. "Hell hath no fury," he murmured before he shut the door to the office and returned to his work counter.

"Can you repair it?" Margaret asked as she followed him.

He nodded as he held the ring between a thumb and forefinger. After carefully placing the emerald into the setting under the three undamaged prongs, he moved the ring so it was behind a magnifying glass and then picked up a tiny tool from the counter. He began bending the prong back into place as Margaret watched in fascination. Although she had seen him work like this many times, she was always amazed at how easily he could work with gold and silver.

"I'll smooth the tool marks out of the gold after I've heated it," he said in a whisper. "And then it will be good as new."

"You're a genius, Father," Margaret remarked, amazed the prong didn't show evidence of how much it had been bent out of shape. There were scratches in the metal from the tool he had used, though.

Adam sighed. "I rather wish you'd been old enough to help me choose gems back in those days," he murmured. "We might have had the best jewelry shop in Ludgate Hill."

"We *have* the best jewelry shop in Ludgate Hill," she countered emphatically. "We just don't have a Royal Warrant," she added sadly.

"We need more aristocrats as customers," Adam mused as he used a tong to grip the ring and then held a fabric-wrapped metal tool over an open flame. He then applied the tip of the tool to the metal, gently rubbing it over the thin gold prong to smooth out the tool marks.

Usually Margaret would chastise her father for risking a gemstone with the application of heat. The stones would sometimes discolor, crack or shatter. Emeralds were notorious for breaking when heated.

"A respected member of Parliament who will sing our praises to his fellow lords," Adam went on, ignoring Margaret's look of worry.

"And hopefully pay the invoice," she added with an arched brow. "So many of them do not. They expect everything to be done on credit."

Adam blew out the flame and then touched a cotton-tipped tool to the prong, rubbing it with a bit more pressure.

Margaret grinned when he held it out in her direction. "Your eyes are better than mine," he said.

She resisted the urge to take the ring from the tongs, thinking the metal would still be too hot to touch. "It appears you have succeeded," she murmured. "Even the other three prongs look better than they did."

"Lady Framingham deserves a ring that looks as good as the day it was made," he replied with a grin. "I'll compose a note to let her know the ring is in our care. Could you see to it it's stored in the safe?"

"Of course," she replied as she took the ring from his tongs. She pulled a black velvet-covered box from behind the counter and mounted the ring inside. Closing it, she was about to head back to her office when the shop's front door once again opened, the gold bell above it tinkling softly.

At first in silhouette—the late morning sun brightened the street in front of the shop—the handsome young man came into focus as his gaze swept the interior, finally falling onto Margaret. He removed his top hat and tucked it under one arm.

"Good morning, sir," she said, quite sure she recognized him. From where, though, she couldn't exactly say. "May I be of assistance?"

"Good morning," he replied, his attention briefly going to Adam, who was still behind his work counter at the back of the small shop.

Impeccably dressed in a long topcoat of navy superfine, a conservative brocade waistcoat, and light pantaloons, he could have been any one of a hundred gentlemen in London. His darker complexion, nearly black hair, and brown eyes set him apart, though, as did his square jaw, full lips, and high cheek bones. As a living, breathing man, he personified a Greek god. Had he lived two thousand years ago, he would have been worshipped as a god. Had he been carved from a block of marble, he would have been on display for all mere mortals to admire—especially those of the female persuasion.

As Margaret was doing that very moment, now quite sure she knew where she had seen him.

"Did you escape your exhibit pedestal in the British Museum, sir?" she asked in a whisper of awe.

CHAPTER 2
TEASING A YOUNG GENTLEMAN

moment later
Alexander Tennison stared at the comely brunette who stood before him in the jewelry shop. She clutched a black velvet ring box in a hand at the end of an arm that seemed entirely too short, but he quickly shook off the thought when he realized it could just be how it was bent and half hidden in the folds of her yellow gown.

Yellow, he was quite sure, was a color he could see correctly. *Primrose*, his sister always called it. At least until a few months ago, when she informed him it was now *jonquil*.

Fitted at the waist, her skirt formed a flattering bell around her lower half. The bodice was also nicely formed, or rather what was beneath it was, for Alexander found it hard not to stare at what he was sure was a perfect pair of pert breasts. Although it was difficult, he managed to avert his gaze so that it was above that general area. On the intricate cameo at the hollow of her throat.

Mounted on a velvet ribbon, the peach and pearl white pendant was larger than most cameos and had definitely been carved from a seashell.

He concentrated on her eyes. He saw them as gray but then wondered if they were really a clear green—he tended to make that mistake all the time. Then his gaze fell to her lips and how they formed words beyond her initial greeting.

He was so caught up in attempting to decipher her colors, he nearly missed the meaning of her comment.

What had she said?

Did you escape your exhibit pedestal in the British Museum?

Alexander blinked. Then he did something he hadn't had the pleasure of doing for several days.

He laughed.

All the concern and worry he'd felt over these past few months—how he had graduated from Cambridge but not at the top of his class, and why he saw things differently from others—seemed to lift at once, leaving him feeling lighter and of a mind to tease the young woman who stood before him.

He was about to accuse her of having escaped the pedestal next to his at the museum, but she had lifted one of her hands to her mouth, and a look of mortification had replaced the pleasant expression that had been there only the moment before.

"Oh! I am so sorry, sir. Please, accept my apologies."

Alexander gave his head a quick shake. "There's no need to apologize, my lady. Your comment has me realizing I should give more credence to my sister's claim about my appearance."

For a moment, Margaret's attention seemed to be on her mind's eye before she leaned forward and said, "Her claim that you are the epitome of a Greek god?" she guessed in a whisper.

Leaning over the counter, Alexander aimed his whispered reply in the general vicinity of her ear. "Uh, actually she claims her friends say I am gorgeous."

"Oh, well. Her friends are very astute."

He straightened. "I, of course, have ignored her—"

"Even when she is right?"

Alexander had to struggle to maintain a sober expression. "Of course you would side with your sex," he accused.

She allowed a grin. "She is younger than you?"

He nodded. "By three years, yes," he replied. "As are her friends, of course."

Margaret nodded her understanding. "Which means they are about to have their come-outs?" she half-questioned. Given his manner of dress and speech—to the manor born—Margaret was sure he was a gentleman.

"They are," he agreed, just before his eyes widened in understanding. "Oh!" he breathed. "No," he whispered, as if he was envisioning his immediate future and was considering where he might hide from it. "You're referring to the dreaded Marriage Mart."

"You probably have invitations to every ball," Margaret continued, deciding she was rather enjoying their banter. She hadn't had such a fun conversation in a very long time.

"I don't know about *every* ball," he countered.

"Where you'll no doubt have a number of mothers wishing to introduce their daughters to you."

He gave her a look of mock frustration. "Must you make it sound so *pleasant*?"

Margaret blinked. Twice. "You won't be flattered by all the attention?" she asked, her query tinged with disbelief. "All those beautiful young women, worshipping you as you pose on your pedestal?"

Alexander inhaled with the intention of responding, and then he let out the breath as he reconsidered what to say. "I suppose I should be."

"Well, I would hope so," she hedged.

He rolled his eyes. "Being gorgeous is *hard*," he complained. "There's the expectation you'll be *nice* to everyone. That you'll have a pleasant disposition no matter how little sleep you might have had the night before, or despite the disagreement you had with your father over your choice of avocation, or the knowledge that you cannot correctly identify..." He managed to stop speaking before mentioning his problem with colors.

He took a quick breath and tried to lighten his voice. "I suppose this happens to *you* all the time," he said with an exaggerated sigh.

"*Me*, sir?" Margaret tucked her withered arm closer to her body, her fingers tightening on the velvet box.

"Young men. Lining up before you to scribble their names on your dance card," he replied. "Tripping over themselves to take your hand in theirs so they might kiss it whilst they bow." Seeing that her right hand was otherwise engaged with a jewel box, he reached for the other, which was resting on the glass counter. He took it in his kid-gloved hand and lowered his lips to her knuckles. He brushed a kiss over the back of her hand before he lifted his head to gaze at her. "Like that," he added before slowly letting go of her trembling hand.

Margaret's eyes widened as she shook her head. "Oh, no, sir. That's never happened before."

He gave a start and then once again glanced around the shop. "I suppose there must be a first for everything," he murmured.

The sound of her father's throat clearing had Margaret remembering the young man was there for a reason. "May I help you find something, sir?"

Alexander nodded in the direction of the man who had joined them at the counter. "I wondered if you might have any gold for sale? I'm looking to create a new signet ring for my father, but I find I'm short on eighteen karat gold."

Margaret's eyes rounded. She didn't recognize the man as

any of the other jewelers in Ludgate Hill nor those who worked in shops in St. James Street. "You're a jeweler, sir?"

He shook his head. "It's merely an avocation of mine," he replied. "You needn't be concerned. I rather doubt I'll be taking any business from you given I have to spend so much time on that pedestal you mentioned."

Despite their earlier banter, Margaret still blushed. She turned to her father. "Have we some gold we can spare?"

Adam nodded. "Will a couple of ounces do?"

Alexander considered the offer. "Might you have four ounces?" Once he finished his father's ring, he thought to take on the challenge of some pendeloque earrings. He had melted down his last attempt at the pear-shaped jewelry when he couldn't make the hinges that connected the pear to the main body of the earring small enough. He had since decided he could connect the two parts of the earring with a small chain link, although he knew he would have to fuse the edges of the link together. Otherwise the pendeloque, which would contain the majority of gemstones, might separate and be easily lost.

Although Margaret seemed about to put voice to a protest —they didn't usually keep much gold on hand—Adam said, "That would be twenty pounds, sir."

Pulling his purse from his waistcoat pocket, Alexander extracted a few bank notes and some coins. "I should like to buy it then. It looks like I have enough blunt," he said as he offered the money to the jeweler.

Margaret exchanged a quick glance with her father. "Should I get the—?"

"I'll see to getting it from the safe," Adam offered. "You can write up the receipt." He left the counter and disappeared into the office in the back.

As Margaret moved to the end of the counter where a pen, ink pot, and a receipt book was located, Alexander said,

"When I arrived, I couldn't help but notice a man being arrested in front of your shop. Did he try to steal something?"

Margaret nodded as she completed the receipt. "He already had. An emerald ring. He had forced the gemstone from the setting—nearly ruined the ring. He was trying to pawn either the gold or the emerald, but a Runner had been following him and saw to his arrest."

"What happened to the ring?" Alexander asked, his curiosity evident.

"My father repaired it. We're holding it for the owner. Lady Framingham. We were about to send her a note to let her know it's in our possession when you arrived," she explained as she collected the money from the counter. "Sir, might I have your name for our bill of sale?" She held out his receipt.

"Tennison," he said. "Alexander Tennison." When he noticed her sudden smirk, he gave a start. "What is it?"

Margaret tittered. "Of course you would be named *Alexander*," she teased. "It's probably carved in marble at the base of your pedestal."

He rolled his eyes, but joined in her merriment. "Might I know your name, miss? Or will I find that at the base of the pedestal next to mine?"

Her mouth dropping open in astonishment, Margaret self-consciously pulled her withered arm against the front of her body. "I rather doubt that," she murmured, quickly sobering. "My name is Margaret Ewen. My father, Adam Ewen, is the proprietor and jeweler here."

"It's very good to make your acquaintance, Miss Ewen," he replied as Adam stepped forward with a small box. "Mr. Ewen," he added.

Inside the pasteboard box were four very small bars of gold. Adam placed each one on the pan of a scale and waited until the pans stopped moving.

"Four ounces," he announced before returning the bars to the box. He placed a lid over the top and handed the box to Alexander. "I'd be interested in seeing what you make with that," he said.

"As will I," Alexander replied. He turned his attention to Margaret. "When I'm not otherwise engaged on my pedestal," he added, his brows waggling. He reached for her left hand and brought it to his lips, which forced her to lean forward given how short her arm was.

"Good day, Mr. Tennison," she said, her voice sounding breathy in her ears.

"Good day to you both," Alexander said as he tucked the box into a pocket. He gave a bow and took his leave of the shop, Margaret watching his every move.

"Mr. Tennison, did you say?" Adam asked, after the door had closed.

"I did," she acknowledged, before she turned her attention to the bill of sale. She wrote the name of their customer at the top, not noticing her father's expression of delight as she did so.

CHAPTER 3
A BLINDNESS IS REVEALED

ater that day in the front salon of Rosemount House
Alexander lifted his eyes from the microscope and gave his head a shake. "This makes no sense," he murmured. He adjusted a dial on the side of the instrument and once again gazed through the eyepiece.

"I told you," his sister said, her arms crossing in front of her chest. "I think the sample has been compromised."

Jerking from the microscope, Alexander stared at Helen with a look of surprise. He had never heard her use the word 'compromised' before, and he wondered if she had learned it from their father, or if she had been eavesdropping on their mother.

Lately, the countess had been hosting several matrons in her parlor during afternoon tea. Those with young daughters seemed especially concerned their future ladies of the *ton* were in danger of becoming *compromised* by the likes of him and his fellow heirs and spares.

Alexander wasn't about to tell his mother they had no interest in girls who were Helen's age.

Their attentions were on women far older. Well, except

for a couple of his friends. He didn't want to think about them, though. Newlyweds, both of them. His attention was on the specimen beneath the microscope.

"Compromised by what?" he asked. "This was in a glass vial—with a cork stopper—until you took it out. Wasn't it?" He lifted the glass slide from beneath the lens and held it up to the light from the overhead chandelier, as if he could make out what might have caused the discoloration of the leaf's veins.

He really would have preferred spending the afternoon out in his foundry melting down some of the gold he had acquired that morning. Forming it into a substantial but elegant ring worthy of an earl. Embedding a huge onyx stone in the middle and securing it with tiny prongs.

All while thinking of Miss Margaret Ewen.

Why his father had assigned him the task of staring at a leaf's veins through a microscope, he couldn't say.

Helen allowed a sound of disgust. "But *I* wasn't the one who collected the sample. Anything could have happened before it was put into the vial," she argued.

Helen might have been a few years younger than Alexander, but she had surpassed him in their natural science studies long ago. Although Alexander was interested in botany and biology, he preferred to dabble in metallurgy and to study fossils and gemstones. Until he inherited the Everly earldom, he had half a mind to relocate to Lyme Regis on the southwestern coast where he could discover all manner of fossils in the cliffs. He thought they would make excellent stones to use in jewelry.

"True. So... who collected this one?"

"Probably me," their father announced from where he stood on the threshold of their makeshift laboratory—the ground floor salon with a window facing Park Lane. Alexander preferred it for the natural light while Helen liked it for the vantage it provided when someone of the opposite sex might be riding by on their way to the park.

"Father," Alexander said in a scolding voice.

Harold held up a warning finger, grinning when Alexander struggled to suppress whatever he was about to say. "You must consider that the contamination might have been deliberate."

Helen's eyes widened. "Contamination," she repeated in wonder. "That's a far better word than *compromise*."

Alexander huffed. "If I didn't collect it, then am I to assume it might be... contaminated?" he countered.

"You are to assume nothing," Harold argued. "I take it you're looking at the sample of the palm frond taken from Lady Weatherstone's conservatory?"

"Indeed," Helen replied. "When I applied the stain, I would have expected the veins to turn blue, and instead, they're... puce."

Her brother furrowed a brow. "Puce?" he repeated. He took another look through the eyepiece and gave his head a shake. "These veins are clearly *blue*."

Harold made his way to the microscope and peered through the tube. His brow furrowed before he slowly straightened.

"What is it?" Alexander asked as he quickly took another look through the microscope.

"Son, what color is this?" Harold asked as he pointed to a pink peony in the fabric of his wife's favorite chair in the salon.

"Sort of a brownish blue."

Helen inhaled softly.

"And this?" Harold moved his finger to an adjacent green leaf in the upholstery.

"Gold," Alexander replied.

Once again, Helen gasped. "What color is my gown?" she

asked, holding out the skirts of her primrose muslin day gown.

"Yellow."

Helen gave him a quelling glance. "Jonquil, if we're to be exact," she murmured, her blonde brows pinching together in confusion. Then her face lit up with understanding. "You're color blind," she said in awe.

Having already come to that conclusion some time ago, Harold gave his son a nod when Alexander turned to him with a look of horror. "She's right. I've suspected it for some time—"

"Color blind?" Alexander said on a huff. "That cannot be. I... I see colors."

"Not all of them," Harold replied quickly. "Your eyes lack the necessary receptors to properly see red and green," he added on a sigh. When Alexander looked as if he might faint, Harold said, "It's an annoyance, nothing more, son."

But Helen's expression suggested it was far more serious than her father was letting on. "That's why Lady Dahlia was so offended when you commented on her riding habit last week." Her eyes darted sideways. "You mentioned the gray was particularly fetching on her, but her riding habit was hunter green. Although she was over the moon that you *noticed* her, she was of a mind to find a new modiste."

Alexander lowered his head into his bent arm, his fingers spearing his wavy jet black hair in a sign of frustration. When he finally lifted his head, he found his father staring at him with an expression of sorrow.

"This is why, isn't it?" Alexander asked in a hoarse whisper.

"If you're asking if this is why you had trouble in some of your classes at Cambridge, then, yes, most probably," Harold agreed.

Despite his keen interest in gemology and fossils, fields his paternal grandfather had found especially interesting, Alexander had struggled with proper identification of rocks and minerals. The descriptions in the texts didn't always match what he saw when he was given the physical examples to study.

"Well, I suppose it's a good thing I don't need to see at all when I'm in the House of Lords," he said on a sigh.

"You're not *blind*," Harold countered in a quiet voice. "And you do see many colors correctly."

"Apparently not *puce*."

"Well, just between us, puce is a rather useless color," his father said.

"But it's so fashionable," Helen argued. "Why just last week, Mother said..." She stopped speaking when she noted her Father's expression.

"I suppose my clothes have been ungodly colors," Alexander replied. He turned to his sister for confirmation, but she was shaking her head.

"They're rather conservative, actually," she said. "Which is probably why so many of my friends think you're gorgeous."

Having heard the term used to describe him since he was a schoolboy, Alexander rolled his eyes. He secretly knew the color of his clothes had nothing to do with why young girls—and matrons—found him particularly handsome. With a half-Greek mother and an especially handsome British father, he couldn't help that he looked like a Greek god personified.

How his sister managed to be blonde and blue-eyed and look just like their aunt Evangeline wasn't a science he was particularly interested in learning, but his father insisted it was quite normal for his progeny to look so different.

"You're clothes are not more colorful than theirs," his sister said, apparently unaware he wasn't listening. "You never want to wear a waistcoat that's more colorful than a young lady's gown."

"Or any lady's, for that matter," their father murmured, suggesting he might have learned the lesson the hard way at some point during his eight-and-forty years. "So wearing blues and golds is perhaps safest."

Most of Alexander's pantaloons were buff, the trousers were dark blue, the top coats were black superfine, and his waistcoats were...

Well, now he wasn't sure what color his waistcoats were.

"I'm going for a ride," Alexander announced. He strode from the room, his startled sister watching him go while their father stared at something in his mind's eye.

"Did you deliberately contaminate the sample?" Helen asked in a quiet voice.

Harold shook himself from his reverie. "I did, actually, so good on you for catching it," he said in a quiet voice.

She allowed a long sigh, disappointed for her brother. "Will he ever be able to see all the colors?"

Her father shook his head and allowed a sigh of frustration. "No."

"Why is it he's color blind? Did something happen to him to cause it? When he was born... or an injury?"

Shaking his head, Harold said, "I have reason to believe he inherited it."

Helen furrowed a brow. "From you?"

"Not according to the paper Mr. Dalton published some five-and-thirty years ago," he replied, referring to John Dalton's research on the topic. "When your brother was bestowed with those dashing good looks from his mother, he was also bestowed with her father's color blindness."

Helen stared at her father in shock. "My grandfather is color blind?" she asked, referring to Stewart Jones, Duke of Westhaven. Her eyes widened as she considered the implications. "Will *my* children be, as well?" She fell down into one of the pink peony-upholstered chairs, slumping in a most unla-dylike manner.

Harold sank into the chair opposite, his fingers steepling in front of his face. "Possibly," he hedged. "The eyes are not my field of study, so I cannot say for certain."

"But, he's an archaeologist," Helen argued. "He's still able to do his work."

Nodding, Harold said, "Color is not nearly as important in his line of work as it is in mine." He had adopted botany as his avocation long before he inherited the Everly earldom.

The two sat in silence for a long time before Helen could tell her father once again had his attentions on his mind's eye.

"I think I shall go for a ride, too," Helen announced. When her father didn't respond but continued to stare at the salon wall, Helen took her leave and hurried up the stairs.

CHAPTER 4

HARRY'S VERY FIRST AND ONLY ARCHAEOLOGICAL EXPEDITION

Forty-four years ago, Rosemount House parlor, Mayfield

"What do you think you're doing, young man?"

Harold's head jerked up, but his small fingers didn't let go of their grip on the reticule, nor did he offer an answer to Eva Tennison's question. The elaborately embroidered bag was obviously full of something—it's shape suggested it contained a number of oddly configured items—and it was heavy.

The countess allowed a smirk, but before she could tell him to put down the reticule, her husband entered the parlor.

"I wouldn't do that if I were you, son," the baritone voice of Charles Tennison, Earl of Everly, intoned. Although his manner seemed most serious, his lips formed a quirk. "Once you get started, it will be like an archeological expedition. You'll find layers upon layers of history, all manner of artifacts going back to the dawn of civil ..."

"Everly!" Eva admonished her husband. "He'll find no such thing," she added as she leaned over and captured the reticule in one hand. "Everything in here is from just this past year," she claimed, her chin rising in defiance of the earl's words.

"What is archaeolo ..." Harold stopped, his brows furrowing in concentration.

"Archeology is the study of artifacts from prior civilizations," his father explained patiently. "Involves a good deal of digging in the dirt. Or reticules, if a woman ever allowed a man such an endeavor."

This comment had young Harold turning his attention back to his mother. He was never sure when he was being teased or not. "Will you show me?" he asked in a voice not much louder than a whisper.

Ever since he'd been breeched the month before, he had been allowed to spend more time in her presence and had even been invited to join her for tea the day before. Although he could only have one biscuit with his cup of milk, he thanked her profusely for the opportunity to prove he wouldn't spill the milk.

Then he spilled the milk.

Even as his nurse hurried over to wipe up the small splash from his lap, his mother sighed and pretended not to notice.

There was a reason Eva Tennison, Countess of Everly, was considered a gracious hostess.

Eva allowed a grin to appear at hearing his query. "I'd be delighted," she said, giving her husband an arched eyebrow in the process.

Charles' face took on a look of surprise. "What? Why, you would never do *me* the honor of revealing the contents of your reticule in my presence," he complained, his voice suggesting he was rather hurt.

His wife giggled, a sound that had Harold widening his eyes. He had never heard such a sound come from his mother before, but the delight she displayed soon had him grinning as well.

"*You've* never asked, darling," she replied as she moved to give her husband a kiss on his cheek.

Darling.

Harold always liked it when he heard his mother call his father 'darling.' He knew she adored his father. She teased him and he allowed it. He teased her and she feigned offense. But Charles would work his magic with the metals he melted in his small foundry, and every so often, he presented her with all manner of beautiful jewelry and small trinkets. He had even crafted the chatelaine that now dangled from her gown's pocket, its collection of small scissors, a thimble, keys and vinaigrette attached to delicate silver chains with clasps.

"I am asking now," Charles stated. "I should like to watch whilst you reveal the bag's contents to my heir."

The countess rolled her eyes as she moved to the card table at the back of the parlor. She spread open the gathered top edge and proceeded to unload the myriad objects onto the table's surface.

The items tumbled out and came to rest in a series of *thuds* and *tinkles*. A small mirror in a hinged ivory case, a pair of silk gloves, a coin purse heavy with blunt, opera glasses in a silk sleeve embroidered with tiny beads, a pair of earbobs featuring green gemstones, a lace-edged handkerchief with an 'E' embroidered in one corner, and a small pad of paper with a tiny pencil attached to a metal case.

His eyes wide as he regarded his mother's treasure, Harold was about to reach for the earbobs when Eva inhaled sharply. He stilled his hand and dared a look at his father before he angled his head in the other direction in an effort to learn what had his mother gasping in shock.

Eva quickly reached for the earbobs and held them in the flat of her hand. "These aren't mine," she said in a whisper.

A quick look back at his father had Harold catching an

expression he had rarely seen the earl display when he was in his company.

Adoration.

For Charles Tennison was regarding his countess with that look.

Harold glanced back to his mother, who now had tears collecting in the corners of her eyes. "Oh, Everly, you remembered," she breathed. "You made these for me, didn't you?" A moment later, his mother's arms were wrapped around his father, and she was kissing him with a fervor that had Harold raising his hands to cover his eyes.

Shaking himself from his reverie, Harold didn't know whether to laugh or cry at his reaction to his parents' rare show of affection. For a moment, he even wondered why he had thought back to that particular day.

His first foray into exploration hadn't revealed anything about color blindness. Anything that had to do with whatever was going on in the current Everly household.

Then it hit him.

The need for a gift.

There was a special occasion on the horizon.

Stella's birthday?

No, that wasn't it.

Anniversary. Wedding anniversary.

He straightened in the chair and struggled to remember that day's date. To remember the date he had taken Stella to wife.

Their wedding anniversary.

Relaxing a moment when he realized he still had a few weeks to find her the perfect gift, Harold found his thoughts turning to the second time he had ever seen Stella Jones.

Drenched with sea water. Wearing barely anything at all.

A mermaid. Or Aphrodite.

His cock certainly remembered, for it was hardening that very moment. Much as it had the night before, when his thoughts of how elegant Stella had appeared across the table from him during dinner nearly had him forgoing the dessert course and instead having her for dessert.

He had announced he wouldn't be partaking in his usual glass of port and escorted her to his bedchamber shortly thereafter, loving that she didn't question his motives or refuse his amorous attentions. After all, she had been the one to flirt with him, bless her heart.

Instead, she had welcomed his body, cried out his name whilst in ecstasy, and held him as he recovered his wits.

Then she had warned him she wasn't going to be sleeping in her own bed that night. His morning's tumescence certainly appreciated the warmth and wetness it encountered only a moment after he awakened that day.

Harold wasn't sure why he found himself so aroused, but he wasn't about to expend the mental energy to sort it at the moment.

Determined to find his countess, Harold made his way out of the salon and up the two flights of stairs to her bedchamber.

CHAPTER 5
A SISTER'S MACHINATIONS

eanwhile, upstairs in Rosemount House Helen knocked on her brother's bedchamber door several times. "Brother, may I join you on your ride?" she called out, before anyone would have had a chance to open the door.

"Go away," her brother's muffled voice sounded.

Helen was about to reply when the door suddenly opened.

"You're not going to tell anyone." It wasn't a question, and from the severe expression Alexander directed at her, Helen knew he wasn't expecting an answer.

"That you're going for a ride?" she asked in a whisper.

Alexander's face darkened in warning.

Sighing, Helen said, "Of course not. Besides, no one would even know what I was talking about." Her eyes darted to the side before she added, "But at least you know now." When his eyes narrowed further, she went on. "You know why it is you have such difficulty with the identification of agates and gemstones." She held up a hand on which she wore a single amethyst ring her grandmother had given her. "Why you think this is blue instead of purple."

Alexander's gaze darted to the ring, and he let out a huff. "I could have sworn that was a topaz," he whispered. "I could never make my living as a goldsmith."

Helen gave him a quelling glance. "You were never going to," she countered. Alexander was the heir to an earldom, after all.

"Still, I thought it an interesting avocation."

"It can still be," she argued. "You do beautiful work with gold and silver. Better than grandfather ever did. Your designs in gold rival what the men at Rundell and Bridge can do." She leaned in closer. "You very nearly spoiled Mother so that Father can hardly hope to compete. He was considering a parure for their anniversary, but now..." She lifted a shoulder, as if all hope was lost for the earl to please his countess.

His eyes widening, Alexander looked as if he wanted to believe her. "I would do one for him to give to her," he whispered. He paused, his gaze darting to somewhere in his bedchamber before he added, "As long as he paid for the gems and the gold."

He thought of the four ounces he had purchased earlier. He doubted there would be enough to complete more than a necklace and a brooch let alone a pair of earrings and the matching bracelet. He would probably need another three or four ounces.

"You should make him that offer," Helen said with some excitement. Anything to get his mind off his malady.

"On commission, of course," he added, a smirk appearing.

"Alex!" she scolded. "What if he *were* to purchase the gold and the gemstones? Or provide you with the money you need to do all the pieces? Would you do it?"

Alexander leaned against the door jamb, his arms crossing over his chest. "The stones would have to be pre-cut. I don't have the tools here to do that."

"I'm sure you can buy them however you need them. One

of my friends said she bought a sapphire at Mr. Ewen's shop in Ludgate Hill." At Alexander's look of surprise, she added, "She lost the one that came in the ring her father had given to her for her birthday, and she was beside herself with worry. But now it's all fixed, and her father never noticed."

"Probably because he hasn't gotten the bill," Alexander murmured.

"Oh, she paid for the sapphire out of her pin money," Helen countered. "And the girl who waited on her in the shop said she wouldn't tell a soul."

Angling his head to one side, Alexander considered that it was probably Margaret Ewen who had waited on Helen's friend. Given her father's business, Miss Ewen would have to be discreet. Careful not to divulge who bought what and for whom, if she knew.

What if a married man purchased a necklace for his mistress? He couldn't risk having his secret shared with his wife. Margaret probably knew the jewelry secrets of many in London.

The minx.

"So, will you do it?"

Helen's query pulled Alexander from his reverie. "I'll speak with him after dinner tonight."

Nodding, Helen secretly wondered when she might gain a moment alone with their father to let him know what she had arranged in his name. That he was to have Alexander make a parure for their mother for their wedding anniversary.

"May I join you on your ride in the park?" she asked again, nearly bouncing on the balls of her feet. Although the Season hadn't yet begun—it would in a few days—the weather was fine enough that some people would be riding in Rotten Row in the next hour or so.

"Ride?" he repeated. "I think not. I have a parure to design."

Helen gave a start as his bedchamber door slammed shut, only inches from her nose.

"Well," she huffed. Turning to head down the corridor, she stopped short when she noticed another bedchamber's door was open. Just beyond its threshold, Stella Jones Tennison, Countess of Everly, stood watching her with an enigmatic expression.

"Mother? Is something wrong?" Helen asked in a hoarse whisper.

Stella angled her head to one side and gave it a shake. "What ever is going on in that head of yours?"

Helen sighed. "A machination, of course. The experiment worked—one I wasn't even aware was happening—and we've confirmed what Father suspected."

Her eyes widening with worry, the countess asked, "What experiment? Is the salon still habitable?" She backed up and pulled her daughter into her bedchamber, closing the door behind her.

"We didn't explode anything," Helen replied with a shrug. "Well, other than Alex's enlarged head."

Stella sucked in a breath and held it. "What did you do?"

From her mother's cross words, Helen knew she was on the verge of being sent to her bedchamber without dinner. "It seems I helped Father confirm that Alex is color blind."

Stella blinked, but she waved for Helen to join her in her apartment's sitting room. "Reds and greens? Or does he only see grays?"

Helen's mouth dropped open. "You *knew*?"

Settling onto a Greek sofa, Stella allowed a sigh. "I've known since he was a child, of course."

Taking the adjacent Chippendale chair by nearly dropping onto it, Helen gave a huff and then said, "Well, he can see *some* colors. Golds and blues. Yellow." She held out a section of her skirts. "But not purple. Or puce. No reds, I think." She paused and watched as her mother grew sadder before her eyes. "Father said he might have inherited it from grandfather. *Your* father."

Stella nodded. "Westhaven has never seen reds as we do," she said, referring to her father. "But as an archaeologist, he didn't think it a detriment. It didn't seem to affect his work."

"Apparently, Alex thinks it's why he did so poorly at Cambridge."

Giving a start, the countess shook her head. "But he didn't do *poorly*," she argued. "He was near the top of his class."

"Except in geology," Helen reminded her. "His favorite subject."

Stella rolled her eyes. "If only he'd had a penchant for archaeology and wished to follow in *my* father's footsteps," she murmured.

"Instead, he wants to follow in his other grandfather's steps," Helen countered. "And he never even met the man."

"Your Father told him some marvelous stories about the late Earl of Everly," Stella said on a sigh. When Helen asked why, she added, "I think because your grandfather was already dead when you two were born. Everly wanted to... to make him seem real to the two of you. Goodness knows, Westhaven certainly didn't need help in that regard," she said on a chuckle, remembering how her father had described and acted out his trips in search of Ancient Greek artifacts to his grandchildren. The exaggerated descriptions of adventures he had experienced when attempting to recover long lost treasures in the Cyclades and on the mainland of Greece had kept Alexander and Helen enthralled for hours.

"You must have had an amazing life when you were my age," Helen whispered.

Stella laughed, quickly covering her mouth with a hand. "I didn't think it so amazing back then. At least, until I met your father for the second time."

Helen leaned forward. "The second time?"

Stella nodded. "The first time was at a ball. We danced once, but... I'm quite sure he forgot all about it. The second time, I was dressed for diving, which means... well, I was practically naked." She ignored Helen's gasp of shock. "I was in the water, and I came up for air near a beach on the island of... of Delos, I think it was. And your father was holding a seashell to his ear. He had the oddest expression on his face."

"And then he saw you and fell in love?" Helen asked, as if she thought it the most romantic way in which two people could meet.

"In *lust*, is probably more accurate," Stella replied. She giggled then, tears brightening her eyes before she waved a hand in front of her face. "He was looking for Cretan plane trees—and my father, as it happens—while I was searching for statues and vases my uncle could sell to the European tourists. Ancient artifacts were all the rage back then."

"They still are," Helen countered.

"*Everyone* was decorating their studies and halls with statuary and broken columns, pots and vases."

When she didn't continue, seemingly lost in thought, Helen allowed a long sigh. "Father said he thought you were a mermaid, even though he knew... or he was fairly sure... mermaids didn't exist."

"I wasn't *that* naked," Stella said, rather alarmed.

Helen giggled and then slowly sobered. "Alex needs a mermaid," she said on a sigh.

"I'm quite sure there are none to be found here in England," Stella murmured. "But from what I overheard out in the hall, I think he does not feel worthy enough to pursue a wife."

"Because of his color blindness," Helen agreed. "And yet, every daughter of the *ton* thinks he's *gorgeous* and would gladly agree to be his future countess, even if he was completely blind."

"I think he might be too young to marry," Stella said on a sigh.

"That's what we thought about Gabe Wellingham and George Grandby, and they both married before they saw their twenty-second year," Helen argued.

"True," Stella hedged. "And they both ended up with fine young ladies. Still, I think Alex needs some time to determine what he wants in a future countess. In a mother for his children. And in the meantime, he can do his metal work out back and attend every entertainment for which he receives an invitation."

"You're still afraid he's going to burn down the house, aren't you?" Helen asked in a teasing voice.

Ever since Alexander had announced a desire to take up his paternal grandfather's avocation—metallurgy—their father had insisted Alexander work on his creations in the same separate building in the back garden that the late earl had used to create his unusual pieces of jewelry and objets d' art.

"We'd be living in a much older house if your grandfather hadn't burned down most of Tennison Manor," Stella countered.

"He didn't!" her daughter exclaimed, her eyes wide with fright.

"Apparently, he did," Stella countered. "Long before your father was born. Before he had even taken a wife."

Helen shook her head. "I feel as if I ought to have some avocation," she murmured. "You were diving for treasures in the Aegean Sea when you were my age. My only accomplishment is managing to sew without sticking my finger with the needle."

"Oh, but your embroideries are so lovely," her mother

replied. "As are your drawings," she added when she noted how Helen grimaced. "You take after your father in that regard. He used to draw all his discoveries as a means to document them," she explained.

"So he could include them in his book," Helen reasoned.

Stella gave a quick shake of her head. "I don't believe your father knew he was going to publish a book on plants and trees when he was doing those drawings," she replied. "I think he was more concerned about using them in his presentations at the Royal Society."

"What about your diving?"

Angling her head to one side, Stella considered how to respond. "I might have dived for treasure, but it wasn't something I enjoyed doing." When Helen looked as if she didn't believer her, Stella added, "Well, I admit there was that thrill when I found something. A statue or an ancient coin. But I always feared I might drown before I reached the surface. And I feared my uncle's censure even more if I didn't come up with something of value."

"Is that why we've never met Uncle Spiros?"

Stella rolled her eyes. "That, and he died before you were old enough to travel."

"I am so glad, then, that I met your cousin, Jakob. He seemed very... pleasant."

Chuckling, Stella said, "He is. And I've just received word he is a father again for the fifth time."

Helen giggled. "I look forward to our next trip to Mykonos," she said, her voice wistful. "Maybe I'll meet and marry a Greek aristocrat. Live on an island where it's always warm—"

"Hot."

"Hot and sunny. Where it only rains at night."

"And the wind blows."

"It only did it at night," Helen argued.

Stella's eyes once again brightened with tears. "You'll have to have a bedchamber for me to live in my dower years," she warned.

"Oh, you'll have an entire dower cottage," Helen claimed, a wide smile lighting her face. "We can swim every day and eat in the back garden surrounded by nasturtiums and those bright pink flowers that grow on the vines above doorways."

"Well, now that you have me dead and buried," came Harold's voice from the doorway, "How will you expect Alex to have any success as the next Earl of Everly if you two are living in Greece?"

The two women gasped and turned to stare at the earl. Although he attempted an air of humor with his expression, Stella knew he was hurt by their musings. She could see it in his eyes. In the set of his shoulders and the way he appeared uncertain. He'd been doing more of that of late. Looking as if the weight of the world was on his shoulders, and Atlas was no where to be found.

Stella stood up and rushed over to him. "Darling, I would never leave our son, and you know it," she whispered as she stood on tiptoe and kissed him on the cheek. "Well, at least, not until his wife has had quite enough of me and insists I move out."

Harold gave her a quelling glance. "If he marries such a creature, I will see to it he's forced into Parliament with a writ of acceleration, and *I'll* take you to Greece myself."

"Back to where we met the second time?"

Harold's brows rose. "Delos?"

"You remembered," she said on a sigh.

He was about to admit he had been thinking of it only the moment before, but thought better of it. "That is not a day I shall ever forget, my love," he murmured. "The first and only time I ever believed mermaids existed. Or Aphrodite."

"And on that note, I think I shall go change for riding," Helen announced as she stood and fled the bedchamber.

Her parents watched her go before their gazes once again met. "Your mermaid would not object to a quick dip," Stella murmured suggestively.

Harold's eyes darted to the bed. "Does it have to be quick?"

Stella's eyes darkened. "It can be as long as you'd like. I'm not expecting any callers today. Dinner isn't for another... three hours?" she guessed.

Closing the door with a kick, Harold took Stella into his arms and kissed her quite thoroughly.

He did much more after he had most of her clothes removed from her body.

CHAPTER 6
A PLAN FOR A PARURE

ater that night in the billiards parlor, Rosemount House
The *clack* of two billiard balls colliding was followed by the sound of one of them landing in the leather-woven basket in the far corner of the table, and Alexander gave his father a bow.

"Show off," Harold accused as he leaned against the fireplace mantel, his own leather-tipped cue resting against the wall. It had been there for nearly the entire game. "I taught you how to play so I would have more frequent practice," he groused. "Not so you could beat me all the time. Bad enough that Sommers has managed to come up to snuff," he added, referring to his brother-in-law.

"I beat Uncle Jeffrey last week," Alexander said before he sunk another ball. "Aunt Evangeline then proceeded to scold me, claiming he would now spend more time practicing than writing his books."

"Sounds about right," Harold murmured. "And speaking of time—"

"Were we?"

"I've a favor to ask of you."

Alexander straightened from the billiards table and regarded his father with surprise. "Me?"

"It's about your mother and our anniversary."

"You're in need of a parure."

Harold blinked. "Yes. How... how did you—?"

"Helen mentioned it this afternoon."

Scratching an eyebrow with his forefinger, Harold let out a guffaw. "Your sister is quite the schemer," he commented. "She only just spoke with me about it after..." He paused, deciding it best he not bring up the moment Alexander learned he was color blind.

"Her machinations can be annoying," Alexander agreed, "but in this case, I rather liked her suggestion that I design and make Mother's present. I started this afternoon, and I have some drawings I wish to show you."

"Why, that's capital," Harold replied. "But will three weeks be enough time for you to do the work?"

His expression suggesting he was offended, Alexander said, "I'll be able to do the goldsmithing. It's mostly crafting the collets and the means to connect them together for the necklace and bracelet and making the ring and the brooch. The brooch of course will also be the pendant for the necklace." Clearing his throat, he added, "My design requires a number of gems, though."

"I would expect nothing less."

"The earrings each feature twenty-eight stones."

Harold's eyes widened. "You've designed pendeloques?" he asked, referring to the pear-shaped pendants that hung from a smaller, hinged setting on the more elaborate earrings women wore to balls and to the opera.

"Indeed."

"So... more than two-hundred stones all told?"

Alexander's eyes widened, amazed his father would guess

a number close to what he had calculated while dressing for dinner.

"If I keep the collets small," he acknowledged. "If I make them larger, then I won't need as many for the necklace. Still, this will require a good deal of gold. More than I purchased yesterday."

Realizing where Alexander was going with his comments had his father lifting a finger. "Buy what you must and have the bills sent to me," he said.

"Are you sure? I've no idea—"

"Your mother is worth it."

"Yes, sir," Alexander replied. He glanced at the two remaining billiard balls on the table before he cleared his throat. "May I inquire, sir... has something happened with you and Mother?"

Alarmed, Harold straightened. "Happened?" he repeated. He was fairly sure his earlier encounter with Stella hadn't been overheard by anyone. The bed's ropes were especially tight, and he knew the headboard hadn't banged into the wall.

Dipping his head, Alexander sighed. "You're suddenly different with her than you have been for the past few years." Heat permeated his face.

Harold allowed a sigh of relief. "I suppose I have been. A bit of feeling my age of late."

Alexander's eyes darted to the side. "Don't you mean 'feeling your oats'?"

It was Harold's turn to redden. "I guess we haven't been as quiet as we thought," he murmured.

"Did you recently have an *affaire* and then end it? Or did you let your mistress go?"

His father's eyes widened. "Of course not. And I haven't had a mistress since... well, since before I married your mother," he claimed. His brows drew together. "Whatever gave you that impression?"

Shrugging, Alexander said, "I suppose I didn't notice how you two behaved with one another until... well, until you were... misbehaving," he stammered. "It's like you barely tolerated being in the same room with one another for most of my life, and suddenly—"

"That's not true. I've always loved your mother. I have since before I married her," Harold claimed.

"So... what changed?" Alexander asked, deciding their conversation was more important than the game.

Harold crossed his arms and leaned against the fireplace mantel. "The simplest answer would probably be my impending mortality," he said on a sigh.

A grunt of disbelief sounded from Alexander. "What are you? Six-and-forty?"

"*Eight*-and-forty. Older than my father was when he died."

Alexander jerked at the harsh response. "Grandfather didn't die of old age," he argued. "I thought he and grandmother died in a shipwreck."

"They did," Harold acknowledged. "And while my hair has turned gray"—he motioned to his temples—"my wife looks just as beautiful as the day I first thought she was a mermaid."

Alexander considered asking when that might have been, but thought better of it. He feared his father would regale him with some scientific explanation for why mermaids either existed—or didn't. "Did you think *she* was having an *affaire*?" he asked in disbelief.

A look of defeat settling over his features, Harold sighed. "The thought had crossed my mind."

"Father!"

"I see the way my peers look at her," Harold argued. "The members of the Royal Society. As if they're imagining what she might look like in their company. In their beds. Without any—"

"Father! Mother would never!"

Harold swallowed the rest of what he was about to say at the same moment his attention was drawn to the door.

"Mother would never... *what?*" Stella asked, her gloved arms crossed over her bosom as she leaned against the door jamb. She was still wearing her bright blue dinner gown, the Grecian-style column dress long out of fashion but perfect for a woman who still looked as if she could be Aphrodite.

Or a mermaid.

Alexander exchanged a quick glance with his father before he lifted his chin and said, "Have an *affaire.*"

Dropping her arms to her sides at the same moment her mouth dropped open, Stella stared at her son. "*Me?*" She quickly closed her mouth but then added, "Well, I suppose I have been of late."

Harold's pool cue fell onto the floor at the same moment Alexander made the oddest sound in the back of his throat. He watched as his mother made her way to where his Father was using the fireplace mantel to remain upright.

"With your Father," she said, her gaze entirely on her husband. She held a hand up to the side of her mouth as she tipped her head up and whispered, "I'll be in my bedchamber should you wish to continue what we were doing earlier this afternoon." Without waiting for a response, she kissed Harold on the cheek, turned, and said, "Good night, Alex. Don't stay up too late."

She slowly took her leave of the billiards room as Harold watched her go. He made an incomprehensible sound in the back of his throat, not unlike what Alex had done only the moment before, and then he turned his attention back to his son.

"Well, there you have it," Harold said proudly.

"How long was she standing there?" Alexander asked in a whisper.

His father shrugged. "I don't know. But it matters not. I love her, and I've been invited to join her in her bedchamber this evening."

Alexander once again reddened. "I suppose that means you're not of a mind to look at the designs for her parure right now?"

Hesitating, Harold said, "I would prefer to see them by the light of day. Have you a particular...?" He almost said 'color scheme in mind' and thought better of it. "Gemstone in mind?"

"Not yet," Alex replied. "I will once I discover which gown the parure will likely be worn with, so I know what color gems to choose."

"Ah," his father replied. "I think it will be red, but only her modiste knows for sure. Suzanne's. In Oxford Street." Then he remembered his last visit to Ewen & Ewen, the jewelry store in Ludgate Hill. His last conversation with Adam Ewen. "Tell me, were you thinking to shop for gems on the morrow?"

"I was," Alex admitted. "I need to decide on sizes. I rather doubt I'm going to find all I need from a single gem merchant."

Harold nodded his approval. "Might I suggest you pay a call at a particular jeweler with regard to the purchase of the gems?"

"A jeweler?" Alexander questioned. "As opposed to a gem merchant?"

Harold gave a slight shrug. "I have done my jewelry shopping at Ewen and Ewen's for the past decade. Mr. Ewen is good at what he does, and his assistant is especially knowledgeable in the field of precious stones."

Alexander's eyes widened at the mention of Ewen &

Ewen. "I bought gold there yesterday," he said. "And Helen mentioned that shop this afternoon," he added. "But won't you be paying more for the gems given there's a middleman involved?" he reasoned.

"Unlikely. Despite his skill as a goldsmith, Adam Ewen doesn't have a Royal Warrant, and therefore, he does not overcharge for his creations. In the same vein, he is not over-charged when he purchases his gemstones." He paused a moment. "You probably bought the gold for about what you'd pay elsewhere."

Alexander had thought the twenty pounds for four ounces of eighteen karat gold a fair price given twenty-four karat gold was valued at just over twenty pounds per ounce. "I did," he agreed. He furrowed a dark brow. "Are you saying other jewelers pay higher prices for their gemstones?"

Harold nodded. "Some do. Although particular names add value to a product, they are not necessarily worth the higher prices they command."

Nodding his understanding—and deciding he could sort exactly who his father meant by the comment—Alexander said, "Then I shall start at Ewen's with my search."

The idea of returning to the jewelry shop had him suppressing a grin. He and Miss Ewen could continue their witty repartee until he asked to meet with the gemologist. Her father probably held that position, he considered.

"Very good," his father said. "In the meantime, it seems I've an *affaire* to continue with my wife," he added as he took his leave of the billiards room.

Alexander watched his father go before he retrieved his pool cue and sunk the second to the last ball. After he had done so, he settled into the room's only chair and sighed.

What the hell was happening to the men in his life?

Just prior to Christmas last year, George Grandby, Viscount Hexham and heir to the Torrington earldom, had married Ann Wellingham, the daughter of the Earl of Trenton. Their courtship seemed to have lasted all of one day, but the two had apparently been secretly pining for one another for several months prior to George's proposal. After the wedding, the newlyweds and both sets of parents had boarded a ship bound for the Kingdom of the Two Sicilies for the wedding trip.

Although the earls and their countesses had returned to London a few weeks ago, George and Ann were due back on the morrow. Given George had accepted a writ of acceleration—his father, Milton Grandby, had decided to live in Northumberland with his countess for the Season—his arrival back in London was cutting it close. Parliament was due to resume on Tuesday.

Then, while the Wellinghams were off to Italy with the young couple, their oldest son, Gabe, had quite suddenly married one of his colleagues from the British Museum. He and his wife, Frances, who already had a son, were living in Trenton House and continuing their employment at the museum. As a curator of ancient Greek artifacts, Gabe was inundated with pots and statuary that arrived on a daily basis while Frances, a potter, saw to the pottery restoration. The two hadn't yet taken a wedding trip, but would do so when the flow of Greek artifacts slowed down. Alexander wasn't sure when that would happen given their popularity with museum goers.

Now, his father was suddenly in love with his mother again.

Perhaps there was something in the water. Or Aphrodite was up to something. Or Cupid was practicing his archery.

Whatever it was, Alexander vowed he wouldn't be falling in love anytime soon. At one-and-twenty, he was far too young to be considering marriage.

CHAPTER 7
A COUNTESS' SEDUCTION

A few minutes later, in Stella's bedchamber

"Did I thoroughly scandalize my son?" Stella asked when she peeked out from her dressing chamber. "I was certainly scandalized when he asked me about an *affaire*," she added. "Had me wondering if he'd heard some untrue gossip." She didn't tell him about Lord Framingham's proposition in Floris the day before.

Given her bare shoulders, Harold was fairly sure Stella wasn't wearing anything. He closed her bedchamber door and leaned against it, chuckling. "He's merely curious, I think."

"He isn't looking to hire a mistress, I hope," Stella said as she emerged from the dressing room. The silk wrapper she wore wasn't secured with a tie, and the hem and edges floated behind her as she made her way to him.

She wore nothing underneath.

Harold was glad his cock knew what to do, because the rest of him seemed to have forgotten.

What the hell was wrong with him?

Why hadn't he been bedding his wife on a more regular basis these past few years?

This past decade?

"He... he hasn't mentioned it," Harold stammered. He might have said more, but Stella's body was suddenly pressed against his, and her mouth cut off any opportunity for him to respond.

Twenty years ago, he would have been the one to initiate such a scorching kiss. He would have been the one to undo his top coat buttons and those of his waistcoat and pantaloons.

But not tonight.

Before he could even think about buttons—Stella's tongue had slipped between his lips and essentially cut off his ability to think—she had the fastenings undone, the coat off his shoulders, and his pantaloons pushed down past his hips. She might have even had his manhood firmly wrapped in one hand and his balls cupped in the other, except the bottom of his shirt was in the way.

A moment of clear thinking allowed him to lift up the fabric before moving his hands to cradle the globes of her bottom. When one of her legs wrapped around his thigh and it was apparent she intended to do the same with the other, he leaned harder against the door. He lifted her and groaned through the kiss when his cock slid into her and her breasts pressed into his chest.

She broke the kiss to gasp. "I thought you'd never get here," she complained in a whisper.

For a moment, Harold was about to argue—he hadn't taken a detour on his way from the billiards parlor—but he thought better of it. Or his cock did. "Apologies, my lady. You can punish me if you wish."

With her arms wrapped around his shoulders and her legs entwined about his thighs, Stella tittered, "Punish you?" she countered. "Then I think you shall not be allowed to leave this bedchamber before morning."

Harold blinked as he attempted to thrust into her more deeply. "If that is your idea of punishment, my lady, then I accept my fate. Willingly." He lifted her slightly and thrust into her once more before adding, "However, I would request I serve my penance on your bed."

Stella's sound of amusement was muted when her lips met his shoulder. She hung on as he made his way in halting steps to the bed, the pantaloons down around his ankles hampering his ability to move.

He finally lowered her to the counterpane before continuing what he had started while propped against the door, managing to shed his shirt and free his feet of the pantaloons before climbing atop her.

Once he had served his penance and kissed her quite thoroughly, he fell asleep, still sprawled atop her.

Amused, but not surprised, Stella flicked the counterpane so it covered his bare back and settled her head against the side of his. The tattoo of his beating heart slowed to an even thud, and soon she joined him in slumber.

CHAPTER 8
A JEWELRY HEIST OF A
DIFFERENT KIND

The following day, at Ewen & Ewen Jewelers

The very last person Margaret Ewen expected to enter the shop on a rainy Friday morning was Mr. Tennison.

Despite the damp, he was impeccably dressed and dry, as if the sheets of water falling from the sky fell all around him but not down on him.

He probably has some arrangement with Zeus, she thought as she dropped the latest copy of *The Tattler* on her desk and hurried to greet him.

"Ah, Miss Ewen," he said as he tucked his top hat under an arm and gave a bow. He reached for her hand, and this time, she held it out for him. He kissed the back of it as she held her breath.

If she hadn't, she was sure an audible gasp would escape her lips. How could a man's simple kiss send so many skitters of pleasure shooting up an arm that usually felt little if anything at all?

"Good morning, Mr. Tennison. Are you already in need of more gold?"

He nodded. "At least two ounces. And some gemstones. Mayhap as many as two-hundred," he replied. "Or, as few as a hundred if they're larger."

Margaret's eyes rounded. "But, sir. Only yesterday you assured my father you wouldn't be a competitor," she argued, attempting to make her words sound light despite the alarm she felt.

"True," he agreed. "But now I have need of a parure. One I wish to make myself, given the woman is very special to me."

Margaret felt a rock drop into her stomach. "Oh," she breathed, trying hard to hide her disappointment. "How very lucky she must be."

"I hope she feels that way when it's bestowed on her. Her behavior of late has been rather... amorous," he went on, oblivious to Margaret's growing despondency. "So I'm to spare no expense in its creation."

"Of course," Margaret managed to say, mentally chiding herself for her reaction. If Mr. Tennison was frequently on exhibit at the British Museum, posed on his pedestal displaying the very expression he was aiming in her direction, then he no doubt had his choice of mistresses from the hundreds of women who stared at him with their mouths wide open. Their behavior was probably amorous all the time.

They probably even offered him *carte blanche*.

"I've been told there is a gemologist here who comes highly recommended," he said. "Is he available?"

Margaret blinked. "I am." Thoughts of who his mistress might be flew from her head, replaced with the wonder of who might be her new favorite person.

Someone had highly recommended her to the Greek god.

"*You* are the gemologist?" he asked, his head angling to one side as if he thought that he might have the wrong person.

"You are in fact speaking with *her*, sir," Margaret whispered, unable to hide her new-found pride. She gave her head a shake, as if to clear it, and then noticed the sheath of parchment he held in his other hand. "Is that a drawing of a bracelet?" she asked, a dark brow furrowing with her curiosity.

Alexander lifted his left hand and stared at it, almost as if he had forgotten he had one. "Indeed," he replied as he placed the drawings on the countertop.

Margaret studied the top drawing, a rendering of a bracelet made up of a line of collets. Their graduated sizes suggested the bracelet would be a *rivière*—a river of light— should those collets be set with diamonds.

She pushed it aside to reveal one for a matching necklace, the arrangement of the collets the same as the bracelet. In the middle, the collets were interrupted by a link where the clasp for a pendant was attached. About to push aside the drawing of the necklace, she couldn't when Alexander's hand pressed down on the parchment.

"I have assurances from both my father and my sister that you are the one that can assist me with this project."

Glancing up, she saw how he stared at her with an intensity that had her insides doing somersaults. Either that, or the flutterby collection from the local conservatory had escaped and found a new home.

She sighed. "I have been studying gemstones since I was old enough to look through a loupe," she said. "Although now I am more inclined to use a microscope."

"A microscope?" Alexander repeated in surprise.

"Occlusions are far easier to spot under a microscope."

Alexander furrowed a brow. "Did you... did you go to school?"

"I had a governess and then a tutor," she replied. "But I learned about gemstones from my father." She motioned to where Adam Ewen was bent over his workbench, intent on the creation of a new pearl ring. "What sort of stones were you considering for your *rivières?*"

Alexander regarded her a moment, his attention drawn to her left arm. From the way she held the limb slightly bent and tight against her front, he decided she had a withered arm. "I had hoped a gemologist might help me make that choice," he finally replied.

"Have you designed the entire parure?"

The query had him nodding. "I have," he replied, lifting his gloved hand from the drawings. He pulled out the bottom drawing, which featured a ring made up of the same graduated collets and then prongs for three larger gemstones.

Margaret inhaled softly. His mistress would be the best bejeweled woman in all of London! Despite the thought, she found she was intrigued by the project. "What colors would you like to include?" she asked, excitement evident in her voice. "And would you like the settings in silver or gold? Knowing that, I could recommend stones we might use to make it exactly as you envision it."

Alexander inhaled to respond and then sighed. "I only need the gemstones, my lady. I will make the settings myself."

Blinking, Margaret stared at the young man a moment before she nodded. "I apologize. When you bought the gold yesterday, I understood you were working on a signet ring."

His eyes lowering to one side, Alexander said, "I was. I still am, or at least, I'll return to it when this is completed. As I said yesterday, this making jewelry is merely an avocation."

"Still, your designs will make an exquisite parure. The woman will be the envy of anyone who sees her wearing it."

"Thank you."

"Now, might I show you some stones?"

Alexander glanced around again. "If I told you her ballgown will be made from...." He reached into a waistcoat pocket and pulled out a small note. "'Watered silk in shades of scarlet'," he recited, "would that help? This information is by way of my sister, so I suppose we must trust it."

Margaret considered the comment. *Sister?* She had never heard of a mistress befriending the sister of her protector, but what did she know?

She wouldn't know anything at all of mistresses except that so many of her customers were gentlemen who purchased baubles for them—either when they contracted for their services or were about to send them packing. Sometimes they bought them for no reason at all.

Oh, there was probably a reason, she realized, sure her face had taken on a pink cast. Or by now, it was probably bright red.

"We must trust your sister," she announced. "Do you know the name of the woman's modiste? I could pay a call and request a swatch of the fabric," she offered.

Blinking, Alexander said, "You would do that?"

Lifting a shoulder, Margaret said, "Of course. I would prefer to match the reds perfectly." She hoped they wouldn't be using her face for reference. "Perhaps with garnets or maybe rubies, depending on the shade of red," she explained. "Or a combination, should there be a need for graduated reds."

"Rubies?" he repeated. "Rather expensive now, are they not?"

Margaret nodded. "They can be. At the moment, they are more costly than diamonds," she admitted.

"Then perhaps we consider only one for the pendant," he murmured.

"Is the pendant for the necklace also to be a brooch?" she asked, knowing the pieces in a parure were usually made so they could be used in a variety of ways.

"It could be," he hedged, not having done a separate design for a brooch.

She paused a moment. "Are you making your collets in gold? Or silver with a backing of gold? Or foil?"

Alexander's respect for the young woman went up a notch. He could save his father a good deal of blunt if he did the collets and their connections in silver. Then he would coat their backs in gold to prevent any tarnish from staining fabric or his mother's skin.

Harry Tennison, Earl of Everly, had insisted money wasn't an issue, though. His father seemed as if he had fallen in love with his countess. Again.

"Gold," he stated, rather liking how the young woman's eyes widened with what appeared to be increased respect.

Or perhaps she had decided he was ripe for the plucking. Or poking. She certainly wasn't in as teasing a mood as she had been the day before.

"Her modiste is Madame Suzanne in Oxford Street," he added.

"I am familiar with Madame Suzanne," Margaret replied. "Do you have a moment? I'd like to show you some stones. I keep a selection back in my office. Although I'm quite sure I don't have enough for all your pieces, I can certainly acquire them once I know the sizes and arrangements you're in need of."

Alexander was sure he wouldn't be able to discern a garnet from an amethyst—he was only sure of stones that were yellow, gold, blue, or diamonds—but he wanted to spend more time in the young woman's company. "Lead the way," he said, his gaze once again going to her bent arm.

Margaret quickly retrieved the drawings from the counter and then moved toward her office, giving her father a nod when he lifted his head and gave her a questioning glance.

"Please, be seated," she said as she moved to the safe at

the back of the office. She closed the heavy door to hide the safe's only contents—a metal container and a ring box—and then hurried to clear her desk of the stacks of news sheets that cluttered it.

"Did Lady Framingham claim her ring?" Alexander asked, remembering the incident of the recovered ring from the day before.

"Not yet," she replied, "Although I rather imagine she hasn't received the note my father sent yesterday." She took a seat at her desk and arranged the drawings beyond the ledge of a board covered in black velvet.

"I don't have the tools necessary to recut any stones," Alexander said.

"So your collets will require a very exact sizing," Margaret reasoned, pulling a tiny ruler from the top drawer in her desk. "These appear to be drawn to size."

"That's correct," he replied, "but they'll have some wiggle room," he argued. He watched as she measured one of the collets on his drawing of the bracelet. When she didn't say anything right away, Alexander added, "I'll close them tightly around the edges to prevent the gems from escaping."

"Is there a reason you're not doing prongs?" she asked as she removed a slim drawer from a chest adjacent to her desk. She placed the velvet-lined drawer in the middle of her desk and then pulled a second drawer out of the chest.

"I find they can get in the way of a gem's ability to reflect light," he replied, his gaze going to the first tray of red gemstones. He didn't see them as red, but rather as a pale gray with an occasional shimmer.

"So true," she murmured as she studied the gems in the second tray before she stacked it atop the first. "Depending on the color of the watered silk, I'm thinking one of these rubies will be spectacular in the brooch," she commented.

She held one of the larger rubies up to the light, and

Alexander leaned toward her in an effort to see it with the light from the window behind it. He was secretly glad he could tell the difference between it and a garnet, even though they both appeared gray.

"If the watered silk tends to a more rose red color, or has more pink in it, then would you consider red coral? Or pearls, perhaps?"

Alexander shook his head. "I would prefer gemstones," he said.

"Very well," she replied as she once again used the ruler to take measurements from his drawings. "What about diamonds? Are you thinking of using any in between all the red? Or some other stone for contrast, perhaps?"

Watching as she took and then recorded the measurements of the collets on a slim sheet of paper, Alexander wasn't sure how to respond. He hadn't given a thought to including anything but stones to match the color of his mother's gown. "Can you show me an example?"

"Of course." Margaret was about to stand up to retrieve a bracelet from a display case when her father appeared in the doorway.

"What can I bring you?" he asked.

Margaret's gaze darted to Mr. Tennison before she said, "The bracelet you made for last year's competition."

Noting how her father's face brightened at seeing their customer from the day before, Margaret said, "Mr. Tennison, I don't believe I introduced you to my father yesterday. May I present Adam Ewen?"

Alexander stood and held out a hand to the jeweler. "I've not had the pleasure," he said as he shook hands with Adam. "My father recommended your shop, and he told me to be sure you sent him the bill."

"Ah, of course. And may I present my daughter, Margaret?"

About to claim they had already introduced themselves to one another the day before, Margaret's eyes widened a fraction. She knew her father would usually ask *her* if he could present her to a customer. The fact that he was asking the customer meant the Greek god was someone of higher rank.

Much higher rank.

His pedestal at the museum was probably halfway to the ceiling.

It also meant she had to stand and offer her right hand so that he could shake it.

She did so. At least it wasn't her withered arm.

"You may, sir," Alexander Tennison said. As before, he bowed over her hand and kissed her knuckles.

Had she been an insipid chit, she might have swooned. Had she been a young lady fresh from the schoolroom attending her first ball, she might have fainted. As a young woman once again mortified by the circumstances at hand while experiencing the skitters of delight his lips created, she tittered.

When Mr. Tennison raised a questioning glance to meet hers, Margaret raised her smaller left hand to cover her mouth. "I apologize, sir, but I'm not wearing gloves, and it... it tickled," she whispered.

She almost—*almost*—regretted her words, for the look Alexander Tennison returned was filled with far more than good humor. Not the least bit of offense showed in his expression.

But a good deal of lust did.

As if her father had known better than to be present for their pleasantries, he had already moved to the display case in the shop in search of the bracelet in question, leaving Margaret to fend for herself. She dipped a curtsy before she tucked her hand back into the folds of her skirts and returned to her chair.

"Here we are," Adam said when he reappeared with the bracelet.

Margaret watched as Alexander stared at her for perhaps a moment too long before he redirected his gaze on the jeweler and the bracelet he held.

"Oh, I see what you mean," he commented. The bracelet's series of sapphires were occasionally broken by a single mine-cut diamond.

"After every five sapphires, there is a diamond," Margaret explained. "The matching necklace had the diamonds in graduated intervals. Three, five, seven," she added. "I would show it to you, but it was purchased shortly after the competition."

"Pity," Alexander murmured as he studied the bracelet. He finally set aside the jewels and sighed. "Depending on the fabric, I'm thinking the contrasting gems should be something other than diamonds," he said. "Amber, perhaps. Or... citrine. The contrasting colors are more important in the earrings and pendant, of course."

Margaret's eyes widened. "Oh, that's brilliant, Mr. Tennison," she murmured. "Then the jewelry could be worn with a primrose gown," she added, her excitement palpable.

Rather pleased with himself, Alexander gave a nod. "Let us hope you're able to come up with over a hundred garnets, a single ruby, and..." He did a quick calculation in his head. "Fifty citrines. Maybe more."

"Oh, I will, Mr. Tennison," she breathed. "I promise. In fact, I am to meet with a gem merchant later today. I might have what you need by tomorrow. Is there a chance you could return? Sometime after ten o'clock?"

For a moment, Alexander wished he could kiss the young woman whose enthusiasm for his project had him more excited than he had been for anything in a long time.

"There is," he murmured. "I look forward to it," he added

before he kissed the back of her hand. He helped himself to his drawings. "I'll return with these tomorrow. I'm off to make collets."

He enjoyed the sound of her giggle as he took his leave of the jewelry shop.

CHAPTER 9
AN EARL'S SEDUCTION

*L*ater that night, in Harold's bedchamber

Having felt his wife's foot make its way onto his during that evening's early dinner, Harold knew she was thinking the same thing he was.

How much longer did they have to stay at the dining table before it would be acceptable for them to make their excuses and retire to her bedchamber?

They had barely finished the second course.

Harold begged off before the dessert course, claiming he had some reading to do.

Stella watched him go and then asked a footman to see to it their desserts were delivered to his bedchamber. She stayed in the dining room while Alexander and Helen finished their desserts, making light conversation as she drank the last of her wine.

When Alexander finally announced he was going out rather than staying for a glass of port, Helen huffed and asked if she could be excused.

Once the two were out of the dining room, Stella made

her way up to his bedchamber. Anticipation had her steps quickening as she neared her door.

Her expectations were met when Harold, wearing only a banyan, met her at the door and asked her what had taken her so long.

"I couldn't just leave the table as you did," she replied, turning so he could undo the fastenings of her dinner gown.

Harold made quick work of undressing her, his hands smoothing over her heated skin after each layer of clothing was removed. He quit before he made it to her stockings, garters, and slippers. "Will you mind terribly if I do this quickly? I promise I shall be more patient later tonight," he pleaded as he lifted her into his arms and moved her to the bed. He followed her down, shedding his banyan as her stockinged legs bent and gripped his thighs.

"Hurry," she whispered.

Surprised by her reply, Harold paused, the tip of his cock poised at her entrance and ready to plunge into her. He could feel her wetness, smell her arousal. "Hurry?" he repeated.

"Yes." When she saw how he stared at her, she bent her elbows and lifted her torso from the bed. "Please."

The move had Harold's attention moving to her breasts, down to her belly and beyond to the dark curls where his cock fairly throbbed. "I think not, my lady," he murmured as his head lowered so he could kiss her breasts and suckle her nipples.

She inhaled softly, her breaths coming quicker. She nearly fainted when she felt his tongue caress her swollen womanhood. "I thought you wanted to do this quickly," she managed to get out between gasps for air.

He held up a finger as if to indicate he needed another moment, and then he moaned as Stella's back arched. He heard his name in the form of a cry from her lips, saw how her hands clutched the bed linens. He moved atop her and plunged himself into her wet depths, groaning as he did so.

"Oh, this is... this is what you meant... when you said... quickly," she stammered, her voice breathy as he thrust into her over and over again. When he paused and held himself suspended over her, his breath held and the cords in his neck straining, she clenched on his manhood and delighted in watching him as ecstasy took hold. Her hands slid down his sides to the back of his thighs, and she brushed a finger along the back of his sac. The wash of warmth filled her as he quietly cursed and then lowered his body to hers.

Stella smiled as she wrapped her arms around his shoulders. "I don't mind quickly at all," she whispered.

After a moment, she realized he was already asleep. She sighed, deciding that later, she would awaken him and insist he do it again.

Who knew how long this new behavior of his would last?

CHAPTER 10
FRIENDS CONVENE AT WHITE'S

*M*eanwhile, at White's, 36 St. James Street, Mayfair
The note from George Grandby, Viscount Hexham, had arrived via a Torrington House footman a few minutes before dinner.

> *Alex,*
>
> *I'm back in London. My beloved already has an invitation to a ladies' card party this evening, so drinks will be on me at White's. See you at ten o'clock?*
>
> *Hexham*
>
> *P.S. I'm sending a note to Gabe as well. Can you believe the reprobate is now my brother?*

Alexander read the short missive and grinned. Apparently, the newlywed wasn't too exhausted from his travels. The mention of a ladies' card party had him curious, though.

Did ladies play cards without their husbands at such affairs? Did they place wagers? Gamble?

At that evening's dinner, he had broached the subject with his mother, whose impish grin said far more than her verbal response. "Only married women are allowed, and, yes, we do occasionally place wagers on the play," she acknowledged.

"Small amounts? Or...?"

Stella exchanged a quick glance with her husband before she sighed. "It depends on who is present and how displeased they might be with their husbands."

Helen gasped as Harold chortled. "Framingham discovered his wife had lost three-hundred pounds in one of those card games," he commented.

Stella blinked, rather alarmed by her husband's mention of the marquess. "Oh?" she responded. She hadn't been at that particular party. But she had learned something about the marchioness at the last tea party she had attended.

"She found out he was having an *affaire* and took umbrage," Harold went on.

Alexander caught the odd expression that crossed his mother's face at the mention of the *affaire*. Was that glee he saw? Was his mother happy to learn one of her peers had succeeded in her quest for retribution? He couldn't imagine any woman wishing to share a bed with the overweight man whose body odor foretold his eventual arrival well in advance.

But what did he know?

Or perhaps it was a wince she exhibited. Perhaps she didn't agree with the marchioness' idea of revenge. If so, was it because she thought it merely wrong, or because...?

Alexander gave his head a quick shake. Surely his mother wouldn't have had an *affaire* with the Marquess of Framingham. The idea was so abhorrent, he dropped his fork on his dinner plate and regarded his boiled potatoes, momentarily imagining them to be Framingham's bollocks.

He picked up his fork and stabbed one of the potatoes, feeling satisfaction at seeing it cleaved in half just before it broke open, the two rounded sides rocking on his plate as steam wafted from the middles.

For the rest of his life, he would be unable to eat boiled potatoes.

"Ah, the traveler has returned," Alexander said when he found George Grandby, Viscount Hexham, in a small salon at the back of White's. From the way George lounged in the upholstered chair, with one ankle resting on a knee and a glass suspended from one hand, he might have been there all day.

George grinned and immediately unfolded his tall frame to stand before Alexander. The two were nearly of the same height, and they shook hands as they regarded one another.

"Married life seems to agree with you," Alexander remarked, noting how George's complexion had changed from that of a pasty-faced Brit to one with more color. Although he wasn't exactly bronzed from the sun, he was definitely tanned.

"Oh, it does," George affirmed as he moved to take his seat. "Ann is an absolute jewel. On the trip, she never complained until..." He paused when Gabe Wellingham appeared and let out a guffaw.

"About time you're back," Gabe scolded as he stepped forward and greeted his friends. All about the same age, they had attended school together and were all distantly related. George's wife, Ann, was Gabe's only sister.

"We might have returned when your parents did," George replied, referring to the Earl and Countess of Trenton, "but your sister was quite insistent she wished to remain in Italy, and I wasn't about to argue. Gave us a chance to visit Florence." He retook his seat as Alexander and Gabe settled into adjacent wing back chairs. A footman took their drink orders and disappeared from the small room.

"You mentioned Lady Hexham never complained,"

Alexander prompted, curious as to what George had been about to say about the former Ann Wellingham before Gabe had appeared.

"She didn't," George affirmed. "At least, not until this dunderhead sent a letter saying he had gone off and married a potter," he added, directing his attention to his new brother-in-law. "Ann was quite upset she missed your nuptials."

Gabe allowed a shrug. "Couldn't be helped. Once I was finally able to convince Frances to marry me, which was harder than it should have been—"

"No!" George interrupted, feigning shock as a huge grin split his face. "I can't imagine there's a woman who could deny a man who looks like Cupid incarnate," he teased.

"—We made it a double with Cousin Emily and James Burroughs," Gabe explained, ignoring George's jibe. "So we were in good company."

"And this wife of yours? I understand you met her at the museum?" George prompted.

"Frances. She's a colleague. An excellent artisan. Used to be a potter for Wedgwood. She restores pottery at the British Museum."

Even as George appeared suitably impressed, Alexander leaned in George's direction. "In case you hadn't heard, he's already a father," he said in a hoarse whisper, his brows waggling.

"I heard that, too. Ann told me when she received a letter from her mother. She's over the moon about being an aunt and plans to invade Trenton House on the morrow," George murmured. "As for me, I shall be in good company when I join Gabe's ranks in the autumn. Ann is expecting a baby."

The other two hooted their congratulations as George flushed and the footman delivered their drinks. They happily toasted the news.

"Have you let Cousin Thomas know you're back?" Gabe asked of George.

George shook his head. "I sent a note to Arthur's to let him know of my return," he replied, referring to the club that included bachelor quarters on the first floor. "The footman came back within an hour and told me Grandby had gone off and married a duke's daughter. Moved to some estate north of London?" he added, as if he couldn't believe what he had learned about Thomas Grandby. "I was only gone a few months."

"I think he was as surprised as any of us," Alexander murmured. "He married Lady Victoria, Somerset's daughter, and bought Fairmount Park for her. She trains horses there."

George stared at Alexander for a long moment. "Didn't *you* have feelings for her at one point?"

Alexander's eyes widened. "Me?" he replied in shock. As Gabe chuckled, he added, "I hardly know her. Somerset rarely came to London," he argued.

"So... who are *you* considering? Lady Juliet, perhaps? She's—"

"Married," Alexander stated, smirking at his friend.

Nearly choking on his drink, George was attempting to clear his throat when Gabe said, "To Christopher Carlington."

George boggled. "He's old enough to be her father!"

Alexander nodded. "Bumped his head and fell in love. Despite her indifference, he courted her. He cajoled her. Finally convinced her—and her parents—that he was the right man for her."

"He allows her to continue her work with horses—"

"She's good friends with Lady Victoria. Lady Grandby, I mean," Gabe quickly corrected himself.

"—and he is having a huge stables built for her. Bought a

townhouse in Curzon Street, too," Alexander went on, despite Gabe's interruption.

Appearing as if he was still trying to make sense of the changes that had happened since he had last been in London, George regarded Alexander a moment. "So will it be one of the Norwick twins for you?" he asked.

Dahlia and Diana Fitzsimmons, daughters of the late David, Earl of Norwick, lived in Park Lane with their younger twin brothers.

The children in all four families had grown up knowing one another, their aristocratic parents attending all the same functions while the boys attended the same schools. Nearly all the girls had stayed in London for finishing school.

Although Alexander couldn't tell the twins apart, he was fairly sure it was Dahlia who had stared at him for most of the last dinner party they had attended at Torrington House. That was the night George had proposed to Ann, and Lady Angelica, George's sister, had agreed to marry Sir Benjamin, an astronomer of some renown.

Alexander recalled the hint of disappointment he had felt at learning Angelica was to marry another. There was a time when he pined for the blonde, blue-eyed daughter of the Earl of Torrington—despite her independent streak and the way she would punch her brother in the arm should she disagree with him.

As for Dahlia, he didn't think he would ever have feelings for her. Not that he didn't like her—he did—but not in the way he thought he should feel for a woman with whom he was supposed to live the rest of his life.

A waving hand in front of his face had Alexander giving a start.

"It wasn't a hard question," George teased.

Alexander blushed as he rolled his eyes. "I rather doubt either one of the Norwick twins will still be available when I finally decide to marry," he argued. Unbidden, an image of Miss Ewen flashed in his mind's eye. He shifted in his chair.

"I'm glad I didn't wait," Gabe said suddenly. "I rather adore having a family."

"I didn't wait because I feared Ann might end up married to someone else," George said, his manner sobering. "I couldn't abide the thought of her with another man. I had a hard enough time in Italy with the men who merely glanced in her direction."

Wincing at the edge in George's voice, Alexander was secretly glad he didn't have such violent feelings for anyone. He supposed George's would temper over time, once the novelty of marriage wore off and he and Ann settled into a routine.

"If you're not of a mind to court anyone, what's keeping you occupied these days?" Gabe asked.

Alexander brightened. "I'm making a parure, actually." At Gabe's look of surprise, he added, "Necklace, bracelet, earrings, and a brooch. Possibly a ring. You cannot say anything to anyone, though. It's a surprise. My parents' wedding anniversary is in a few weeks."

George and Gabe exchanged quick glances. "Sounds expensive."

"I'll know just how expensive on the morrow. I've a meeting at Ewen's to choose the gemstones and to buy some more gold."

"Why there?" George asked, leaning forward, his curiosity apparent.

Inhaling, Alexander said, "Father recommended it, and he's footing the bill, so..." He thought of his mother's comment about Miss Ewen. "The gemologist there is apparently who the women of the *ton* employ to replace the missing stones in their jewelry."

Gabe straightened. "My mother just discovered she's lost

a sapphire from her favorite bracelet," he said. "I could ensure my continued status as favorite son if I were to see to its repair. Not sure when I could manage it, given my schedule at the museum, though," he added as he considered how he and Frances usually weren't able to return to Trenton House until an hour before the dinner bell rang. They barely had time to spend with her son, David, before they had to change for dinner.

"If you'd like, I can stop at Trenton House on my way to the shop in the morning," Alexander offered. "Take the bracelet with me."

"Would you? Have the bill sent to my father, of course," Gabe replied. "It's very sporting of you to offer."

"Think nothing of it. Now, have you two received your invitations to Weatherstone's annual ball?"

George allowed a shrug. "Probably. I haven't had a chance to get through my correspondence yet."

"Ours arrived two weeks ago," Gabe said. "We're going. And you?"

"I am. I was wondering... do either of you know how I might secure an invitation for someone else? I haven't seen Bash since October," he said, referring to Sebastian Peele, the heir to the Weatherstone earldom. "I paid a call at Weatherstone Manor a couple of days ago but was told he was out."

"He's in town," Gabe claimed. "Been racing with the Four-in-Hand Club. Last I heard, they found a particularly good road out by Richmond Park and have been frightening the locals ever since."

George guffawed. "Although I might have felt a bit of jealousy at hearing of such exploits in the past, I find the prospect of breaking my neck no longer holds any appeal."

"I share your thoughts on the matter," Gabe agreed. "But Bash isn't of a mind to take on responsibility just yet."

"What is he? Thirty?" Alexander guessed.

"Older," George said, one of his brows arching. "Nearly five-and-thirty, I should think."

Alexander winced. Bash was certainly of an age to marry, and given the Earl of Weatherstone's advanced age, he would need to see to a wife and an heir and spare before long. Sebastian Peele was the only heir to the Weatherstone earldom.

"As for an invitation, Lady Weatherstone loves hosting a crush. If someone's been overlooked, she would wish to know," George said with some authority. His own mother, Adele Grandby, was older, and she was good friends with Lady Weatherstone. "A mention from your mother, and I should think an invitation would be dispatched immediately."

Alexander nodded. "I'll speak with Mother when I return home," he said. He noted George daring a peek at his pocket watch and chuckled. "Oh, dear. It seems we're keeping you from your bride," he teased.

"You are," George replied with a grin. "But I'm also fighting the urge to yawn. It's been a long day."

"I'll see to the drinks," Gabe offered. "And join you in taking my leave."

Shaking hands with his friends, Alexander thanked Gabe for the drink and watched as they departed.

For a moment, Alexander experienced a pang of jealousy at realizing both young men had wives waiting for them at home. Women who apparently looked forward to their return. Women who would welcome them into their beds. Women with whom they could make love before falling into satisfying slumbers.

I'm too young to take a wife, he thought as he finished off his brandy.

Then he remembered George's comment. The one about marrying Ann to prevent someone else from ending up as her husband.

When he did finally decide to marry, none of the young

ladies with whom he currently attended dinner parties—the young women with whom he had grown up in Mayfair, the ones whose parents were friends with his parents—would still be available to marry.

Had his future wife even made her come-out?

The thought had him realizing the young women he would have to choose from were probably Helen's age.

Helen's friends.

The ones who thought him gorgeous.

He would no doubt be dancing with a few of them at this Season's balls. Insipid young misses who had been so sequestered growing up that they had no idea how to converse with a gentleman. He would have to ask all the questions.

He rolled his eyes as he made his way back to his coach, his melancholy replaced with a lighter feeling when the memory of Miss Ewen's teasing replayed itself over and over in his head. Given the way she could hold her own in a conversation, she would be an excellent dance partner.

The idea of dancing with her nearly had Alexander stopping in his tracks.

The first ball of the Season was Tuesday night at Weatherstone Manor. He had an invitation. Nearly every peer of the realm was invited to the annual fete.

Although many bankers were invited, jewelers were not.

So how could he see to an invitation for Margaret Ewen? And then ensure she attended?

Alexander spent the entire trip back to Park Lane sorting what must be done, and who could do it. Although he wasn't pleased at the thought, it seemed he would have to rise early and make his case known.

To his mother.

CHAPTER 11

A MOTHER LEARNS
TOO MUCH

The following morning, breakfast parlor, Rosemount House

"Morning, Mother," Alexander said when he entered the breakfast parlor. Despite having stayed at White's until nearly eleven and then working in his foundry for a couple of hours after that, he had risen early and paid particular attention to his morning routine.

His father's valet, Dumphries, had chosen clothes appropriate for his appointment—buff pantaloons, a navy blue topcoat, a waistcoat embroidered with gold birds, and a white cravat. When he asked about the color of the waistcoat, Dumphries assured him it was not dark gray but rather scarlet. From the way he replied to the query, Alexander knew his father had apprised the valet of his color blindness.

"Good morning," Stella said, her eyes widening when she looked up from her correspondence. She glanced at a clock on the sideboard. "You're up rather early."

"I've an appointment... with my tailor," he replied, hoping she wouldn't notice his white lie. He had an appointment, but it was with Miss Ewen at the jewelry shop. "Weatherstone ball and all," he added as he took his seat.

A footman brought him a plate loaded with various breakfast foods while another saw to his coffee. "Will your gown be ready in time for the ball?"

Stella regarded her son with a furrowed brow. "I've an appointment with my modiste this afternoon for the final fitting," she replied. "And since when do you care about my ball gowns?"

Alexander sighed. "Oh, I don't, really," he once again lied. "But you would be vexed if it was not ready, and I shouldn't want to be in the same room if you discovered you would have to wear one from last year."

"Alex!" she scolded. "Although the fashions have changed somewhat since last spring, I don't really care if the old biddies find fault with what I wear."

Perhaps because she had spent so much of her young life in Greece and had been given the cut indirect as a result of her lineage, Stella had developed a rather thick skin when it came to the opinion of her peers. Knowing what his friends' mothers had to put up with when it came to gossip, Alexander liked that about her.

"What color did you decide to wear this year?"

At first, she aimed a curious look in his direction, but then seemed to understand why he asked. As if he was concerned he might call it by the wrong name in public. "If you really must know, I have Suzanne creating two new gowns for me."

Alexander gave a start. "Two?" he repeated. He was only making one parure.

Stella furrowed a brow. "Last year I had four made," she replied, her tone defensive.

"And you were stunning in all of them," he commented. "I remember Lady Framingham making a comment that your blue gown might go missing from your dressing room."

Boggling at his comment, Stella was about to put voice to

a protest, but then she hadn't been present to overhear the marchioness make such a claim. "Oh?" she finally replied, curious if Alexander mentioned Lady Framingham for any particular reason—other than the gown.

He shrugged. "So what are you having made for this Season?"

Stella relaxed when she realized the marchioness was no longer a subject of their conversation. "On the one that will be ready today, I would describe the main color as scarlet. Some might call it burgundy, but it doesn't have any purple in it. So... dark red," she said with authority.

"And the other?"

"Won't be done for another fortnight. A satin gown in primrose trimmed with roses above the hem and tiny roses around the neckline."

"Primrose?" he repeated. "According to Helen, that's the same as yellow?" he half-asked. "Jonquil?"

Stella angled her head to one side and allowed a long sigh. "Yes, and now I understand why it is you ask me," she said.

"You do?" Alexander asked, nervous that she had guessed what he was doing on behalf of his father.

"Well, of course. You wish to know the colors to save yourself from calling them by the wrong names. You're right to ask."

Relief settled over Alexander. "Yes, yes, that's it exactly, Mother. Thank you," he murmured.

With any luck, Miss Ewen would have had a chance to secure a fabric sample from Suzanne's for the red gown. If the modiste was astute, she might remember to include a swatch of the primrose satin as well.

"I may not usually care about what to wear to a ball," Alexander said, changing the subject. "However, I am interested in who's *at* the ball. In ensuring someone receives an invitation," he stammered.

Straightening in her chair, the letter she'd been reading forgotten, Stella said. "Oh?" as a grin appeared. "And who might she be?"

At that very moment, Alexander realized his plan to have his mother approach Lady Weatherstone about inviting Miss Ewen to the ball was flawed. How would he explain having met the young woman without giving away why it was he had come to meet her?

He could tell her he had been at Ewen's to purchase gold for the signet ring, he supposed, but that would hardly account for it.

When he didn't answer right away, Stella's interest increased. "Oh, come now. You cannot say such a thing and then not tell me who it is," she scolded.

"Miss Ewen," he blurted. "From the jewelry shop."

Stella leaned back in her chair, surprise apparent in her expression. Before she could say anything, Alexander added, "After what you said the other day—about how she was the one you went to for a replacement pearl—I paid a call at the shop and introduced myself. Bought some gold for father's signet ring. I thought I might purchase gems from her at some point in the future, you see, and it seems she's quite... *knowledgeable*."

"And you'd like to dance with her," Stella said, not making it a question.

Alexander frowned, amazed how his mother had jumped to the correct conclusion so quickly. "I would," he admitted.

"An invitation to your sister's come-out?"

The breath he'd been holding blew out in a huff. "Uh, yes," he finally agreed, having completely forgotten there was to be a ball in his sister's honor. "And perhaps the Weatherstone ball as well?"

Setting aside her letter, Stella regarded Alexander a moment before she said, "You'd like me to pay a call on Lady

Weatherstone and request that Miss Ewen be sent an invitation?" she clarified.

"Oh, could you?" he countered, with entirely too much enthusiasm.

Jerking back, Stella seemed to think on the idea a moment before she said, "I... I could, actually. Later this morning, in fact. Your father promised Lord Weatherstone he would deliver a bulb from one of the flowers in the conservatory." After a moment, she asked, "Are you quite sure Miss Ewen can dance?"

Alexander shrugged. "I... I think so. I am allowed two dances with the same partner, am I not? Thought I could make at least one of them a waltz."

"You *have* met Miss Ewen?" his mother asked. "Spent time in her company?"

Shrugging again, Alexander said, "A few minutes, yes. She was... very amiable. Teased me about having escaped my pedestal at the British Museum." He paused when he noticed how her eyes darted to one side, as if she might have been the one to have mentioned such a possibility in the first place. "I can understand why it is the ladies of the *ton* like to go to her." When his mother's expression didn't change but she continued to stare at him, his eyes rounded. "What is it?"

Stella sighed. "Perhaps you didn't notice her...?" She allowed the sentence to trail off as a blush colored her face. She meaningfully waved her left hand above the table, her elbow tucked into her side.

Alexander's eyes rounded again. "She's *married?*" he asked in alarm.

Rolling her eyes, Stella said, "No. No. I'm quite sure she's *not*. I was referring to her *arm*."

Alexander blinked. "Oh, her withered arm, you mean?"

It was Stella's turn to blink. "You noticed, and yet you... you offered her two dances? A waltz, even?"

Realization dawned on Alexander then. "Not exactly. But surely she can dance."

"Well, possibly," Stella hedged. "But a waltz? You'll have to..."

"Hold her closer than I would anyone else," he finished for her, imagining how Miss Ewen's right hand would rest on his shoulder. He'd have to bend his right arm a bit more than usual for her shorter left arm to reach his hand, which meant her entire body would be mere inches from his. He allowed a brilliant smile. "Why, Mother, you make it sound as if it will be quite scandalous," he accused.

"Some might think that," Harold said from where he'd been leaning against the door jamb. He had arrived about the time Alexander had mentioned the pedestal at the museum and, rather curious as to what that was all about, Harold had paused to eavesdrop before making his presence known.

"Father!" Alexander said as he gave a start and turned in his chair to regard the older man. "Would you?" he asked. "Think it was scandalous?"

Harold moved to kiss his wife on the lips—Alexander quickly averted his eyes—before settling into the chair next to hers. "I wouldn't, but then I am not an old biddy prone to gossip."

"What do you suppose caused her arm to be like that?" Alexander asked.

Inhaling slowly, Harold was about to answer when Stella said, "Forceps."

Harold and Alexander both turned to stare at her.

"Her mother died in the childbed, and whoever delivered her—a midwife or a physician—had to use forceps to pull her out," Stella explained. "Her left arm was partially crushed in the process," she added, as if she had been present for the delivery.

Alexander sucked air through his teeth.

"She probably suffered damage to the nerves," Harold commented, his brows furrowing. "It's a wonder she has use of her arm at all."

"She didn't when she was very young," Stella replied, her comment once again making it sound as if she were intimately familiar with Miss Ewen.

"How... how do you know all this, Mother?"

Stella gave him an assessing glance. "She told me." When he seemed surprised, she added, "Because... well, I asked," her manner suggesting she was embarrassed. "Apparently no one else had, or... or they just assumed she inherited it, or thought she was cursed in the womb. She seemed most relieved to tell *someone* what had really happened," she added on a sigh. "What's even worse is that her mother died giving birth to her."

Harold regarded Stella with a look of sadness, as if he might have known the woman in question. "How is it you were in her company to even ask?" he queried, as a footman delivered his breakfast.

"She is the one who replaced the pearl in my ring," Stella replied. "Nike came with me that day," she added, referring to her best friend. "She was terribly curious. Nike has never seen anyone with such an infirmity before, and despite my scolds, she couldn't help but stare at the poor woman's arm."

Having been born and raised on Mykonos, Nike Xenakis had come to England on the arm of Alex Bradley, a then-agent of the Foreign Office. The two had fallen in love when Alex, in his guise as Captain Jack Crawley, had been dispatched to Mykonos to help in the search for the missing Duke of Westhaven—Stella's father.

"Rather awkward for Miss Ewen if she noticed Mrs. Bradley staring at her," Harold murmured.

"Indeed, but I may have commented on the dexterity she

exhibited whilst she worked," Stella admitted. "And so she explained what had happened."

Alexander swallowed, reminded of Miss Ewen's fingers. Reminded he had imagined them trailing down the front of his body, through his dark curlies, along the throbbing vein on the back of his... He gave his head a shake, hoping his reddening face wouldn't be noticed by his mother.

Of course she noticed.

"Alex, are you all right?" she asked, about to reach out with a hand to place it on his forehead. "You look as if you have a fever."

He blinked. "I'm fine, Mother," he lied before clearing his throat and shifting in his chair. "I do hope Mrs. Bradley didn't offend her with her stares," he said, knowing Nike Xenakis Bradley's occasional queries—all innocent and usually borne from ignorance—could leave a new acquaintance uncomfortable in her presence. As a result, Nike was rarely invited to tea parties, but given her husband's position at Whitehall, she was frequently in attendance at Society events and the theatre.

"Not only was Miss Ewen not offended, I do believe she was glad to finally share her story with a sympathetic ear, as if she was unburdening herself of some terrible secret," Stella said in a quiet voice. She turned her attention to her husband. "Alex has asked that I pay a call on Lady Weatherstone—"

"Mother," Alex interrupted, his almost-olive complexion once again taking on a reddish cast.

"You wish to dance with Miss Ewen?" Harold asked.

Alex swallowed, amazed at how his father could take disparate bits of information and come to a logical conclusion —much like his mother.

Either that, or he had been eavesdropping on them before he made his presence known in the breakfast parlor. "I do," he admitted.

His father gave him an appreciative glance. "If your mother is unable to pay a call on Lady Weatherstone today, I can certainly do so. I'm going to take a flower bulb over to Lord Weatherstone," he said, his lips quirking with his amusement. "We're designing a new section of gardens on the west side of his property. To take advantage of the afternoon sun," he added. "He's a soft heart for young love, which is why I think he's become such a consummate gardener."

"Father...," Alexander started to protest.

Harold held up a hand. "No thanks are required. We shall see to it you have your dance with Miss Ewen."

About to mention he expected *two* dances with the gemologist, Alex thought better of it and merely returned his attention to his breakfast.

He sighed when he realized his eggs had gone cold.

CHAPTER 12

A JEWELER AND A GEMOLOGIST HAVE A HEART TO HEART

n hour later, at Ewen & Ewen, Ludgate Hill

Stifling a yawn, Adam Ewen stepped into his daughter's office and glanced around. His eyes rounded. "Were we robbed?" he asked in alarm.

Margaret looked up from the collection of garnets on the black velvet-covered board on her desk. She had arranged them in rows by size and set aside a few that were either too large or too small to fit in collets. "Not that I'm aware of," she replied, quickly coming to her feet to look around. She was about to move to the safe to ensure that it was still locked, but her father held out a staying hand.

He allowed a chuckle. "You must have an impending appointment," he said, an eyebrow waggling suggestively.

The office, which usually appeared disorganized, what with papers and tools scattered about and thin drawers of gemstones stacked willy-nilly, was now the model of neat and tidy. Gone were the piles of news sheets that once littered the desktop. Only scraps of a scarlet watered silk, a yellow satin fabric, and her black velvet board covered with garnets were atop the desk.

Giving him a quelling glance, Margaret settled back into her chair. "It was past time I do some housekeeping in here," she said. "Take inventory, which I did yesterday afternoon, so I would know how much I needed to procure from our supplier. I'm very glad I sent Mr. Goldman a note in advance to let him know of the need for garnets. I think he brought me every one he had in his possession whilst you were running your errands this morning."

"For what project?" Adam asked, realizing she must have taken an order he knew nothing about.

"Mr. Tennison's parure," she replied. "He's coming to choose garnets, a ruby, and some contrasting stones later this morning," she added.

"Tennison?" Adam repeated. "As in... Harold Tennison?"

Margaret shook her head. "No. Alexander Tennison." She wondered at her father's upraised eyebrows and expression of approval. "The one who was in my office yesterday. The one who looks like a Greek god," she added with an arched brow.

"No doubt," her father replied with a smirk.

Her eyes widening, Margaret regarded him with an expression of confusion. "What do you know of him?"

One shoulder raised in a shrug. "Nothing, really," he replied. "Other than he was being teased mercilessly by you," he accused. He chuckled when his daughter blushed. "His father has been in on occasion. Harold Tennison, Earl of Everly," he added as he leaned against the door jamb and crossed his arms. He waited to see her reaction and then nearly had a laugh at her expense.

Margaret stared at him a moment before she lowered her head to the desktop and pounded her forehead onto the velvet a couple of times, careful to avoid coming into contact with any of the garnets.

Adam chuckled again. "Oh, my darling daughter. What ever did you say to him?"

A moan erupted from Margaret, but she didn't raise her head. "I asked him if he escaped from his pedestal at the British Museum."

His chuckle turning to outright laughter, Adam said, "Well, he is part Greek, and he does look like he could be a son of Zeus." He sobered. "Hephastus," he murmured, referring to the Greek god of the foundry. "It's a good thing he's the heir, because he's quite accomplished when it comes to metallurgy, and I shouldn't wish to have him as a competitor when it comes to making jewelry."

Lifting her head from the desk, Margaret glanced over all the garnets and then turned her attention on her father. "But he already is," she replied, a hand waving over the gemstones. "He's designed a parure. Obviously for his mistress," she added, as she experienced a moment of disappointment at hearing her thoughts spoken aloud.

"A mistress, you think?" Adam asked. "Well, don't fash yourself. He's welcome to buy his gems here," he assured her. "Charge him whatever you would for any other customer. But no more," he added in warning, as if he thought she might be tempted to do so given his father's title.

Or because she thought the parure was for a mistress.

"Yes, sir," she replied. Then her eyes rounded once again. "Did you say *Everly?*"

Adam nodded. "I did."

She exhaled a long breath as she held her withered arm before her, her expression sorrowful.

"What is it? What's wrong?"

She shook her head. "Lady Everly was here a few weeks ago. Remember the pearl you had to set in that gold ring?"

Adam grinned. "I do. But then, I made that ring many years ago. For his lordship."

"She had a friend with her. A foreign woman, I think," Margaret said in a quiet voice. "She asked about my arm, and so I told them everything." She covered her eyes with open palms. "How could I have been so stupid?"

Adam sat in the chair next to her desk, his arm resting on the edge as he leaned toward her. "It was not stupid of you," he assured her. "Better they know the truth than to assume you were born with some sort of defect. Some sort of malady you could pass along to your children."

The mention of children had Margaret wincing. "I rather doubt I'll ever have children," she whispered, her eyes brightening with unshed tears.

"Oh, now," her father said in a quiet voice. "You needn't cry, daughter. As I've said before, there is a gem for every ring, and a man for every woman. You are no different."

Margaret quickly dried her eyes. She was fairly sure if there was a man for her, he wasn't living in London. He was probably in Greece or some far off land she would never in her life have the privilege of visiting.

He certainly wasn't standing on a pedestal in the British Museum.

CHAPTER 13
A VISIT TO WEATHERSTONE MANOR

*M*eanwhile, in Park Lane

When Alexander had finished his breakfast and left Stella and Harold alone in the breakfast parlor, the two glanced at one another before Harold leaned over and kissed her on the cheek.

"Thank you for spending the entire night with me," he whispered.

"Thank you for having me," Stella replied, her arched eyebrow suggesting her comment was meant as a double entendré. "I'm quite sure we've scandalized my maid since my bed isn't mussed."

"Oh, I'm sure we can probably see to unmaking it at some point today," he replied.

A blush colored Stella's face. "Harry," she murmured.

He regarded her a moment, a smirk lifting the corners of his lips. "On the one hand, I wonder what's happened to us these past few days, and on the other, I am of a mind not to question my good fortune."

Stella leaned over and kissed him on the cheek. "It's good to have you back." At his questioning glance, she added,

"Sometimes you're so involved with your plants, I think you've become one of them."

Sighing, he found he had to agree. "That one experiment? The one that confirmed Alexander's color blindness? I admit it had consumed my attention for several months, but now that it's done, I am... well, I am yours." He paused, his brows furrowing. "Well, at least until Tuesday. Parliament resumes, but I won't be gone all the time."

Stella's eyes darkened. "Well, I certainly know what to do with you for part of the days until then," she replied. "What will you be doing with the rest of them?"

"Perhaps..." He paused and moved his chair closer to hers. He took one of her hands in his. "Perhaps we might help our son."

Stella furrowed a brow. "You mean, because he's not taking this news of his situation very well?"

Harold started to reply and then exhaled. "I was thinking more because he seems to have taken an interest in a young woman. I've never heard him say he *wants* to dance with anyone before."

"Well, he's not going to be dancing with Miss Ewen unless she's at the ball," Stella argued. "Seems I have a service to perform in that regard, and it requires I pay a call on Lady Weatherstone."

"Ah," Harold replied, understanding her meaning. "I sent Peters to Lord Weatherstone with a note that I would be paying a call this morning," Harold said. "He's already returned with word that the Weatherstones are awaiting our arrival."

Stella's eyes widened. A quick look at the clock on the sideboard showed it wasn't even half-past nine. "He must really want your bulb," she commented.

"He does. When he learned we had *Fritillaria meleagris* in our conservatory, he very nearly had a coronary."

Her brow furrowing slightly, Stella asked, "Is that the droopy purple tulip with the little checks all over it?"

He grinned before he took a sip of coffee. "Indeed. We have several pink ones as well, but I think I shall wait a year or two before I make their presence known to him," He inhaled slowly. "Will you go with me? It's a glorious day. We could walk."

"That's a capital idea," Stella replied. "I can be ready in five minutes."

"Make it ten," he countered. "I still have to dig up the bulb."

Fifteen minutes later

The early spring day might have been bright and sunny, but there was a nip in the air as Harold and Stella made their way to Weatherstone Manor. The walk was short —not even a half-mile separated the two residences—and the couple covered the distance quickly as Harold cradled his rag-wrapped *F. meleagris* bulb in one arm. When he noticed how Stella kept glancing in his direction, he finally said, "A penny for your thoughts."

One of her arms already linked with his, Stella placed her other hand atop it. "I'm considering how I might bring up the topic of Miss Ewen with Agnes. I've never done this before, but given I'll be hosting a ball in not even three weeks for our daughter, I can already imagine how I might feel should someone ask me if I might include an additional person."

"Would you feel put out?" he guessed. "Or flattered?"

Stella inhaled softly. "Flattered?" she repeated.

"That your ball is so well regarded that others wish to attend? I should think Lady Weatherstone will be happy to learn there is a young man who is attending for the sole purpose of dancing with a particular young lady," he explained.

"But that's not his sole purpose for attending," she argued. "He would go even if Miss Ewen was not there."

Harold's gaze slid to the side as he made an odd keening sound. "But what if she was the *reason* he planned to attend? And if he learned she wasn't to be there that he might instead spend a night at his club?" His brows waggled as his face displayed a huge grin.

Stella gasped. "Are you suggesting I employ... blackmail?"

He continued to grin. "Something like that. I understand our son is gorgeous. Seems Lady Weatherstone would want to do whatever is necessary to guarantee a gorgeous man's attendance."

Stella's mouth dropped open in shock. "You men are incorrigible," she complained. "I would never," she added as they approached the double doors of the Weatherstone mansion.

Harold chuckled as he used the brass knocker. Expecting a butler to answer, he was surprised when Lord Weatherstone answered the door and waved them in. "I know you were expecting us, but—"

"Is that it?" the elderly earl asked as he reached for the fabric covered parcel in Harold's arm.

"It is," Harold replied as he allowed William Peele Sr. to take it, handling it as if it were a newborn babe. "Fresh from the ground, but already well on it's way to bearing flowers. I expect if you plant it today, you may have a bloom or two next week."

His cap of snowy white hair floating about his liver-spotted forehead, Lord Weatherstone's face lit up in delight. "Will you join me in the west gardens?" He turned and seemed to finally notice Stella. "Oh, forgive me, my lady," he said as he gave her a deep nod.

Stella curtsied. "Of course, Lord Weatherstone. I'm quite used to being a wallflower when it comes to live plants."

"As am I," Agnes Peele, Countess of Weatherstone, announced as she breezed into the hall, apparently from the breakfast parlor. She allowed Harold to take her hand and kiss the back of it even as she waved Stella to join her. "Come, join me for tea while these two dig in the dirt. I require a younger woman's thoughts on Tuesday's ball."

Stella grinned at Harold as she was swept away by the elderly matriarch.

Harold watched her go, his gaze lingering a moment before he finally turned his attention back to the earl. "Lead the way to your west garden, my lord."

Lord Weatherstone regarded him a moment, his bushy white brows waggling. "Haven't seen a man look at his wife quite like that in a long time," he murmured.

Pretending ignorance, Harold asked, "Quite like what?"

Chuckling as he led Harold down the corridor toward the back of the house, his ancient body bent forward, Weatherstone said, "Like he's in love and in lust, all at the same time."

Deciding not to argue, Harold said, "Well, that's probably because I am."

"Good. Now is not the time in your life to be taking a mistress," Weatherstone warned. "Much as you might be tempted, they're just a bother. My son is discovering it. Probably for the fourth or fifth time," he groused.

"Is Sebastian even married?" Harold asked. He knew the earl's only son had recently returned from the Continent. He had spent several years on a late Grand Tour.

"No," Weatherstone replied, obviously annoyed. "But he's getting to the age where he has to think about starting a nursery. He's already five-and-thirty, but you would think from the way he drives a coach-and-four and how much time he spends in the company of Cyprians that he's still a young buck."

"Oh, he'll settle down," Harold replied as they made their way through the earl's study and out an exterior door.

"Some poor woman is going to have to lock him up to a real ball and chain for that to happen," Weatherstone groused.

Harold tried to imagine the rather tall and well built Viscount Cougham with a shackle around one of his Hobys and found he had to struggle to keep a straight face. Cougham would hardly notice such an impediment.

"And then she'll have to secure the ball in some sort of immovable object so that he can't simply pick it up and carry it around with him," Weatherstone continued, as if he had guessed what had Harold so amused. "I cannot begin to imagine there is a woman in this country who could abide being married to him."

"All it takes is one," Harold replied, deciding not to mention it might have to be a Welsh milkmaid or a butcher's widow.

The west garden, already partially dug up, was backed by a yew hedge and featured some newly-planted rose bushes. Given the morning sun hadn't yet climbed high enough to clear the mansion's roof, the grounds were in shadow. "Point me to where you'd like that to go, and I can dig a hole for you," he offered.

The earl toddled to a place where there was already a hole in the newly-turned earth. "I've already beat you to it," he replied as he unwrapped the sprouted bulb and then gently lowered it into the hole. He made sure the green leaves and stem were protected as he did so.

Harold watched in fascination as Weatherstone used his bare hands to pack the loose soil around the base of the green shoots and then press it down with his booted foot. He lifted a nearby watering can and poured its contents onto the base of the plant.

"When you said you were ready for it, I did not realize how ready you were. I apologize for not having come earlier this morning," Harold teased.

Weatherstone waved a dirt-stained hand. "You timed it right," he replied, pulling a handkerchief from his pocket to wipe his hands. "I will admit I've been anxious to learn the results of your latest experiments, though. What had you so engrossed you couldn't be bothered to attend the last meeting?"

He referred to the group of gardeners who occasionally met at a local coffee house to discuss the latest news on plants and to share their grafting discoveries. "My son's inability to see certain colors," Harold finally replied. "The latest experiment confirmed what I've feared. He is color blind."

Weatherstone's bushy brows took on the shape of a cater-pillar across his forehead, and he gave his head a shake. "But not completely color blind?" he asked.

"True. He cannot make out reds or greens."

The older earl sucked air through his teeth and gave his head a shake. "Such a shame. He knows?"

Harold nodded. "He does. He's understandably upset about it, but... I have employed him to make some jewelry for our wedding anniversary, and I think the project has him suitably engaged."

"He'll need help," Weatherstone said, his tone serious.

"He's... he's working with Ewen's daughter to choose the gems."

"Ah! Good choice," Weatherstone replied, his attention turning to a rosebush. "I hope Ewen can stave off Baumeister's attempts to buy him out and buy her in the process. Nasty man, he is."

Harold turned from examining a tulip. "What's this?"

Weatherstone looked up from an early rose bud. "Samuel

Baumeister. He's a gem merchant that wants his own gift shop. Jewelry, gold and silver, much like Rundell and Bridge," he explained.

"So... he wants to be a competitor?"

"Oh, no. Rather than open one of his own and pay a jeweler and craftsmen and such, he wants Ewen and Ewen."

Uneasiness swept through Harold. "When you say he wants Ewen and Ewen—"

"He wants the shop, and he wants Ewen making the jewelry, at least as long as he can," Weatherstone replied. "He wants the jewelry, and all the gems, including Adam's daughter. Although I think he only wants her because she knows her stuff when it comes to the stones. Can't imagine he'd ever allow himself to be seen in public with her given her shrunken arm, poor girl. And because of that, he wants a bargain."

Harold straightened and regarded Weatherstone with a look of alarm. "You mean, he wants all that as a *dowry*?"

"Something like that," Weatherstone replied. "Ewen doesn't really want to sell, but times have been tough. He's never been asked to make jewelry for the monarchy, and without a Royal Warrant, he can't command the kind of prices Rundell and Bridge do."

Harold considered the comment, his brows furrowing. "His pieces are sometimes finer."

"I know. Agnes has a jewel box full of them," Weatherstone said proudly.

"I think my son is in love with her."

The older earl blinked. "With Agnes? Well, he can't have her. She's mine," he said before he burst into laughter that was soon interrupted by a fit of coughing.

Harold hurried to assist the older man, but Weatherstone waved him off. "Ha! Best laugh I've had in a week," he said in delight, wheezing slightly.

"I meant he's in love with Miss Ewen," Harold said quietly. "Or, at least as in love as a very young man can be," he amended. "Which is understandable given her knowledge of gems and his ability to make jewelry." He was about to add that she could see colors, but thought better of it.

"You *have* met Miss Ewen?" Weatherstone asked.

Harold nodded. "Of course. As has Stella. She has said many of her friends go to Miss Ewen to help them choose stones to replace missing gems in their jewelry."

Weatherstone leaned in and asked, "Her arm is not an issue for your son?"

Thinking this conversation sounded an awful lot like the one he had overheard earlier that morning, Harold allowed a shrug. "Apparently not. Especially once he learned it isn't a defect but rather a side effect of a bad birth."

Weatherstone angled his head to one side, his appearance suggesting he was plotting something. "Perhaps your son should see to some sort of... *partnership* with Ewen. Something that can stave off Baumeister and provide him with a gemologist who can see colors."

"My thoughts exactly," Harold replied. "Which is part of why Stella joined me today. She's hoping Lady Weatherstone will see to an invitation for Miss Ewen to attend your ball."

Weatherstone's bushy brows waggled again. "If a footman hasn't already been dispatched to the jewelry shop, then I shall see to it," he said as he turned to make his way toward the east gardens. "As I mentioned earlier, it's time we make some changes, and Agnes is of a similar mind."

"I admit I was rather surprised when our footman returned to say you were ready to receive us so early today," Harold remarked.

"Agnes was nearly as anxious for your arrival as I was," Weatherstone said. He surveyed the rest of the west garden before heading back toward the house. "I know she was looking forward to spending time with your countess. They both have balls to see to."

"I suppose you're expecting a crush," Harold murmured as he bent to examine a rose bush.

"Probably," Weatherstone replied. "Although things are different these days. Those in power seem to be changing."

"Oh?" Harold responded, his attention turning from the plant to regard the old man. "How so?"

Weatherstone was studying the new shoots of some tulip bulbs. "Time we get some new blood into these events, and I don't just mean these young girls having their come-outs this year."

"Then who do you mean?"

Straightening as much as his bent back would allow, Weatherstone said, "The rest of what we used to call the *ton*," he replied. "Money talks, Everly. Bankers, the wealthy tradesmen—"

"Jewelers?" Harold offered, wondering if Stella was having any luck with her request of Lady Weatherstone.

"Goldsmiths, yes," the earl said. "Not just the titled folk."

"For their youth? Or for their money?" Harold quipped.

"Both, actually," Weatherstone said as he moved to another plant and stood over it. "The future of the aristocracy is at risk. Our lands can't always be counted on to pay the bills," he explained. "Horse racing is too unpredictable. Any sort of gambling will have you losing your unentailed properties if you let it get out of hand. Although I want my son to marry a daughter of the aristocracy, I have half a mind to tell him he should marry the daughter of a wealthy tradesman. Someone who can see to shoring up the coffers in the event we continue to have crop losses and inflation."

Harold understood the older man's concerns. Although most aristocrats could afford a year or two of losses, at some point their properties would suffer from deferred maintenance. He already knew of aristocrats whose tenant cottages had been in need of repair or replacement for over a decade. "I suppose owning a jewelry store might be a logical way of diversifying," Harold murmured. The information would have be to be kept quiet, though. The *ton* didn't look favorably upon aristocrats owning businesses, even if many of them did.

"Now you're thinking for the future," Weatherstone said.

His brows arching with his agreement, Harold considered why it was an earl in his seventies seemed to embrace the future while the younger members of the aristocracy seemed intent on living in the past. In resisting the change that was bound to happen. "Even if Alex doesn't pursue Miss Ewen for more than a professional relationship, I think I shall look into the investment."

The older earl winked. "If you do not, please do inform me. I shouldn't like to miss the opportunity to own a jewelry shop."

"How long do I have?" Harold asked, his query made in a teasing voice.

Weatherstone considered the question a moment. "Three weeks," he stated. "If you haven't secured the promise of a sale by then, I shall make an offer Mr. Ewen cannot turn down."

Startled, Harold blinked. "I accept your terms," he replied, rather shocked he had just agreed to make an offer on a jewelry shop.

CHAPTER 14
AN APPOINTMENT TO SECURE A DANCE OR TWO

A half-hour later, Ewen & Ewen, Ludgate Hill

Alexander paused before entering the jewelry shop, gazing at his reflection in the mullioned window panes. Behind one, there was a brooch featuring what he supposed were multicolored gemstones. He could make out sapphires and citrines and the occasional topaz. The rest appeared gray.

He tried to guess the identity of the gray gemstones. Garnets, rubies, emeralds, mayhap?

Behind another window pane was a diamond necklace. The gems had been backed with foil in an attempt to increase their sparkle. He had never been impressed with diamonds, knowing they couldn't be properly cut to reveal the brilliance that was buried within. This particular necklace had him changing his opinion, though, as the gems seemed to gleam in the morning sun that pierced the window.

He tucked his top hat beneath one arm as he entered the shop. Immediately moving to the necklace, he pulled it from its display to examine it more closely.

"The diamonds are double mine cut," a feminine voice

said from his left. "And they're set with a silver foil backing to give the stones more fire."

Alexander afforded Margaret Ewen a quick glance before placing the necklace back on the display shelf. "Careful, Miss Ewen, or you will change my mind about what to use for a contrasting stone in the parure we're designing," he commented. He reached for the hand she held tucked against the front of her waist, noting it covered the hand of her withered arm. Although he felt a slight resistance at first, she allowed him to lift it to his lips as he bowed. "How are you on this glorious sunny day, Miss Ewen?"

Margaret managed an awkward curtsy once she had her hand back in place, momentarily stunned by his greeting and by the scent of his cologne. Notes of amber and citrus and something far more masculine combined to make for a welcome change from the Bay Rum and spice so many young men seemed to prefer these days. "I am well, thank you. And you, Mr. Tennison?" She turned to face the direction of the small office at the back of the shop, one of her shoulders nearly close enough to touch his.

"Better than I have been for several days," he replied.

Margaret's expression changed to one of curiosity. "You didn't seem ill when you were last here."

"Oh, it was nothing," he replied, "Just poor spirits at the time." He noted her expression of concern. Touched, he added, "I had learned something about myself that is unfortunate but not fatal."

Thoughts that his mistress might have left him with a sexually transmitted disease had Margaret momentarily feeling triumph. She shouldn't know of such things, of course, but how could she not when most of her clientele purchased jewels for their mistresses? When they spoke of their deepest, darkest secrets while her father took their orders and assured them he would create a memorable bauble?

It served him right. Mr. Tennison deserved whatever he had contracted by way of the overpaid tart.

In her mind's eyes, his pedestal at the British Museum lowered in height by several feet.

"You're not going to ask me what had me so blue?" Alexander asked, his voice tinged with disappointment.

Margaret gave a start. She inhaled, preparing herself for his answer. "It's really none of my business, Mr. Tennison, but since you seem inclined to share, then please do so."

Whatever could he say that would shock her at this point?

"You won't tell anyone else?"

The whispered question sent the most unusual sensations coursing beneath her skin. "I will keep your secret, of course," she assured him, her voice breathy.

Who would she tell?

Alexander inhaled and bent so his head was closer to hers. "I am—"

"Margaret?" her father said as he entered the shop from the back. "Oh, pardon me. I didn't realize you were with a client," he said as he stepped behind his workbench.

Alexander immediately straightened while Margaret's attention went to Adam. "Yes, sir. Mr. Tennison has an appointment to look at gemstones today," she reminded him, hoping the flush of red she felt on her face wasn't too apparent. For a moment, she was sure Alexander was about to whisper in her ear, or perhaps even kiss it. Flutterbies swirled around her insides at the thought of what his secret might entail.

His desire to kiss her, perhaps?

Or something that no one else knew?

Glancing around as if he wanted to be sure there wasn't anyone in the shop besides Adam Ewen, Alexander nodded. "Might we go somewhere more private? Your office, mayhap?"

Nodding, Margaret led him to her office and closed the windowed door once he had passed over the threshold. "You may speak freely," she encouraged. "No one can hear us in here."

Alexander inhaled and then blurted, "I have a difficult time identifying gemstones." He held his top hat in front of him as if he were using it as a shield.

"As do most people," Margaret replied with a slight shrug. Disappointed his secret was so mundane, she added, "That's why some of our competitors' clients come to me. To ensure that what they have paid for are indeed real." After a pause, she said. "And it helps when I'm dealing with gem merchants. Not all of them are trustworthy."

Some were downright dastardly.

"I can identify most gems," Alexander argued, "but sometimes they appear... gray to me," he added on a sigh.

Margaret blinked. "This is... is a new malady?"

He shook his head. "Not that I'm aware. No matter how hard I studied, I found it difficult to tell garnets from rubies, or emeralds from some other stones. It explains much, including why I did not do well in my geology class at Cambridge."

"No doubt," Margaret murmured, feeling sorry for the young man for the first time since he had arrived that day.

"Since I cannot be trusted to choose the correct stone, I am at your mercy. I am hoping you will agree to be my partner in this regard."

Margaret inhaled softly. "I will assist you, of course," she replied. When she saw how his expression didn't change, she added, "In fact, I believe I have already discovered what gemstones will work best for your designs."

"My father is of the opinion that I needn't allow this... *malady* to change the way I live my life," he murmured, as if he hadn't heard her.

"Of course, it shouldn't," she replied. "Why, *she* probably hasn't even noticed," she added, thinking a mistress wouldn't have any reason to note such a defect in her protector.

Alexander blinked. "Oh, my mother knows," he replied. "Apparently she has known since I was young. I seemed to have inherited it from her father," he explained.

Margaret allowed a nod, not quite sure what he was talking about. "I was... I was referring to your mistress."

Alexander blinked again. "Mistress?" he repeated, his brows furrowing. "But... I don't *have* a mistress."

Falling into her chair—his words had been that unexpected—Margaret stared at her client. "Oh," she managed to say in a quiet voice. For a moment, her body felt as if a giant weight had been lifted from it. As if Atlas had appeared and taken the world onto his massive shoulders.

Well aware of his stare, she allowed a shrug. "Well, if not your mistress, then for whom are you making this parure?" she asked, as she indicated the gems that were lined up on the black velvet board on her desk.

Alexander settled into the chair next to her desk and said, "My mother, of course," he replied. "Which has me realizing I have not been entirely truthful with you. I meant no offense. I wasn't deliberately keeping the information from you," he assured her. "But my mother cannot know I am making this for her. My father intends to give it to her for their wedding anniversary. As a surprise. In less than three weeks. I expect he'll do so before the ball at which my sister, Helen, will make her come-out."

Feeling as light as she had the first day they had met, Margaret smiled. "She will be thrilled," she said as she gripped his hand with one of hers. "That you have made her a collection of jewels she might wear for the rest of her life? With your own hands?" She glanced again at the garnets arranged in two lines on the velvet board on her desk. "I am quite jealous."

"Are you?" Alexander asked in a hoarse whisper.

She inhaled as if to respond and then noted how he regarded her, as if he *wanted* her to feel jealousy. She nodded. "Of course. Any woman would be. How could *I* not be?"

"Does that mean you will dance with me?"

Margaret blinked as she stared at him. "Dance?" she repeated.

Whatever did dancing have to do with making a parure for his mother?

"I have it on good authority that you will receive an invitation to Lord Weatherstone's annual ball. Probably later today," he replied, his sudden enthusiasm infectious.

"Me?"

"Yes."

"But, I've only ever helped Lord Cougham choose baubles for his mistresses," she protested. "Lord Weatherstone hasn't been a client of ours in well over a decade," she added.

A pang of jealousy had Alexander wondering how long she had been in the company of Sebastian Peele, Viscount Cougham. He was older and far more worldly than Alexander. Some considered him a rake. He had recently returned from his Grand Tour of Europe having left a string of broken hearts from the tip of Italy's boot to the top of France. "I do hope Lord Cougham was on his best behavior in your presence," Alexander murmured.

Margaret furrowed a dark brow. "I hardly think the viscount even noticed me," she replied. "He seemed more concerned with the stones in the bracelet he purchased. And if they could be easily replaced with paste versions."

Alexander made a sound of disgust.

"Oh, not that *he* wished to have them replaced, but he seemed to think the woman he was going to give them to might do so..." She stopped speaking. "My apologies. I've said entirely too much," she whispered in dismay.

A smirk teased the edges of Alexander's lips. "He does seem to have bad luck when it comes to mistresses," he whispered, leaning in closer to make the comment. "Which may be why I haven't been tempted to take on such a creature."

Margaret inhaled softly, at once relieved and disappointed all at the same time.

He wouldn't be offering her *carte blanche*.

"So why is it I'm to expect an invitation to Lord Weatherstone's ball?" she asked, remembering what had set them on this line of discussion.

Alexander straightened. "Oh, well, before anyone else has a chance to secure a dance with you, I should like to ensure you will allow me a waltz. And at least one other dance," he replied, his excitement palpable. "Even the second waltz if you're so inclined. I've already seen to it you will receive an invitation to my sister's ball, as well."

Margaret stared at him. "*You* have seen to it I will receive these invitations?" she asked, reeling from his words.

This was not what she had imagined they would be discussing this morning. Her eyes once again darted to the line of garnets.

"My mother and Lady Weatherstone are good friends," he explained. "My father is giving Lord Weatherstone a rare flower bulb today. Something for his famed back gardens. Why, they might have already completed their errand," he said with some urgency. "I expect that at any moment..." He was interrupted by the sound of a knock at the door. He looked up at the same moment Margaret did.

She waved the man in. "May I help you, sir?" she asked.

"Morning, ma'am. I'm to deliver this to a Miss Margaret Ewen," he replied, as he held out a folded missive.

"I am Miss Ewen."

The liveried footman gave her the note, bowed, and closed the door.

Having recognized the Weatherstone livery, Alexander grinned. "He timed his arrival perfectly," he said in a quiet voice.

Margaret stared at him as she popped the wax seal from the back of the note and unfolded it. She quickly read it, her dark brows rising in surprise. "It *is* an invitation," she murmured.

"To Lord Weatherstone's ball?" Alexander asked with a grin.

"Indeed."

"Do I have your promise of a waltz and one other dance?"

About to claim she couldn't promise such an arrangement —she barely knew any of the dances performed at a ball— Margaret noted his look of enthusiasm and lowered her eyes. "You do if you agree to buy all these garnets I have acquired on your behalf."

Alexander's attention went to the lines of gemstones on her black velvet board. "They all appear gray to me," he replied as he doffed his gloves. "But if you can assure me they will fit in my collets, then I shall purchase every single one of them," he said. He reached for the primrose satin fabric swatch, one brow rising. "Yellow satin," he commented. "Is this for my mother's second gown?" he asked, his fingers smoothing over the slick fabric. He imagined Margaret wearing a gown made of it. She would look stunning in such a color—at least to his eyes.

He thought of what it would be like to slide his hands down her sides, up and over her breasts, down her back and over the swell of her derrière.

Aware of how his thoughts had his cock responding, he quickly changed his train of thought to something more mundane. Such as how many more collets he would need to produce for the parure.

CHAPTER 15
CONTRASTING COLORS

*M*eanwhile Margaret struggled with how to respond to Mr. Tennison's query about the swatch of yellow satin for the second gown. She had merely mentioned his name when she had asked Suzanne about procuring the fabric swatches. The modiste seemed to know immediately whom she meant and had pulled the samples from where two seamstresses were stitching on large swaths of the fabric.

Now that she knew Mr. Tennison was the son of an earl, she felt ever the fool.

"It is for the second gown," she finally replied. "I do believe your idea of contrasting stones in either amber or citrine was an excellent idea." She pulled open the top drawer of her desk and pulled out another black velvet board. "I am of the opinion these citrines will be the perfect complement to complete your parure."

Alexander stared at the collection of gems, all yellow and all lined up in graduated sizes. "You're a genius," he murmured in delight.

"Only if you can set them perfectly in your design," she countered, unable to hide her grin at hearing his compliment.

"I shall do so. I promise," he replied as he began counting the gems.

Margaret reached into one of the small drawers in the gem cabinet and pulled out a teardrop-shaped ruby. "What do you think of this for your brooch? The rose red is perfect with this portion of the watered silk," she added as she held the fabric swatch next to the gemstone.

His count forgotten, Alexander stared at the ruby. "The size is certainly appropriate for a brooch. For a pendant. Do you have two more? Like that one, but... smaller? For the earrings?"

Pulling out two matching stones to the larger one she already held in one palm, Margaret said, "Why, sir, it seems I have at least two."

Alexander allowed a brilliant smile. "You *minx*," he replied in delight. He reached for the gemstones, the tips of his fingers lingering on her palm as he lifted first one and then the other from where they rested.

The oddest sensation shot through Margaret. No one had ever referred to *her* as a minx before. She had heard the expression, of course. On the occasions when a couple came into the shop and perused the selections. The man was already predisposed to purchasing something for his lady—and she always seemed to know it. A dance of seduction and denial would ensue, and before they departed, the woman would be bestowed with a brooch or a bracelet, a ring or a necklace.

For a moment, Margaret thought to simply enjoy the rare treat of a man's touch. To revel in the sensations his simple accusation had set off by hearing it repeated over and over in her mind. But she found there was an entirely different situation to consider when she noticed her client had leaned closer to her, his lips hovering near her cheek.

She turned to face him, entirely unprepared for the kiss he bestowed on the corner of her mouth.

Margaret inhaled sharply, but dared not look at him when he finally pulled away.

"Apologies," he whispered. "I was... I was supposed to ask permission to do that, but I fear words escaped me just then."

Margaret regarded him as she swallowed, shocked to discover he was still staring at her. "I am sorry I was... I was unprepared, sir," she stammered in a quiet voice.

Alexander glanced around. "Do you mean because you do not have a weapon in your possession that you could use to clobber me? Or that...?"

He couldn't finish the comment. Margaret's lips had captured his and cut off the words.

The attempt at a kiss was awkward at first. Neither of them was at the right angle to engage in such an intimacy. Within a few seconds, though, Alexander managed to angle his body in his chair, and she did the same. Her withered arm reached up, her hand gripping his lapel as one of his hands moved to hold her cheek.

Never having kissed a young woman before, Alexander was at a loss as to what exactly to do after their initial pressing of lips. He soon opened his mouth, gratified when she did the same. All at once, they both seemed to understand what to do, sliding their lips into place and suckling one another's lips as quiet mewls sounded from the back of Margaret's throat.

A distant *thud* and a faint tinkling had them quickly ending the kiss. They stared at one another in shock for a moment before Margaret leaned forward and looked beyond the glass in the office door. A man stood at the jewelry shop entrance, glancing about as if he were searching for someone.

Alexander followed her gaze. He didn't recognize the middle-aged man, but he could tell from Margaret's reaction that she did. "Customer? Or a friend?" He paused a moment. "A lover, then?" He meant for the last question to come out as a tease, but it was hard to make his voice sound lighthearted when part of him wanted to throttle the man for having interrupted their kiss.

Margaret tore her gaze from the new arrival, her eyes wide. "Mr. Baumeister? Hardly," she replied in a huff, finally giving her head a quick shake as if she had eaten an especially sour pickle. Her expression eased when she saw that her father had stepped from behind his workbench and had made his way to the front door. "Father will wait on him," she murmured, relief evident in her voice.

Alexander furrowed his brows, noting how her demeanor had changed with the man's arrival. "Are you all right?" he asked, his hand moving to take hers.

Her attention went to their hands, to how he held hers. "I am," she replied. She sighed, though, the sound indicating frustration. She carefully extracted her hand from his hold, "You no doubt think me fast—"

"I think nothing of the sort," Alexander stated. "I should, in fact, apologize for my—"

"Please don't," she said in a hoarse whisper.

Alexander blinked, suddenly sober. A moment later, and a grin teased the corners of his lips. "Then I shan't," he said with a good deal of relief. "But you are going to dance with me?"

Margaret dipped her head, her attention going to the invitation she still held in her hand. "I suppose this is a rather grand affair."

"The first ball of the Season," Alexander replied lightly. "The Weatherstone ball is always a crush."

"I might have something appropriate to wear," she murmured.

Alexander's immediate thought was that she looked lovely wearing what she had on. Given her dark hair and gray—or were those green?—eyes, she would look stunning in nearly any ball gown. Probably in any color, but then, what did he know about colors?

But wearing nothing at all?

He remembered his father's mention of mermaids. That he had thought Estelle Jones a mermaid when she first appeared from beneath the water near a beach on Delos.

A mermaid. Or Aphrodite.

A goddess of love.

Alexander imagined how his fingertips might skim over Margaret's sun-warmed skin, how her nipples would pucker into delectable buds, ripe for kissing. How his hands would smooth down her back, his fingers caressing the bumps along her spine and then circling the dimples at the base of her long back.

His palms would round the globes of her bottom to the back of her thighs before one hand would slide along a rounded hip to her front and then delve into the space between her thighs.

He imagined how she might inhale softly. How that simple act would have the tips of her breasts combing through the black hair that covered his chest. How she would beg for him as his fingers separated the dark hair of her mons to slide along her womanhood. How his fingers would become drenched with her ambrosia as he slowly, carefully brought her to ecstasy.

Margaret seemed to guess some of what he was thinking, for she let out a gasp of protest. "Mr. Tennison!" she scolded.

Blinking several times, as if he might be able to erase the erotic image that had formed in his mind's eye,

Alexander asked, "Are your eyes green? Or... or are they gray?"

Not expecting the question given what she had imagined he was thinking, Margaret stared at him a moment before she said, "Gray. They're gray. With darker gray rims."

Alexander let out the breath he'd been holding. "Well, at least I see *them* as I should," he murmured. Then he inhaled, his eyes darting about as if he couldn't decide what to do. When they returned to her, he found her attention was once again drawn to something beyond the office door. He turned his head to the right to follow her line of sight in time to see the retreating back of the man who had entered only a few minutes earlier. The door to the jewelry shop closed with a resounding *thud*, as if it had been slammed shut. The gold bell above it shook so hard, he was afraid it might come loose from its hook.

Margaret exhaled softly and seemed to relax. Alexander could tell from the lower set of her shoulders that the man's presence had caused her concern.

"I could challenge him to a duel, if you wish," he offered, his tone light.

Margaret stared at him before she visibly swallowed. "Mr. Baumeister would not be worth your time nor your trouble, sir."

Alexander's brows furrowed. "My lady?"

She shook her head. "He is an annoyance. Nothing more." Turning her attention back to the gems on her desk, she said, "Shall we be sure I have the numbers right? That there are enough for your designs?

His gaze going to the black velvet board, Alexander nodded. "Of course." In truth, he would have liked to learn more about Mr. Baumeister.

"Do you have your drawings with you?"

Pulling the four sheets of drawings from a waistcoat

pocket, Alexander spread them out on the desk to the right of the velvet covered board. "How do you suppose I should include the yellow gems?"

"Why, that will be up to you, of course," she replied.

"But... if this were for you, what would be your preference?" he countered. At her look of startlement, he added, "I ask because I trust your judgement and because... I *need* your assistance with this. I wish this to be a creation utilizing both of our skills. Yours as a gemologist and mine as a fledging metallurgist."

Margaret stared at him a moment, at once thrilled to hear he respected her and yet hesitant to agree. If he opened his own jewelry concern and became a competitor, she would have been complicit in helping him do so. "I am flattered, sir, truly," she replied.

"If you are concerned I will take work from your father—sales from your shop—please rest assured I am only doing this for my mother."

"Of course," Margaret replied, allowing her relief to show. She glanced at the lines of gems, a pattern of garnets and citrines forming in her mind's eye. She opened her desk drawer and captured a wood pencil between two fingers. She handed it to him. "You'll need to mark your design as I call out each gem," she explained when she noted his questioning look. "Then I will place the gems into separate boxes for each item so you can keep them straight."

"Capital," he said as he watched her start a new arrangement on one of the velvet boards, alternating the garnets with an occasional citrine until there were enough for the bracelet. "Even in dark gray and yellow, this pattern appears pleasing to the eye," he said as he watched her fingers pick and place the small gems in a row.

"If only you could see the red," she whispered. "If you're truly making your collets in gold—"

"I've completed nearly half of all that I'll need."

"—Then this will be a stunning bracelet."

"I shall be sure you receive the proper credit for the design," he said.

Margaret once again thrilled at hearing his words. Then she pointed to the drawing of the bracelet, indicating the leftmost gem, and began reciting what gem should go into the corresponding collet. "Garnet, garnet, garnet, citrine..."

It took Alexander a moment to write Gs and Cs above each collet as she continued calling out names. When she finished, she counted and recorded the numbers of each gem and then collected them into a small box. She handed it to him. "Mark it with a B for bracelet," she instructed.

He did as he was told as Margaret returned her attention to the velvet board. She held the drawing of the necklace in one hand as she arranged gems with her other, moving them around until she had a similar pattern to the one she had created for the bracelet.

"What of the ruby?" Alexander asked.

"Do you want it to be separate? To use as a brooch?"

"I like that idea, yes."

"So there will be citrines at the top with the ruby hanging beneath?"

Alexander frowned, remembering how he intended to do the earrings. He pulled that drawing forward. "Perhaps," he hedged.

Margaret noted his hesitancy. "Then on the necklace, we shall include more garnets in the middle, so there are an odd number of stones on either side of where the pendant will hang. The citrines at the top of the brooch will provide the contrast in the middle of the necklace when it's added as a pendant." She moved the gems into place and set the ruby where it would hang.

"I think I should like to make the brooch to look like a

larger version of the earrings," Alexander murmured. He used the pencil to show that the larger rubies would be taking the place of seven stones in the new design.

She glanced at the drawing of the earrings. "Which means we'll require four citrines—"

"Five," he interrupted. "I'd like a garnet in the middle. So it… so it looks like a flower." This was to be a gift from his father. It only made sense that there was a hint of his avocation included in the design.

"Six, then. It will make it easier to execute the pattern when you attach the collets in a circle," she replied. She pulled a small piece of parchment from her desk drawer and sketched six circles in a round pattern and then drew a larger one in the middle. "Like this?"

"That's it," Alexander agreed. "You don't think it will be too many stones above the single ruby?"

Margaret shook her head. "The ruby is brilliant enough to hold its own," she assured him as she arranged the gems in the pattern she had drawn. Then she placed one of the smaller rubies where it would fall in the pendeloque design.

"I like it," Alexander said with a nod.

"Do you like the size of the gems?"

"I do," he replied. He watched as she set up the design for the second earring to match the first, making sure the stones were equal sizes and that their cuts were equivalent.

She returned her attention to the design for the brooch, choosing larger stones for the flower. "You'll need eight citrines for this one, I think, with a larger garnet in the middle." She showed how, despite the larger gems, the circle of stones would be spread too far apart around the central gem. When she had the flower pattern complete, she sat back and regarded him with a raised brow. "Well?"

A slow smile split his face as Alexander studied the design. "You're brilliant," he murmured. "I only hope I can do these stones justice," he added. He watched as she counted the stones and marked the numbers on the receipt. She scooped up the gems for the earrings into another small box and handed it to him. "Earrings," she said.

She returned her attention to the necklace design, mirroring the placement of garnets and citrines to match the first half that she had already completed. A few stones remained off to the side of her velvet board, the gems either the wrong size or color to work in the design.

Moving the gems to place the brooch in the middle, she regarded the design a moment before pushing a few stones around, rearranging them until she finally allowed a long sigh. "What do you think?"

"I think I should like to take you on a ride in the park," he blurted.

Margaret straightened in her chair. "Sir?"

"And for an ice at Gunther's," he went on, oblivious to her stare of shock. "Is there an afternoon you might be available for me? Next... Thursday, perhaps? Two days after the ball?"

The query had a combination of flutterbies and fear tumbling about in Margaret's stomach. Her gaze went back to the arrangement for the necklace.

If she turned down his offer, would he rescind his agreement to purchase the gems?

"I apologize. I merely wished to spend more time in your company," Alexander said in a quiet voice. "And although I will probably make a bauble of some sort for my sister's come-out, I don't wish to wait a fortnight to see you again."

"I must speak with my father," she said finally.

"As will I, of course. To ask his permission," Alexander said. He reached into a waistcoat pocket and extracted the bracelet he had been given by Sarah, Countess of Trenton, earlier that morning.

Gabe had been right in mentioning his mother's bracelet

was missing a sapphire. When Alexander had paid a call at Trenton House prior to his arrival at Ewen & Ewen, the countess seemed especially touched that he would see to the stone's replacement. She claimed she would be too embarrassed to pay a call on a jeweler. From how scratched the gold appeared, Alexander knew she had probably worn the bracelet nearly every day since her wedding to Gabriel Wellingham, Earl of Trenton. She had, in fact, been wearing it when he arrived.

"Might you have a sapphire for the Countess of Trenton's bracelet?" he asked as he held it out for her perusal. "She asked that she be sent the bill for the repair," he added.

Margaret gave a start at the change of subject. She stared at the bracelet a moment before lifting it with two fingers until it dangled freely. Angling her head to one side, she waited until the bracelet hung motionless. Laying it onto the velvet board below the string of garnets and citrines, she regarded it another moment before she pulled open one of the small drawers to her left.

Alexander's eyes widened at seeing the collection of sapphires that lined the drawer. Blue was a color he could see directly, and he nearly laughed. "They're gorgeous. All of them," he murmured.

"But only one of these will work in this bracelet," she replied before she plucked a round cut sapphire from one corner of the drawer. She held it up to the light from the window before placing it next to the bracelet. The cut was the same as the other sapphires in the bracelet, as was its size and fire.

"It's perfect," Alexander whispered. "Can your father do the setting?"

"Of course," Margaret assured him. "Thank you for bringing this business to us."

He regarded her with a grin. "When I tell you it is my pleasure, please know that I mean it," he replied.

The strange sensations in her middle returned, and Margaret inhaled sharply before she returned her attention to the line of garnets and citrines. "Are you ready to record your necklace's design?"

Alexander cleared his throat and pulled the parchment forward. "Ready," he replied, holding the pencil above his drawing.

She called out the gem's names, one after another, and then swept them into a small box once she had completed her count. "To whom shall I send the invoice, sir?"

"Rosemount House, Park Lane. To the attention of Harold, Earl of Everly," he recited. "Or, if you have it ready now, I can take it to him. Ensure my mother doesn't accidentally see it."

Margaret had begun to write the address at the top of the receipt, but upon hearing the words *Earl of Everly*, she was reminded of what her father had told her. She stopped and stared at Alexander. "You *are* the son of an earl?" she said in a whisper. "I wondered if my father was teasing me."

Alexander nodded. "Please don't hold it against me," he replied.

She swallowed. "I would never," she murmured. Before she knew quite what was happening, he once again leaned over and kissed her, this time on the cheek.

"If you require a chaperone for the ball—"

"I will, of course," she replied, disappointment sounding in her voice. "I am not yet an old maid," she added with a crooked grin. She hadn't given a thought to propriety when she decided she would go, and now she questioned the wisdom of attending such a grand affair.

"I'm quite sure my mother will oblige you," Alexander said. "Do you live here? Above the shop?" he guessed.

She nodded.

"We shall come for you Tuesday night. Half past eight o'clock?"

Margaret inhaled softly. "I will be ready," she replied.

"Capital."

She finished completing the receipt and handed it to him. He gave the total a quick glance, apparently surprised by the amount.

"Are you sure this is right?" he asked.

"You think it too much?" she asked in alarm.

"I think it quite a bargain, actually," Alexander replied as he added the figures in his head.

"You already paid for the gold you took the other day," Margaret reminded him.

Alexander looked up from the receipt. "Still, my father will be pleasantly surprised to learn that my project isn't going to cost him an unentailed property."

"If that's what he expected, then he's been shopping with the wrong jeweler."

Taking one of her hands in his, Alexander kissed the back of it. "Until Tuesday, Miss Ewen," he said. He stood and gave her a bow before collecting the small boxes into his arm.

Margaret watched him go, aware that he headed toward her father's workbench rather than to the front door. When she glanced up again, it was to see him winking at her before he took his leave of the shop.

She wasn't the least bit surprised when her father opened her office door, leaned against the door jamb, and crossed his arms.

CHAPTER 16
AFTERNOON DELIGHT

*M*eanwhile, in Park Lane

Stella's hand on his arm and an ornate cane gripped in his gloved hand, Harold walked proudly down Park Lane. They had just completed their call on the Weatherstone's and were feeling especially happy.

"I don't believe I've ever seen the earl so excited to see a plant before," Stella remarked.

Harold chuckled. "Had I any idea he wanted that particular flower, I could have seen to giving him a bulb a year ago," he replied. "They practically grow like weeds in our conservatory." He paused before he asked, "Were you able to accomplish what you set out to do?"

She nodded. "I did. From Lady Weatherstone's reaction, I had to believe she was truly happy to invite Miss Ewen to the ball."

"Why wouldn't she be?"

Stella gave him a quelling glance. "Invite another unattached female when there are always far more of them then there are bachelors?" she countered. "Perhaps she's expecting more men this year than usual, but there seemed to be some other reason she was happy to learn of Miss Ewen."

Harold considered the comment. "As a gemologist, Miss Ewen has no doubt been involved in the creation of a number of sets of jewels over the years. Perhaps she expects the earl to buy some bauble for her."

"Perhaps," Stella hedged. "Or maybe she wants to have all her jewels replaced with paste so she can sell the gems and run away with some young buck." Although the comment was made with a straight face, Stella couldn't help the grin she finally allowed when her husband displayed an expression of shock.

"Lady Weatherstone must be in her sixties—"

"Seventies," Stella whispered.

"You are joking, I hope."

"About her being in her seventies?"

"No! About selling off her gems and running off with a young buck," he countered with a grin.

"I am," Stella assured him. Before he could ask, she added, "I promise I shall never do that to you."

"Whew!" he replied, his breath sending a curly lock of hair from his forehead up against the bottom rim of his top hat.

"Speaking of baubles," Stella said in a quieter voice. "Do you have any idea what our son is up to in his foundry? I think he was out there all night last night."

Harold pretended ignorance, and then his eyes widened. "He's been working on a new signet ring for me," he replied. "I think he's having trouble with how to set the stone, though."

Stella furrowed a brow. "Is that all?"

Not about to mention the *other* project he had asked Alexander to create, Harold shrugged. "Perhaps he's working on a necklace for his sister's come-out."

"Oh!" Stella breathed, her expression brightening. "I do hope he is, although he cannot know what her gown will look like. What color..." She paused, exasperation sounding. "I suppose it wouldn't matter if he did know what color it was if he can't even see it," she murmured.

"It's not that bad," Harold assured her. "He's not *blind*. And besides, he knows her gown will be white. They're all white at her age, aren't they?"

Stella's gaze went to the pavement in front of them, her mood sobering. When she didn't say anything for a few moments, Harold dipped his head in an attempt to catch her attention. "What has you so quiet, my sweet?"

She blinked several times, as if she was staving off tears. "I cannot help but think it is my fault he is—"

"It is *not* your fault," Harold said firmly.

"He inherited it from me—"

"*You* could not help it."

"And now Helen's sons will be—"

"*Might* be," he interrupted. "And they might *not*," he added, again with authority. He wrapped an arm around her shoulders and pulled her against his side. "It's a blessing, Stella."

Her eyes rounded as she turned to stare at him. "How can you say that?"

Harold sighed as he hurried them to the front door of Rosemount House. "Our son is perfect in every other regard," he replied. "I've heard the young women speak of him as if he were a deity—"

"Well, he does look like one," Stella agreed.

"A deity they wish to worship, and not in the usual manner."

"Harry!"

The front door opened, and they shed their coats into the butler's arms.

"It's true. If he didn't have some defect, his head would grow too large for his body, and we'd have a monster on our hands. Or a son like Sebastian Peele," he murmured, remembering Lord Weatherstone's comments about his heir.

"Alex would never be a monster," she argued.

"Now we're assured he will never be. He's humble, and he's kind, and he has interests that don't include brothels and strong drink, or racing a coach-and-four at high speeds and gambling until four in the morning."

"True," Stella agreed as they climbed the stairs, remembering Lady Weatherstone's descriptions of what her son seemed to enjoy despite his five-and-thirty years on the planet.

When did men outgrow the need for speed and derring-do?

"When Alex is a year or two older, I think I shall encourage a writ of acceleration. He will make a fine addition to Parliament," Harold commented. They paused on the landing before ascending the next flight of stairs, as if one thought the other might be headed to one of the rooms on the first floor.

"Not until he's done with his avocation, though," Stella warned. "It might keep him up all night, but at least we know where he is."

"He can make jewelry even when he's a lord. My father certainly did," Harold argued. They stepped off the second flight of stairs and made their way down the hall, both coming to a halt outside of Stella's bedchamber. They glanced at one another and then looked around, as if making sure no one saw them. Then they both disappeared behind the door.

Stella tittered when Harold locked the door and leaned against it. "I thought perhaps you would like a luncheon before..." She allowed the sentence to trail off.

"Maybe later," he whispered. "In the meantime, how might I serve you, my lady?"

Stella glanced at him before her lips curled up in a teasing grin. "I fear it's a task that might be too difficult."

Harold frowned. "Can I do it in bed?"

Her expression suggesting she had to think on it a moment, Stella finally giggled. "You could," she hedged.

"Name it."

"Remove all the pins from my hair."

Harold blinked. "You make it sound as if it's a herculean task," he muttered. He straightened and moved to stand behind Stella as she took a seat at her dressing table. Instead of removing hairpins, though, he undid the buttons down the back of her gown. He pushed down the sleeves of her carriage gown and chemise and then kissed her bare shoulders.

Stella straightened, pulling up the gown's bodice to hide her corset. "There are six-and-fifty pins," she stated.

Pausing as he extracted three from the edge of her elaborate coiffure, Harold asked, "How do you know that?"

"It's how many I own, and Anderson used all of them when she styled my hair this morning."

"Oh, Zeus!" he complained, pulling out a few more pins. Several locks of her auburn hair tumbled down past her shoulders. He used a finger to trace the line of her bun, stopping to pluck out the pins when he felt their curved ends. "This is truly like finding needles in a haystack," he groused.

Stella angled her head so her chin rested on one shoulder. "Are you calling my hair a haystack?"

Harold plucked several more pins before he said, "Of course not. It's merely a metaphor," he replied. Soon, he was forced to lean over and use both hands so his fingers could comb through her hair in search of stray pins.

Purring, Stella closed her eyes. "Perhaps I should require you to wash my hair, too."

"Another day, my sweet," he replied absently, his brows furrowed when he realized he was still missing a few of the metal U-shaped hairpins. "Are you quite sure she used all six-and-fifty?"

Stella assured him that was the case, even as she noticed a few in the opposite corner of her dressing table. The sensation of his fingers caressing her scalp was not one she wished to have ended anytime soon, though.

"Oh, dear. I fear I have failed," Harold whispered.

"Why do say that?"

"There are only fifty... fifty-three pins here."

"Hmm," she replied as she leaned back against him until her back was pressed against the front of his chest. When one of his hands pushed aside her long, wavy hair, his lips took purchase on the side of her neck. "Then I suppose that's all there were."

Harold chuckled as he clutched the pins in a fist and then leaned around her to drop them onto the dressing table. "Minx," he whispered.

"You haven't had your hands in my hair in an age," she murmured.

"I always feared I would muss it."

"You didn't used to," she countered.

"I was ignorant back then. I had no idea how long it took your lady's maid to pin up your hair." When Stella didn't say anything in reply, Harold pulled her up from the chair and removed the gown from her body. He continued to undress her until she wore only stockings and garters.

Meanwhile, Stella undid all the buttons of his various garments, pushing and pulling them off his body in an increasingly frantic manner.

"Are you in a hurry, my lady?"

Stella paused, her hands beneath the top edge of his pantaloons. "Maybe?"

Harold chuckled as he struggled to remove a boot. "Have you an appointment this afternoon?"

"No," she lied, remembering she had promised to pay a call on Lady Sommers. There were arrangements that still needed to be done for the ball she and Evangeline were hosting for Helen's come-out. "Maybe."

His eyes darting to the side, he leaned down to remove the other boot. "With Evangeline?" he guessed.

She nodded as she threaded her fingers through his dark hair. "I can send my regrets with a footman—"

"I'll be done with you in a couple of hours."

Stella blinked. "Oh?" A hint of disappointment sounded in her voice.

Chuckling again, Harold pushed down his pantaloons—a move made difficult by his erection—and stepped out of them. "We'll both be hungry," he reminded her.

Eyes widening, Stella understood his meaning. "Of course, you are right—"

"I must admit I'm flattered by all the time you're affording me," he murmured. He lifted her into his arms, grinning at hearing her squeak of surprise, and placed her on the bed. He followed her down and kissed her mouth.

"Likewise," she whispered, before she nipped one of his earlobes.

Although he intended to be slow in his ministrations, her pleas and small gasps had him mounting her for what became a frantic rush to their mutual ecstasy.

When he finally caught his breath, he lowered himself to the bed and rolled over onto his back. His arm slid beneath her shoulders, and after a few minutes, he managed to lift himself onto an elbow. He gazed down on her, grinning at the sight of her mussed hair spread out in an auburn halo around her face. "You're even more beautiful now than when you were a mermaid," he whispered.

She grinned, her face taking on the blush of a young maiden. "Are you saying that because you wish to make love to me again?"

Harold furrowed a single brow. "I'm saying it because it's true," he replied carefully. "But should you be so inclined to make love to me, I will not object. In fact, I shall willingly subject myself to your every whim and fancy,"

"Every whim and fancy?" she repeated as she beamed in delight. She sobered when she noticed how his hand smoothed over her belly and then up and over a breast. "What is it?"

"I like your breasts like this." He lowered his lips to kiss a nipple. "All rounded, like you've eaten too many cakes at tea," he whispered. He leaned over and kissed the other nipple.

Stella inhaled softly. "I have put on a bit of weight. But you don't think it's too much?"

"Oh, no," he said, the response coming from the back of his throat in the form of a loud purr. His mouth descended onto one of her breasts, and she nearly shrieked as he suckled it.

"I'm so relieved," she whispered. Grinning, she pushed him off of her and followed him over until he was on his back. She climbed atop him, straddling him before she gripped his manhood in one hand. Staring down at him, she said, "My turn."

Harold blinked, but he wasn't about to argue. "Do you have any idea just how... how delightfully *scandalous* you look right now?" he whispered. He inhaled sharply when she leaned forward so his manhood could slide into her wet warmth.

"Are you accusing me of looking like a mistress?" she asked as she placed her hands on his shoulders.

"I'm sure I wouldn't know," he managed to get out. His hands on her hips, he helped lift and lower her until the familiar rhythm was established. He used the flat of his hand to smooth over her rounded belly, his fingertips sending tickles beneath her skin.

When he rubbed a thumb over her womanhood, she inhaled and whispered his name over and over as the waves of her orgasm had her slowly collapsing atop him.

Harold waited as long as he could before he finally allowed his own release, the sound of his deep groan ending the quiet in the room.

Her breaths labored and her hair splayed out over his chest, Stella settled her head onto one of his shoulders and closed her eyes. She could feel the pounding of his heart beneath her ear, how his chest rose and fell in time with her own.

When she awoke, she was mostly on her back, her head nestled against his chest as Harold leaned on an elbow. His hand was smoothing over her belly, his fingertips occasionally drawing circles on her skin.

"That tickles," she said as she covered his hand with one of hers.

"You're all soft and round," he whispered. He lowered his lips to her belly and kissed it. "You really have been eating too many cakes at teatime. Not that you're plump, exactly," he quickly added. "Or... or that I think you've grown fat, because... I don't."

"You truly don't mind?"

He shook his head. "You haven't been like this since you were expecting Helen," he said on a sigh. He lowered his body back down to the bed and then pulled her against his side. He stayed like that for nearly an entire minute before he suddenly sat up straight.

"What is it?" she asked in alarm, pushing herself up onto an elbow.

Harold turned to stare down at her. "You're pregnant."

Stella returned his stare before she rolled her eyes. "And if I am?"

His eyes widening in delight, Harold let out a hoot.

CHAPTER 17
A FATHER PREVARICATES

Meanwhile, back at Ewen & Ewen

"I cannot decide if I should scold you or kiss you," Adam Ewen said as he regarded his daughter from the office doorway. "Is it true? You've received an invitation to a *ton* ball?"

Margaret sighed as she lifted the engraved pasteboard from her desk and waved it. "Lord Weatherstone's ball. Mr. Tennison insists I attend," she replied. "He wishes to dance with me." She self-consciously hid her left arm beneath her right and allowed a sigh.

Had Madame Suzanne known something Margaret hadn't that day she had procured the fabric samples from her shop? Why else would she have encouraged Margaret to buy a gown? At least the simple sapphire satin gown was one she could afford. Margaret hadn't felt the least bit of guilt in buying something she had no plans to wear anytime soon. "I take it you gave him permission to take me for a ride in the park?"

He nodded. "I did, of course. He's a fine young gentleman, Margaret. You would do well to encourage him."

Her eyes rounding, Margaret said, "I don't believe he's *courting* me, if that's what you're thinking."

Frowning, Adam said, "What's he doing then?" His eyes rounded. "He'd better not have offered *carte blanche*," he warned.

A blush colored her face before she said, "Of course not, Father." She allowed a sigh. "I cannot say for certain, but I think he's merely... lonely."

"Lonely?" Adam repeated. "He has mates. Lots of them. He must have mates from at least—"

"They're married," she said in a quiet voice.

"What's this?"

She rolled her eyes. "I know you don't like that I read *The Tattler*," she said, referring to the London gossip news sheet, "but in the past few months, there have been a number of articles featuring several of Mr. Tennison's friends. They've all married, and two were his age."

"Which is?"

"One-and-twenty."

Adam gave a start. "He tell you that?"

"No. I looked it up in *DeBrett's*," Margaret replied. "You should have told me his father is an earl."

"Hmm. Thought I did," Adam hedged.

"When Mr. Tennison was here the *first* time," she argued. "He says he has difficulty identifying certain gemstones, which is why he required my help with choosing the stones for his project," she explained. "He said the garnets appear to him as gray."

Adam furrowed a brow. "I'm sorry to hear that, but it does explain why he was in there so long with you."

"He assures me his father will pay the invoice in short order."

"Good to hear, but his payment might arrive too late."

Adam's eyes filled with worry. "Baumeister was here," he added on a sigh.

"I saw him arrive. I *heard* him leave," Margaret replied, remembering how the entire shop seemed to shake when he slammed the door to the shop. Her gaze darted to the bell above the door, thinking it might have broken. "What did he want this time?"

"This time?" her father repeated. "Same as always. Payment in full. Ownership of the shop. And you."

Margaret hissed. "Please, promise me you won't make me marry him," she whispered.

"You know I cannot promise you anything," he replied.

"Mr. Tennison assures me his father will pay for the jewels he took today in a timely manner. You can give Baumeister those funds, and we'll simply pay Mr. Goldman later," she reasoned.

"That only delays the inevitable that much longer," Adam replied, his pained expression having become more and more common. "But a delay is better than today."

Margaret plucked the bracelet from her desk and held it up. "The Countess of Trenton's bracelet is in need of a sapphire." She held up the one she had found in her stash of gems. "Fix it today, and we can deliver it. Mr. Tennison says the countess will see to the payment herself."

Adam took the bracelet and gem from her, admiring the workmanship before he glanced at the sapphire. "Good match," he remarked. "This wasn't made by anyone in London," he murmured. "And it looks as if it's old, given how worn it appears."

"The design isn't that old, though," Margaret argued.

"You think it's from the Continent?"

"The jeweler's mark is beneath the clasp," she replied as she reached for a small chipboard-clad book. "It was made here in England," she added as she flipped the yellowed pages of the thin tome. "Here it is," she said as she pointed to a drawing of the same jeweler's mark as what had been stamped into the sapphire bracelet. "Hind in Birmingham."

"It's only a couple of decades old," he murmured. "Do you suppose she wears this every day?"

Margaret angled her head to one side. "If I had such a bracelet, I certainly would," she said with a grin. "Not to flaunt my title, though," she added, her brows furrowing.

"Oh?" her father prompted.

"I would wear it as a reminder of my title," she explained. "Humble beginnings and all." She paused, a thought of what Mr. Baumeister might have her wear in the way of jewelry should she ever end up married to the cur. "Or because my husband required it of me."

It was Adam's turn to hiss. "I truly hope it does not come to that," he said on a sigh. "I'll set this stone right away. Smooth out the gold as best I can and deliver it later today."

"I'll see to the invoice," Margaret replied.

Despite the promises of quick payment, Margaret found she was fighting back tears as she completed writing out and copying the invoice for the sapphire and its resetting. Her father was right in mentioning a delay was better than today when it came to Samuel Baumeister. She had no desire to end up married to a vindictive man who was old enough to be her father.

CHAPTER 18
PILLOW TALK

eanwhile, in Stella's bedchamber at Rosemount House

"How long have you known?" Harold asked as his expression changed from one of delight to one of confusion.

"A couple of months, I suppose," Stella replied. "I didn't tell you because... well, I wasn't completely sure, and I worried I might have a miscarriage—"

"You haven't before, have you?" he asked in alarm.

"No, but... it's been so long since Helen was born," she explained. "I wasn't sure—"

"That's on me," Harold said as he stared at something in his mind's eye.

"How so?"

He shook his head. "All these years, I only ever made love to you on Saturday nights."

"So?"

"I should have been sleeping with you every night," he announced.

"You were frequently preoccupied," she reminded him.

"Your experiments. Your plants. The garden. The conservatory. The Royal Society. Parliament."

"Still, I should have been doing my duty. Seeing to another heir, at least," he reasoned.

"True," she whispered. "For a time I thought you might have taken a mistress."

"Never," he replied. He furrowed a brow. "For a time, I was afraid you might have taken a lover."

Stella sat up and stared down at him. "Never." The memory of Lord Framingham had her wincing, though.

"What is it?"

She shook her head. "It's nothing."

"You did have one?"

"No," she insisted, her eyes wide. "But recently, I was approached..."

Harold sat up, his eyes blazing. "By whom?"

"It's nothing," she said in a quiet voice. "I took care of it."

"Tell me who," he demanded.

Stella sighed. "Earlier this week, Lord Framingham spoke with me when I was in Floris—"

"That *ass*? I am challenging him to a duel!" Harold stated as he started to get off the bed.

Stella reached out and grabbed one of his arms. "Harry, no. I already told him what you would do to him."

Harold paused and furrowed his dark brows. "And what did you tell him? So I'll know exactly what to do to him."

Wincing, Stella said, "I told him you were a terrible shot, but that you were quite good with a sword. I may have implied you would..." She made a flicking movement with one wrist. "slice off his prick with your foil."

It was Harold's turn to wince, but after a moment, a brilliant grin appeared. "Did you really say 'prick'?"

Grimacing, Stella said, "Yes."

"To him?"

Her gaze darted to one side before she nodded. "Yes."

Harold's laughter filled the room and caused the entire bed to vibrate. "Oh, I should have liked to have seen his face," he murmured between chuckles.

"He was quite shocked, I think," Stella said, not exactly sharing in her husband's humor.

"No doubt," Harold replied, his chuckling continuing. "In fact, I think I shall approach him on Tuesday—"

"Oh, don't, Harry," Stella pleaded.

"He needs to know *I* know, and he needs to know he cannot proposition you," Harold stated, finally sobering.

"Oh, if you must, but do try to keep your distance. The man's odor is quite pungent, and I shouldn't want you to faint. I know I nearly did."

"True," Harold agreed. His gaze dropped to her breasts and continued down her seated figure until it reached her toes. He repositioned himself on the bed, returning to her side. "I would kill for you," he murmured.

"Harry," she breathed in alarm.

"I love you that much."

Stella reached out and wrapped her arms around him as best she could, heartened when he gathered her against his body and held her for a time. She would have been comfortable remaining in the same position for the rest of the day, but the telltale sensation of pins and needles suggested one leg was about to go to sleep. On the verge of saying an apology, she held it when Alexander's voice sounded from somewhere far away.

"Our son is looking for you," she whispered.

Harold nodded. "I heard," he said on a sigh. "Not that I want him married off, but there are times like this when—"

"Harry," she scolded.

Harold gave a start and let go his hold on Stella. "I do need to speak with him," he said suddenly. At her look of surprise, he added, "Something Weatherstone spoke with me about today. About earldoms. About our future. "

"Oh?" she asked as she stepped off the bed. She pulled on a silk wrapper, ignoring her husband's sudden pout. "What exactly was it about?"

"Diversification," Harold replied as he finally got off the bed and began picking up his clothing.

Alexander's voice sounded again from just down the hall. "Father?"

Harold moved to the door and opened it a fraction. "I'll be down in a moment. Meet me in the study."

Pausing in his approach, Alexander heard the censure in his father's voice and said, "Yes, sir."

Closing the door, Harold turned to resume dressing. He noticed how Stella was grinning and asked, "What?" as he glanced down at his mostly naked body.

"I don't think I've ever heard you use that tone of voice with our son before," she said as she moved to stand before him. She reached up and kissed him on the corner of his mouth. "Please don't take out your anger toward Framingham on Alex."

Harold inhaled softly and then kissed her quite thoroughly. "I won't," he promised.

CHAPTER 19
A FATHER SON TALK

few minutes later, Rosemount House study, ground floor
Alexander stood before his father's desk and lined up the boxes he had brought home from the jewelry shop. Placing the invoice on the desk blotter, he made sure to turn it around so it would be readable from the other side. He was removing the lids from each box when his father appeared.

"Looks as if you've been shopping," Harold commented as he peeked into one of the boxes on his way to his chair.

"Indeed. I'm anxious to get started. I have enough collets ready for all of the necklace—"

"Your mother mentioned you were up all night."

"Not quite," Alexander replied. "But I might be tonight."

"You have more than a fortnight to finish," his father reminded him. "And you don't have to have all the pieces done."

"True," Alexander agreed as he took a seat in front of the desk. "I was thinking I should make something for Helen. Something with pearls, perhaps."

Harold sat down, nearly falling into his chair at hearing his son's last comment. "A necklace for your sister?"

"Do you think that would be appropriate?"

A sound of disbelief emanated from the earl before he said, "Yes. Yes, of course. I'll even buy the pearls for you."

"Well, before I do anything on *that* project, I hoped you might see to paying the invoice for the gems I purchased today." He indicated the four boxes before him. "Miss Ewen had obviously spent a good deal of time—and blunt—with someone to acquire these gems—"

"Mr. Goldman, no doubt," Harold murmured as he lifted the invoice and glanced at the total. "This is all of it?" he asked with a hint of surprise.

"It doesn't include the gold. I bought that separate with the money you gave me a few days ago."

"Still—"

"The rubies *are* expensive," Alexander continued. "Miss Ewen says they're more valuable than diamonds right now."

"I wasn't complaining in the least," his father said as he studied the rest of the numbers. "It appears as if she's given you a bargain, and I don't know that Ewen and Ewen can afford to do so." He picked up one of the boxes and peered into it.

Alexander gave a start. "Wh... What do you mean?"

Harold sighed. "Your mother and I paid a call at the Weatherstone mansion this morning," he said as he returned the box and looked into another.

"You must have been there awfully early. Miss Ewen's invitation arrived whilst I was at the shop."

"Really?" Harold replied, impressed. "Weatherstone must have a very efficient footman." He returned the box to its original position and took another to examine.

"I must thank mother for her help. Miss Ewen was very surprised—happily so—at receiving the invitation."

Harold furrowed a brow. "You're quite serious about Miss Ewen?"

Alexander blinked. "What do you mean?"

Leaning back in his chair, Harold asked, "Are you courting her?"

"No," Alexander replied. "I merely like spending time in her company," he added when he noted his father's look of disbelief. He watched as Harold set the box next to the others.

"What if I told you I was considering making an offer to Adam Ewen? To buy his business?"

Alexander's mouth dropped open. "But, why?"

Harold placed his arms on his desk and leaned forward. His voice lowered, he said, "Apparently there is a gem merchant who claims he is owed a good deal of blunt from Mr. Ewen. He'd be willing to take his payment in the form of the shop, the inventory, and Miss Ewen." He held out a hand when Alexander looked as if he might launch himself from his chair. "Weatherstone will buy it if we do not. He's determined to keep it out of Baumeister's hands."

"Baumeister?" Alexander repeated, his eyes rounding. "He was there. Today, while Miss Ewen was arranging the stones." He paused as he recalled how she had tensed upon seeing the middle-aged man. "What did you mean when you said he would take Miss Ewen?"

Angling his head to one side, Harold considered the query. "He wants her and her father to continue working there, and he'll marry her. The shop will be the dowry, so to speak."

"No." Alexander said, his head shaking violently. "No. No, no, no, no, no. We cannot let him have her. She despises him. I could tell," he added. "And he's old enough to be her father."

Attempting to suppress his humor at hearing his son's protestations, Harold said, "I don't know what it will take to buy the place, or if it's even worth it. If it can even provide any income for the earldom—"

"It can. If she's the one buying the gems. She said she prefers working with Mr. Goldman for stones. Mr. Ewen can probably continue working another five or ten years, and I can do commissions—"

"Yes, yes, of course," Harold said as he held up a hand again. "We needn't make a decision this very minute," he added quietly. "I just wanted to get your opinion before I looked into it further."

"What kind of claim does Baumeister have on Ewen?" Alexander asked. "How much is he owed?"

Shaking his head, Harold said, "I don't have that information." When he noticed Alexander's look of worry, he added, "I take it you're in agreement if I decide to pursue this? And there are no guarantees Mr. Ewen would even consider an offer."

"He will if the alternative is Baumeister," Alexander countered. He didn't know it for certain, of course. He was only basing his claim on Margaret's reaction to the gem merchant's presence in the shop that morning. "And, yes, I agree that we should pursue it."

"It won't be an entailed business, but you'll have to oversee it after I'm dead."

Alexander winced, but after a moment, his expression softened. "It's really a perfect situation for me," he murmured. "My own jewelry shop. An experienced gemologist. A jeweler. A place to sell my own creations."

"There's an apartment above the shop where the Ewens live."

"They can continue to live there, of course," Alexander said.

"I'll make an appointment to speak with Ewen on Monday," Harold said. "See if I can't get the purchase started before Parliament meets on Tuesday." He leaned back in his chair, his expression suggesting he was happy with their decision.

About to get up from his chair, Alexander paused. "May I ask you about... about you and Mother?"

Harold blinked. "What about your Mother and me?"

Inhaling as if he was about say something, Alexander instead sighed. He finally said, "You two have been so *different* with one another these past few days. I'm half-expecting Mother to announce she's having a baby."

For the second time that day—the first time had been earlier that afternoon in his countess' bed—Harold laughed. Even as he sobered, a grin teased the corners of his lips. "I suppose I have been more open with my intentions towards your mother these days," he admitted, deciding it was too soon to mention that there would be a younger sibling in less than five months. A change of topic was necessary. "Will we be seeing Miss Ewen at the ball Tuesday night?"

Alexander gave a start at hearing the change of subject. "She has agreed to go," he replied. "I've secured her promise of two dances at both the Weatherstone ball and Helen's come-out ball," he went on. "But mother will have to be her chaperone since she doesn't really have anyone who can act in that capacity."

The last comment had his father arching a brow. Although he knew Adam Ewen was a widower, he hadn't considered if there was an aunt or another relative who might have seen to raising Margaret. "I'm sure your mother will agree to it," Harold said as he pulled his book of bank drafts from a desk drawer. "In the meantime, let me see to paying this invoice. I don't want Mr. Ewen's circumstances any worse than they might already be."

"I really appreciate this, Father. I can see to delivering it. Now, in fact."

Harold paused while writing the draft, the dot of ink at the end of his pen threatening to drip. "Today is Saturday," he remarked. He completed the draft and set it aside. "Ewen won't be able to deposit this until Monday, so perhaps it's best left here until then."

"But... they have a safe. In their office."

Quirking a brow, Harold gazed at his son for perhaps a moment too long, for Alexander quickly dipped his head. "You feel affection for her," the earl accused.

Embarrassed, Alexander kept his eyes downcast. "I do like her."

"Have you kissed her?"

His head jerking up, Alexander stared at his father before swallowing. Hard. He was about to answer but thought better of it.

"That's a yes, then," Harold whispered, not making it a question.

"I'm too young to marry," Alexander stated.

"Says the one whose friends have all been caught in the parson's trap since last December."

"True," Alexander hedged.

"Perhaps you should court her. Take her for a ride in the park," his father encouraged.

"I am. Next Thursday. Her father gave me permission."

Harold blinked. And blinked again. "I suppose you're planning to take her for an ice at Gunther's afterwards?"

"Of course," Alexander replied with a nod. He rolled his eyes when he realized to what he had admitted.

"I suppose she'll require a chaperone."

Alexander swallowed. "Do you think Mother will be amenable?"

A quiet knock at the door had them staring at each other. Alexander quickly put the lids on all the boxes in front of him. He pushed them to the side of the desk while Harold stood and moved to the door.

He opened it to find Stella fully dressed but her hair still down past her shoulders. "How do, gorgeous?" Harold opened the door wider so she could see that Alexander was in the room. Their son stood upon seeing her and gave her a nod.

"Afternoon, Mother."

"Bounder," she whispered, giving her husband a wink before she leaned in and said, "I just wanted to be sure all was well?"

"Our son has secured two dances with Miss Ewen," Harold replied as he waved her into the office. "For both balls."

Stella paused on the threshold before she hurried into the study. "Why, that's wonderful!" she gushed as she reached up and kissed her son on the cheek. "I was about to pen a note to let her know I could act as her chaperone, but I wanted to be sure she had agreed to go to the ball."

"I believe I have convinced her," Alexander said, wishing he hadn't told his father anything about his meeting with the gemologist. He was sure his face was as red as the rubies hidden in the boxes on the desk.

His glance in his father's direction reminded him he needed to ask about her availability for additional chaperoning duties. "Might you be available Thursday afternoon? For a ride in the park with Miss Ewen and me? I'll treat you to an ice at Gunther's."

Stella stared at her son a moment before a brilliant smile appeared. "You kissed Miss Ewen, didn't you?"

Harold had to stifle what would have been his third laugh of the day.

"In all fairness, it was supposed to be a peck on the cheek," Alexander claimed.

"But then she turned her head," Stella said on a happy sigh.

"How did you know?"

She gave him a quelling glance. "Oh, please, Alex. We might be taught to be demure, but we're not stupid," she replied. "Kisses are so rarely bestowed, we must do whatever we can to help them along."

Alexander dared a glance in his father's direction, noting how the man stared at his countess as if she'd cast some sort of love spell on him. "I don't believe Miss Ewen is that calculating, Mother." Then he remembered her comment about hoping he didn't think her fast. "Nor fast," he quickly added.

"Of course she isn't. Now, how long do you suppose she'll be in the shop today?"

"Probably until ten o'clock," Harold offered, his good humor still evident as he moved to stand next to her. "We'll have a footman deliver your note whenever it's ready," he assured her, lifting one of her hands to his lips to kiss the back of it.

Stella turned her attention back to Alexander. "I'll let her know I can join you two on Thursday."

"Thank you, Mother."

"You're welcome. You must know I would do anything for my favorite son."

Alexander blinked. "I thought I was your *only* son."

When it appeared his countess might be about to tell Alexander about the baby, Harold quickly intervened. "You are," he stated. He placed one of her hands on his arm and escorted her to the door. In a lowered voice, he said, "We're discussing... diversification."

Stella stopped on the threshold and arched an elegant brow. "I can hardly imagine there's a downside to diversification," she murmured. "Although I truly have no idea what it is."

"There might be benefits you will especially enjoy," he countered, thinking he might allow her to borrow some pieces on occasion. "Helen as well."

One of her brows furrowing, Stella seemed to think on his response a moment before a brilliant smile appeared. She stood on tiptoe, and kissed him on the cheek. "It sounds as if I'll rather like diversification."

With that, she took her leave of the study, and Harold closed the door behind her.

"Do you suppose she suspected anything?" Alexander asked as he indicated the boxes. Although he had tried to hide them by standing in front of them whilst Stella had been in the study, he feared she might have spied them during their conversation.

"If she did, the comment about diversification would have put a stop to her curiosity," Harold replied with a grin.

Alexander gathered up the boxes. "I'm going to hide these in my foundry," he said. "There's still some room on my workbench."

"When you're done out there, join me in the kitchens. I don't know about you, but I'm starving."

Fairly sure he knew what had caused his father's increased appetite, Alexander suppressed the urge to make fun of his father. "And after you've had your fill?"

"I'll be off to see my solicitor. I want to... inform him of what I'm considering with regard to the shop. Get his opinion." In reality, he wanted to have his will updated to account for a third child.

"If it's all right with you, I think I'll spend the afternoon in the foundry," Alexander said. "My enthusiasm for this project is high given what Miss Ewen came up with for the designs."

"Very well," his father replied, secretly glad his son had a hobby.

With that, Alexander left the study, unaware his father collected the bank note from his desk and slid it into a waist-coat pocket.

Some deliveries were too important to entrust to a servant.

CHAPTER 20
FATHERS DISCUSS
IMPORTANT MATTERS

n hour later, Ewen & Ewen, Ludgate Hill

When Thorton, one of the Rosemount House grooms, opened the town coach door for Harold, he said, "If I may say, m'lord, your countess is a very lucky lady."

Harold paused once he was standing on the pavement in front of Ewen & Ewen. Curious as to the servant's meaning, he regarded Thorton a moment before he responded. "Oh? Why do you say that?"

"Third time I've brought you or your heir to this shop in the past week, guv'nor," the groom replied as he waggled his bushy brows. "Don't need to be clever to know there are jewels in the countess' future."

Relieved the groom didn't refer to something else, such as the possibility that Stella might have lost a gem and was attempting to have her jewelry repaired without his knowledge—or his blunt—Harold nodded.

He had never told her he knew about the time when she had come to Ewen & Ewen to have a missing pearl replaced. At least Helen had told him about it, although his daughter hadn't meant to tattle on her mother. She was simply explaining to him why Stella had been so taciturn over dinner the prior evening, as if she had a secret and couldn't bear to share it.

Once she knew about the pearl, Harold had simply seen to adding to Stella's stash of pin money.

Now he wondered if she had even noticed.

"A new Season is about to begin, Thorton," he said. He leaned in closer and added, "Lady Helen will be making her come-out, and there's a wedding anniversary coming soon, so there are some gifts in my ladies' futures."

"Ah, her ladyships will be most pleased." After a beat, Thorton added, "You needn't worry, guv'nor. I'll never give away your secret. My lips are sealed."

Harold nodded his appreciation and turned around. Before entering the shop, he spent a moment examining its exterior. The Portland stone façade was as white as could be expected given the shop was located in the city. There were only a few places where it was apparent rain hadn't washed away the most recent layer of winter soot.

The mullioned window panes were all intact with no visible cracks. Behind one and hanging from a brass chain was a sign bearing the word 'Open' in an elaborate script.

None of the painted shutters hung askew or otherwise appeared broken. But the shingle above the door, hung from gold chains and painted to appear as if it were a locket made of gold, looked as if it had faded. A small crack in the wood interrupted the last 'n' of 'Ewen & Ewen,' and a bird had deposited its droppings along the top edge.

Two flower boxes hung from the first floor windows above the door. Only a hint of greenery showed at their edges, but given it was still March, he didn't expect there to be any blooms.

Before opening the arched door, Harold studied it. Painted black to match the shutters, it featured two mullioned windows in the top half. They were of a height that allowed him to look into the shop—and those within to look out. An elegant brass handle protruded from the middle, and a brass kick plate had been installed at the bottom.

He had a thought the door should be some color other than black. Red, perhaps, or a dark green. Either would help the door to stand out from the neighboring shops.

Then he remembered his son's color blindness and realized that both colors would appear as shades of gray to him. A sapphire blue would still work with the gold and brass, and he made a mental note to mention it as a possible upgrade if Ewen rebuffed his offer.

Turning the handle, Harold discovered the door opened easily. He waited for a telltale squeak or moan to indicate the hinges needed oiling, but the only sound was the tinkling of a gold bell. He stepped in and shut the door.

Before he had his hat removed from his head, a young woman, who appeared to be in her mid-twenties, approached him from an office at the back of the shop.

"Good afternoon, sir. May I help you?" she asked, dipping a curtsy when she was closer. Her arms were crossed at her waist when she straightened.

Harold bowed. "I am hoping to help you," he said as he reached into his waistcoat pocket and retrieved the bank draft. "Miss Ewen?"

Margaret blinked. "I am."

"Ah, it's good to meet you. I'm—"

"Lord Everly," Adam said as he stepped from behind his workbench and hurried to greet the earl. "It's so good of you to come."

"Mr. Ewen," Harold acknowledged. "I trust you're well?"

"Indeed. May I present my daughter, Margaret? I don't believe she was here when you last paid a call."

"It's very good to meet you," Harold said, reaching for her hand.

Margaret unfolded her arms and offered her right hand as she once again curtsied. "And you, my lord." She dared a glance at her father as she returned her arm to her waist in an effort to cover her shorter, left arm. Although he had told her Mr. Tennison was the earl's son, she hadn't imagined she would ever meet the Earl of Everly.

"You must be the gemologist in the family," Harold said, his attention still on the brunette. He understood immediately why Alexander was so taken with her. She was attractive. Not a classic beauty, but her soft features were enhanced by eyes so gray, they almost appeared silver.

"I am, my lord," she replied, taken aback at his comment. "Are you in the market for a particular gem? Or a piece of fine jewelry?"

"I will take a look at your offerings appropriate for a young lady's come-out," Harold replied. "But first things first." He held out the bank draft. "My son was here earlier today to purchase some gems for a project I've commissioned him to create. I wanted to see to it you were paid."

Margaret's eyes rounded. Mr. Tennison had only left the shop a couple of hours ago. When she saw the amount written on the draft, she inhaled softly. "That's very kind of you, my lord." Her eyes rounded again. "I can hardly believe Mr. Tennison is your son."

"He is," Harold hedged. "Oh, dear. Has he done something for which I should—?"

"Oh, no, my lord. I... you... it's just that you don't appear old enough to be his father, is all."

Harold blinked and then turned to regard Adam. "Whatever you're paying her, you need to double it," he teased.

Adam dipped his head. "I would if I could, my lord."

Hearing the sound of frustration in the owner's reply,

Harold thought better of what he planned to say next and instead turned his attention back on Margaret. "I do hope Alexander didn't command too much of your time with this project."

"Oh, not at all," she assured him. "Unlike my father's designs, Mr. Tennison's drawings were quite well done," she said as she aimed a teasing grin in her father's direction. "Having fabric swatches for your countess' gowns made the task of choosing gems rather easy."

Harold furrowed a brow. "Swatches you no doubt secured from her modiste," he half-asked.

Margaret appeared unsure of how to respond. "It was no trouble, my lord. Madame Suzanne's shop is not far from here."

About to counter her claim, Harold thought better of it. This was the kind of service he wanted his employees to provide if he owned the business. "I am glad to hear it. Except for this Tuesday's ball, I rather doubt I'll see much of Alex for the next couple of weeks. He practically lives in the building that houses his foundry while he works on projects like this."

"A man after my position, it sounds like," Adam groused.

"Not at all," Harold assured him. "In fact, I wondered if we might have a word?"

His brows furrowing, Adam exchanged a quick glance with Margaret before he said, "Of course." He gave the earl an expectant look, as if he thought Harold would divulge his information in front of Margaret.

Immediately understanding the earl wished to speak with her father in private, Margaret motioned toward the back of the shop. "Do feel free to use my office. I was about to rearrange the necklace display," she claimed.

Harold gave her a nod. "I appreciate it. I shouldn't take much of your father's time." He made his way to the office and then preceded the jeweler into the small space. He waited until Adam was about to be seated at the desk before he took the adjacent chair.

Scanning the area around him, Harold tried to imagine spending most of his day in such close confines, and he nearly shuddered at the sensation of claustrophobia that engulfed him. "If what I'm about to offer is in any way an affront to you, please know I mean no offense," he said by way of a preamble.

Adam's eyes widened, and he removed the gold-rimmed spectacles that hung from the end of his nose. "My lord?"

"You and this shop were part of a discussion I had with Lord Weatherstone earlier this morning. A discussion that involved the mention of a certain gem merchant who seems determined to take your livelihood."

Adam stiffened, immediately understanding Harold's comment. "And my daughter."

Harold gave a start, expecting the jeweler to put voice to a protest of some sort. To deny his claim. "So what Weatherstone said about Mr. Baumeister is true? He's trying to take your shop from you?"

Adam dipped his head. "He is. It's all my fault, though. Margaret had nothing to do with what happened."

"What happened?"

Sighing, Adam seemed to ponder how to reply before he finally said, "I had a terrible time last year. I sold a good deal of jewelry, but nearly all of it on credit. No one would pay with blunt. I was buying gems from Baumeister on credit—"

"Which included a good deal of interest, no doubt," Harold murmured.

"Indeed. Ten percent."

Harold's eyes narrowed. "Per year?"

"Per *month*," Adam whispered hoarsely. He ignored the earl's sound of disbelief and added, "Half of what he sold me were rubies of poor quality, and he would not take them back. That's when Margaret insisted on taking over the gem purchases. She's learned a good deal about precious stones in the past few years," he explained. "She can tell the real from the paste, and when she realized Baumeister was attempting to foist poor quality stones on us, she arranged for fair terms with a different gem merchant."

"Who is?" Harold prompted.

"Mr. Goldman. He's honest, and he's fair with his terms."

Harold nodded his understanding. "And your outstanding invoices?"

"Although some clients have since paid, it's not been enough to pay off Mr. Baumeister. Since we haven't bought more gems from him, he knows we're buying from someone else, and he's... well, he's *offended*, my lord. Quite incensed, in fact, which is why he's made the threat to take the shop."

"How much time do you have?"

Adam furrowed a brow. "He was here this morning," he said on a sigh. "He offered a compromise. He would gladly take the shop and keep me employed, as well as my daughter, in exchange for sole ownership. Obviously he would supply all the gems for whatever jewelry is made once he is owner." He inhaled and said, "I have a fortnight to either pay in full, or he will use the courts to take the shop."

"And the amount I have paid you today? I take it that will not be enough to cover your debt to him?" Harold asked.

Shaking his head, Adam said, "Not by half, sir. Not even a quarter. Margaret knows the exact amount. She's the one who sees to the bills these days."

Harold nodded his understanding. "Would you be willing to accept an offer from me if I assured you a position for your daughter and an income for you until you are of a mind to retire? I would see to it Baumeister is paid in full, of course, and warned to keep his distance."

The jeweler regarded the earl for a long time, his brows still furrowed with worry. "You're offering to buy this shop?"

"I am."

"But... why?"

Harold was about to ask himself the very same question. When he had spoken with Weatherstone earlier that day, the purchase of the shop seemed like a good idea. An opportunity to diversify. A place from which his son could practice his passion for making beautiful things. "As a peer with a son whose avocation is metallurgy and jewelry making, it would be in my best interest to own a business where he can sell his creations. A business that would provide income for the earldom. One that he can inherit upon my death."

Adam winced. "We've not been as profitable as we once were, my lord," he whispered.

Harold struggled to display an impassive expression. "Why do you suppose that is?"

Shrugging, Adam said, "Competition can be fierce, especially with Rundell and Bridge selling such a variety of gifts. We only make jewelry—no watches or clocks—and we don't have a Royal Warrant."

"Rundell and Bridge needn't have all the jewelry business, Royal Warrant or not," Harold replied, thinking some advertisements in the news sheets could drive business to the small shop. News sheets like *The Tattler* and respected newspapers like *The London Times*. "Besides, I don't like bullies. And it sounds as if Mr. Baumeister is a bully."

Nodding, Adam said, "He *is* a bully, my lord. My poor Margaret. The things he says about her arm? And then he has the nerve to claim he'll take her to wife. Take the shop as her dowry."

His head jerking as if he'd been slapped, Harold stared at the jeweler. "He wants to *marry* her?"

All at once, Harold was imbued with what could only be

described as horror. In fact, he could not abide the thought that Adam Ewen's daughter might end up married to Samuel Baumeister.

He was fairly sure Alexander would find the possibility untenable.

Buying the jewelry shop, no longer a lark based on a comment by Lord Weatherstone, was suddenly uppermost in his mind.

CHAPTER 21
A SON CONFRONTS HIS MOTHER

eanwhile, at Rosemount House, Lady Everly's salon
"Mother, may I speak with you?" Alexander asked as he leaned around the edge of her salon door. He had just come from the small building that housed his foundry. Once he had lined up the boxes of gems on his workbench, he had spent some time working on the pendants for the necklace and the earrings.

Excited at how well the gems worked in his collets, he experienced a setback when one of the rubies for the earrings cracked while he was heating the setting.

He was sure his curse could have been heard all the way down Park Lane. He had probably awakened the dead and anyone engaged in an afternoon nap. Half of those in Hyde Park had probably cowered in fear. He even had half a thought that Margaret might have heard his cry of frustration all the way in Ludgate Hill.

His first thought had been to blame the gemologist. It wasn't her fault the expensive stone had cracked, though. He should have known better than to have overheated the setting with the stone already in place. He could only hope

Margaret would have another ruby in her stash at the shop. Something close in color and shape. If not, she would have to find him another, or the earrings would require a complete redesign.

When Alexander emerged from the foundry, he discovered the back gardens were as quiet as when he had first disappeared inside. Perhaps his curses of frustration hadn't been as loud as he imagined. Perhaps he was merely overtired. Perhaps his worries over his parents' recent change of behavior had him overwrought.

That was it, of course. He was sure his mother was having an *affaire*. At any moment, his father would find out, and all the collective calm and quiet of Rosemount House would be shattered. With Parliament starting in only a few days, his father would be gone—and probably stay gone—for entire days at a time. His excuses would range from needing to attend meetings at the Royal Society to having drinks with fellow lords at his club.

The only thing Alexander could think to do was confront his mother. Get it out in the open. Put her on report that he knew of her infidelity. Perhaps she would promise to break off the *affaire*. Apologize profusely and swear fidelity to his father.

He could only hope.

Stella looked up from the letter she'd been writing to her father. At seventy-two years of age, Stewart Jones, Duke of Westhaven, really shouldn't still be digging in the dirt. Nor should he be engaged in *affaires* with marchionesses half his age, but it was really none of her concern.

The week prior, she knew he had been in Athens on another of his archaeological expeditions. He was due to return to London sometime soon, though, and Stella wanted the letter to be waiting for him at his townhouse when he arrived.

She was about to let Alexander know she would be done in a moment, but she noted the expression that darkened his face. She dropped her pen on the parchment. "Of course. What is it?" she said in response to his question about speaking with him.

Alexander slipped into the room and closed the door behind him. He leaned against it, his hands clasped behind his back. He didn't look at her when he finally asked, "Mother, are you having an *affaire*?"

Stella's head jerked back as if he she'd been slapped across the face. Then she rolled her eyes. "If you're referring to the way your father and I have been behaving these past few days, then, yes, I am having an *affaire*," she admitted, a grin lifting the corners of her mouth. "With my husband. And I am not about to apologize for it."

Alexander cleared his throat. "I... I wasn't referring to *Father*," he said with a shake of his head, although his expression had softened somewhat at hearing of her devotion to the earl.

Her eyes widening in horror, Stella shook her own head. "I've never been with anyone *but* your father," she whispered. "Oh, dear. Whatever gossip have you heard?"

Alexander's shoulders slumped, and one of his hands moved to his head. His fingers speared his hair and scraped through the wavy locks, leaving his freshly-combed hair looking as if he'd had a bad night. "That evening, when Father mentioned Lord Framingham—"

"That despicable man!" Stella interrupted as she pounded a fist on her writing table. She stood up and began to pace the floor of the small carpeted salon. "I made it perfectly clear that I was *not* interested in engaging in an *affaire* with him," she said as a hand went to her forehead. "I cannot even abide being in the same *room* with him, he smells so bad, let alone the thought of sharing a bed with him." She shivered with her disgust.

"So... he offered you *carte blanche?*" Alexander asked, his brows arching.

Stella stopped her pacing and stared at her son. "He propositioned me in *Floris*, of all places," she replied, deciding it best she tell him everything. "When your father mentioned Framingham's marchioness had lost three-hundred pounds playing cards, all I could think was that she had done it deliberately, and that he had it coming to him, the *rake*," she spat out.

There was another reason, but she didn't mention it. Alexander didn't need to know that his grandfather had been engaging in an *affaire* with Caroline Framingham.

For a moment, she wondered if Lord Framingham had propositioned her in retaliation for what his wife was doing with her father.

Or had been doing. Stewart Jones, Duke of Westhaven, had been away from London on another archaeological expedition for the past four months. He was due back in the capital any day, though.

"You say you turned him down?" Alexander half-asked.

"I told him your Father might not be a perfect marksman, but he is an excellent swordsman," Stella said, "and he would see to removing the man's prick should he learn the marquess had offered an *affaire*." Stella's eyes widened when she realized what she had said. Aloud.

Alexander's eyes rounded with humor. "You said that?"

"Well, I... I don't think I said 'prick,' exactly," she amended, even if she had. "But he knew which body part I was referring to."

Her son began chortling as he watched her face redden

with embarrassment. "Oh, Mother. I wish I had been there. Whatever did Framingham say in response?"

Stella angled her head to one side and said, "Something about keeping it between the two of us. I thought he heard my message loud and clear." She paused before a look of worry crossed her face. "He hasn't said anything at his club, I hope?" she asked in a whisper. "I would hate to think he's... retaliating for my refusal by spreading horrible gossip about me."

Alexander thought back to Friday night and his visit to White's. He couldn't recall seeing the marquess there, but then he was fairly sure the man didn't have a membership. Brooks's, perhaps. "I haven't heard any rumors, if that's what you're asking," he replied.

"Well, that's a relief. I really don't know what your father would do to him."

"He would probably just poison him," Alexander remarked, his comment said in jest. "He no doubt knows of some lethal plant extract he could dump into the man's drink."

"Alex!" Stella scolded, even though she secretly liked the idea of the marquess suffering an abdominal ailment for what he had done. "I can't imagine what life must be like for his wife," she murmured. "To be married to someone who is so repulsive?" She shivered again, her shoulders shaking in response to the thought.

Alexander wasn't about to say what he knew about the marchioness. That she apparently had a cozy relationship with a widower and was rarely in the company of her husband. Instead, Alexander said, "I cannot fathom it myself, but Framingham's odious odor is a reminder to all my sex that we must strive for cleanliness."

"And fidelity, I should hope," Stella murmured.

Dropping his head, Alexander said, "You have nothing to

worry about when it comes to Father. It would seem he rather adores you." He watched in wonder as a serene expression settled over his mother's features, and he felt a good deal of relief at knowing his words had assured her of his father's love for her.

The expression she displayed reminded him of someone else, but he had already taken too much of his mother's time.

He would make additional inquiries later.

"I need to go back to Ludgate Hill," he said.

"Oh?" Stella asked, surprised by the change of subject.

"I, uh, came up a bit short of gold to finish father's signet ring," he stammered. "And I've decided to make Helen's gift out of gold instead of silver."

Stella placed a hand over her mouth. "I can hardly wait to see what you make for her," she gushed.

"Me, as well," he replied before he gave her a nod and left the salon.

CHAPTER 22
SATISFYING A VENGEFUL MARCHIONESS

Meanwhile, at Ewen & Ewen, Ludgate Hill

Adam nodded when Lord Everly asked the question that had him wincing as if he'd eaten an especially sour pickle. He was just as appalled at the thought that his daughter could end up married to Mr. Baumeister.

"It would not be a love match, my lord," Adam assured Harold. "In fact, I would do anything I could to see to it Margaret is saved from such a fate as marriage to Mr. Baumeister."

Daring a glance out the office door window, Harold spotted Margaret greeting a matron who had just arrived. Her manner was as pleasant as it had been with him, and soon the older woman was fingering a necklace on a black velvet display.

Harold would have continued to watch the two women, but Adam's words had him thinking. Had him more determined than ever to see to it Baumeister was prevented from owning the shop—and Margaret Ewen.

"So you'll sell me the shop?" Harold asked, wanting to come to an agreement.

"You'll be changing the name, no doubt," Adam murmured.

"Why would I?"

The comment had Adam giving a start. "You would keep my name—and hers—on the shingle?"

Harold nodded. "I will. No one even need know I own it," he replied. "Except Mr. Baumeister, of course."

"You're ready to discuss numbers now?" Adam asked hopefully.

Glancing back into the shop, Harold watched as Margaret placed the necklace into a velvet lined box and gave it to the customer, her face beaming in delight and the customer apparently just as happy. The woman even paid with cash, which had him curious as to her identity.

"That's Lady Framingham," Adam said with a nod, noting how Harold watched the proceedings. "Which reminds me. I have something that belongs to her," he said as he stood up and moved to the safe.

"Lady Framingham?" Harold repeated in surprise. He didn't recognize the marchioness given the angle of her hat on her head. Her features were hidden behind a riot of silk roses and satin ribbons.

Adam nodded. "She's a frequent customer. Claims she buys something expensive whenever her husband has done something unforgivable. Pardon me a moment while I give this to her." He rushed out of the small office in an effort to catch up to the marchioness, holding out the black velvet ring box as he did so.

Lady Framingham paused at the door and regarded the ring box for a moment. When she didn't immediately reach for it, Adam opened it to reveal the emerald ring. "This is the ring I wrote you about," he said. "The one your nephew stole from you?"

"Oh, as I told Miss Ewen, I'm quite sure there's been

some mistake," she murmured. "Although it is a very lovely ring, it is not mine." Her gaze seemed to linger on the ring as if she was tempted to take it, but she turned and took her leave of the shop, the gold bell tinkling as the door closed behind her.

Margaret and her father exchanged curious glances. "I mentioned we had it in the safe when she first arrived," Margaret said in a quiet voice. "I thought it was why she had come in. But she said it wasn't hers, and that she didn't have a nephew." Margaret's expression was enough to indicate she didn't believe Lady Framingham's claim, at least the one about her not having a nephew. "If it doesn't belong to her, then the Runner must have been mistaken," Margaret added, her consternation evident.

"Indeed," her father replied. "I'll see that it ends up in the hands of the rightful owner," he added on a sigh. "I can at least do that."

Margaret gave a start. "But... how can you know who the current owner is if it's been so long since you made it?" she asked.

Her father allowed a shrug. "I suppose I don't. But he'll know. Trust me. It will end up on the right finger."

*H*er brows furrowing in confusion, Margaret watched as her father returned to the office and his meeting with the Earl of Everly. For the briefest of moments, she had seen a wistful expression on the marchioness' face as Lady Framingham regarded the ring. A sort of longing. Desire, even.

Margaret was sure Lady Framingham was about to take the ring, but then she had simply turned and left the shop.

Whatever would have a woman denying she was the owner of such a beautiful emerald ring?

Heartbreak?

Bad memories?

Guilt?

Then Margaret remembered what her father had said about the ring. That he had cut the gem and fashioned the gold setting a long time ago. It was one of his first creations.

So if it hadn't been made for Caroline Framingham, and Lord Framingham wasn't a client, then who had commissioned it?

*H*arold arched a brow, wondering if the Marchioness of Framingham's purchase had been made as a means of revenge. Had she learned her husband had propositioned Stella?

Although he would prefer the honor of skewering the earl with a sword, his marchioness stabbing him in his pocketbook might be more effective.

The thought had Harold more determined to purchase the shop.

When Adam returned to the office, ring box still in hand, Harold held up a finger to stave off anything the jeweler might say. Harold hurried out, intending to introduce himself to Lady Framingham. She had already taken her leave, though, and he paused next to where Margaret stood. "She seemed to be a satisfied client," he remarked.

Margaret angled her head slightly. "I make sure she never leaves in the same mood in which she arrives," she replied, although her expression betrayed her confusion over what had happened.

"Which was?"

Margaret inhaled softly, her eyes lowering as if she were struggling for a way to answer without divulging the truth.

"Vindictive?" Harold offered.

"That is usually one of her moods, in fact," Margaret admitted with a sigh. "I find diamonds help in that regard."

"And when she's angry?"

Margaret stared at him a moment before she said, "Something with rubies. They're rather expensive right now, so they can be quite effective in bringing a smile to her face."

Appreciating her candor, Harold asked, "Has she ever been... jealous?"

"Frequently," Margaret replied. "I've sold her an entire parure featuring rubies over the course of the past year."

That parure had been the beginning of the shop's downfall, though, and she struggled to display an impassive expression at remembering what the purchase of the rubies were costing the shop—in more ways than just money.

Harold resisted the urge to laugh for the fourth time that day. "And when she is sad or unconsolable?"

"Sapphires, my lord. Earbobs and brooches, usually, but once she purchased a bracelet of blue sapphires."

"What if she was in love?"

Margaret sucked in a breath, and one brow furrowed as if she were trying to remember if there had ever been a time when Lady Framingham bought jewels because she was in love. "Is this a trick question, my lord? Because... I don't recall a time when her ladyship came here on that account."

The ring came to mind again. The look on her face. If the emerald ring had been given to Lady Framingham by a lover, then the *affaire* was obviously over.

Margaret couldn't help but feel curiosity over who that might have been. She was sure she would have read something about it in one of the gossip rags.

Harold nodded his understanding. He couldn't comprehend how any woman would love the odoriferous and rakish Lord Framingham. "But if I did? If I came seeking the perfect jewel for my countess—because I loved her—what would you show me?"

An impish grin appearing, Margaret said, "Why, garnets and rubies of course, my lord. An entire parure, fashioned in a most elaborate design. To be created by the hand of your heir."

"You *minx*!" Harold accused, a smile lighting his face.

Margaret gave a start. Mr. Tennison had said the same about her, a few minutes before he kissed her. She couldn't help the bloom of color that suffused her cheeks.

Before she could say anything, though, Harold laughed for the fifth time that day. "Oh, do not be vexed on my account. I shall not kiss you, my lady," he said with a teasing grin. "I save all my kisses for my countess."

Her face now displaying the pinkest of blushes, Margaret finally dipped her head and said, "Of course, my lord."

"Thank you for agreeing to dance with my son."

The change in topic had Margaret giving a start. "Mr. Tennison was quite insistent, my lord. I could hardly deny him, given he had a hand in arranging the invitation," she replied.

"And if he had not? Would you still grant him a waltz?"

Margaret's eyes lowered before she said, "How could I not? I've imagined dancing with him every time I've seen him on his pedestal at the British Museum." The words were out of her mouth before she could stop them, and she inhaled sharply.

Harold stared at the gemologist for several seconds before he burst out laughing for the sixth time that day. "No wonder he feels affection for you," Harold remarked happily. He quickly sobered when he noted her reaction to his comment.

Shock.

Disbelief.

Awe.

A look that suggested she was about to faint.

"If you dare tell him what I just said, I shall have to deny it or claim I'd drunk too much wine at luncheon," he warned, a grin lifting the corners of his lips.

Margaret dipped her head again. "It will be our secret, of course, my lord," she replied, unable to hide her embarrassment.

"We shall come for you Tuesday evening. Give you a ride to the ball," Harold said. "At half-past eight o'clock?"

Margaret's eyes widened. Alexander had mentioned a ride in the Everly town coach. He had even stated a time when he would collect her, but at that moment, she hadn't thought she would be attending. Not really. Now it seemed that she would have to. An earl was giving her an invitation she could not turn down. A new gown hung on a peg in her wardrobe. "I would be most appreciative," she replied.

"Should I inform your father?"

She shook her head. "I will tell him." She glanced back toward the office. "Have you already finished your business with him?"

Harold sighed. "Not yet. Tell me... as the one who sees to the invoices and payables, how would you value this shop? "

"Value it?"

"How much is it worth?"

Margaret dared a glance toward the office, noting how her father seemed to be staring at something in his mind's eye. "Property, building, jewels, gems, and all?" she countered.

Harold cleared his throat. "If someone made an offer to buy it, what amount would have *you* selling it? Without question?"

Inhaling deeply, Margaret leaned in and whispered the amount she had determined only the night before. An exercise that had left her both vexed and saddened. How had her father's business—once vibrant and profitable, become such a sad concern? "That includes the amount plus interest owed to Mr. Baumeister, a gem merchant—"

"I am well aware of Baumeister's claim on you and your shop," he whispered hoarsely.

Margaret gasped. "My lord, are *you* considering saving the shop?" *Saving my father and me?* she nearly added

Harold furrowed a brow. "Even if I could not, I think *you* could," he replied. "You are no fool, Miss Ewen. Nor are you likely to agree to a marriage that would see you no better than chattel."

Stunned at hearing his assessment of her, Margaret stared at him for a moment before she allowed a nod. "You seem to know me well, my lord."

Harold regarded her for a time before he said, "If you feel the least bit of affection for my son, please show it when he takes you for a ride in the park." Harold leaned in and added, "He is of the opinion that he is too young to marry, but that does not preclude the option of him securing a woman's hand well in advance of a wedding."

Margaret's eyes rounded in surprise at hearing the earl's words. "Yes, my lord," she replied. A whirlwind of thoughts had her feeling light-headed. For some reason, a mention of her age seemed to offer a means to ground the heady experience. "In the interest of full disclosure, I should warn you that I am..." She paused, an expression of uncertainty crossing her face. "I am not nearly as young as Mr. Tennison."

Harold gave a start. "Oh?" he managed, not about to ask her age. He knew better. Stella had seen to that lesson long ago. Besides, the young woman had already seen to boosting his ego with her earlier comment about his age.

"I am five-and-twenty, sir," she admitted in a whisper.

"Oh," he replied with a good deal of relief. "For a moment there, I thought you were going to tell me you were five-and-*thirty*, even though you do not look it."

Margaret tittered nervously, secretly thrilled at hearing the earl's assessment. "There are days when I feel as if I am," she admitted.

Lately, she had felt old nearly every time she rose from her small bed. Older when retired for the night. She held out her withered arm. "And although you and your son haven't said anything, perhaps it's best he direct his attentions elsewhere. I shouldn't want him to suffer the cut direct for his consideration of me."

Harold glanced at her arm before she tucked it back against her waist, understanding her meaning. "I would never warn my son off considering a clever young woman for friendship or for matrimony. Especially when she shares an interest in his avocation."

Margaret gazed at him in wonder, stunned by his words. "I hardly think I am a match for a man who could be part of the exhibit of Greek gods at the British Museum, my lord."

Remembering Helen's claim that her friends thought Alexander was gorgeous, Harold allowed a smirk. "I thank you for your candor." He gave a nod—as much as a dismissal as it was a bow—and made his way back to the office.

*O*nce the door was shut, Harold announced an amount about fifteen percent more than what Margaret Ewen had stated and felt a good deal of satisfaction when Adam said, "I accept your offer, of course, my lord."

Surprised at the lack of negotiation—at the lack of an attempt at haggling—Harold let out a breath. "Well, then. I'll have my solicitor draw up the papers," he said. "See if we can't have this all settled in the next fortnight."

Adam glanced out the office window, his attention on his daughter. "And Mr. Baumeister?"

"I'll see to paying him off as part of the purchase," Harold replied. "Should he come around before that happens, do send him my way, won't you?"

The jeweler regarded him with awe. "Yes, my lord."

"He's not to go anywhere near your daughter."

Nodding, Adam said, "Of course not."

"If he pays a call and is difficult, do send word. I have a friend at Whitehall who can help in situations like this," Harold murmured, thinking of his friend, Alexander Bradley. He thought of all they had shared when they'd been on Mykonos, back when Alex had met Nike Xenakis and Harold had found Stella while searching for her father.

"Whitehall?" Adam repeated, his eyes round.

"Indeed. Alexander Bradley will do whatever I ask," Harold claimed, attempting to shake off the brief reverie that threatened to keep him in the past. "Mr. Baumeister needs to know he cannot threaten you or Miss Ewen," he added.

Adam nodded, now well aware the Earl of Everly was capable of vengeance if the circumstances demanded it. "I accept your offer of protection for my daughter, my lord," he stated.

Harold nodded to Adam, his gaze going to the red swatch of fabric on Margaret's desk. He raised a brow. "Is that the fabric my wife's ballgown is made from?"

"Indeed, my lord. Margaret fetched it from the modiste, Madame Suzanne. Feel free to take it," Adam encouraged. "Your son already has nearly every red stone we had in our possession."

Grinning, Harold helped himself to the square of red watered silk. He held out his right hand, and Adam shook it. "If you'll excuse me, I need to secure a pair of red slippers for my countess," Harold said.

"Very good, sir."

Harold took his leave of the establishment, well aware his exit was watched by two very relieved people.

CHAPTER 23
AN EARL RECALLS DARING DEEDS AND A DANCE

few moments later, in front of Ewen & Ewen
Even before Harold made it to the coach, Mr. Thorton at the ready with the door held open for him, Harold's attention was on his mind's eye.

Although most thought his son, Alexander, had been named for Alexander the Great, he had in fact been named after the Foreign Office operative who had been instrumental in Harold's rescue of Stella's father from the island of Delos over two decades ago.

Bradley's alter ego, Captain Jack Crawley, a pirate of some renown, had sailed the *Molly* all over the Mediterranean and the English Channel in pursuit of smugglers and missing persons, pirates and foreign operatives.

Married to Stella's best friend, Nike Xenakis, for longer than Harold had been married to Stella, Bradley now piloted a desk at Whitehall. His years of experience as a pirate and field agent meant his current operations were just as successful, even if he wasn't the one standing at the stern of a ship or operating behind enemy lines.

Harold remembered the sense of danger and derring-do

he had felt back then when he and Stella were on Mykonos and Delos. Remembered the moment when Nike had been shot, taking a bullet intended for Bradley. Remembered how Bradley's love for Nike had been apparent from the moment he had seen the two together for the first time.

Had others thought the same about Stella and him as they had about Alexander Bradley and Nike Xenakis?

Harold frowned when he remembered what had happened the very first time he had ever met Stella. Their initial interaction hadn't exactly ended on the best of terms. Out of a sense of duty, he had danced with her at her come-out ball. *Trod upon her feet* was a better way of putting it.

He had been a terrible dancer back then.

Sure he had ruined Stella's slippers that night, he decided he still owed her a pair of shoes. She might have purchased a few dozen pairs during the course of their marriage, but he had never actually replaced the pair he had trod upon that night.

Armed with the swatch of red watered silk, Harold knew exactly where he would be paying a call after he left the jewelry shop.

He tried to imagine how Stella might react when the slippers were delivered.

Would it be like that day on Delos? Like that moment when Stella had agreed to be his wife? That day had been filled with fear and uncertainty, excitement and adventure. Harold had never felt so alive, so in love knowing Stella would have to agree to be his countess or there would be no reason for him to return to England.

The thought had him recalling what they had done together earlier that morning. What they had done when they returned from Weatherstone Manor. What he hoped they would be doing later that evening.

Remembering he was about to become a father for the

third time, Harold nodded to Thorton. "Take me to Lady Everly's favorite shoe maker," he ordered as he stepped into the town coach.

"Yes, my lord," Thorton replied before shutting the door.

Harold considered what he would owe Bradley should the man have to use his influence to see to it Mr. Baumeister was prevented from causing further trouble at Ewen & Ewen.

Another namesake.

If his countess gave him his second heir, Harold would see to it the babe would be named Bradley.

If the child his wife carried was a girl, Harold decided he could always name her Alexandra, if only because he couldn't sort a girl's name from 'Bradley.'

He was grinning in delight when he made his way into the shoe maker's shop.

CHAPTER 24
RED SLIPPERS ARRIVE

The following day, Rosemount House

The Rosemount House butler found Lady Everly in her salon, her attention on the invitation to Helen's come-out ball. Her sister-in-law, Lady Sommers, had provided the original from which she was penning copies. "This box came for you a moment ago, my lady," Jones said as he held out the pasteboard box.

Stella looked up from her escritoire and stared at the box. "Me?" she asked. She reached for it and then held it for several moments before she finally lifted the lid and peered inside.

Shoes. Silk slippers, in fact, in a scarlet she immediately recognized.

Atop the pair of red slippers was a note, and she unfolded it slowly.

To my lovely Countess Everly,

I was reminded on this day that I never replaced the slippers I no doubt ruined during our first dance together at your come-out ball. You probably think I forgot, but a man never forgets his first encounter with his Aphrodite.

I look forward to our next dance. Will you save the first and second waltzes for me at the Weatherstone ball? I promise not to trod upon your feet, although if I do, I shall replace these with yet another pair.

Your loving husband,

Harry

"Oh, Harry," Stella whispered. Fighting back tears, she blinked several times as she reread the missive. She finally pulled one of the slippers from the shoe box, allowing a watery grin and a sniffle as she lowered it to the floor.

Removing one slipper using the toe of the other, she slipped a bare foot into the red slipper and held the foot out from beneath her skirts.

She was sure the jeweled clip that decorated the top of the slipper was made of garnets and citrines. They were probably paste, but they would be perfect with both of the ball-gowns being crafted at Suzanne's for this Season's balls.

However did he know? she wondered as she lowered the other slipper to the floor and tried it on.

The fit was perfect, as was the red silk.

She knew exactly when—and how—she would thank him.

CHAPTER 25
A SON CONTEMPLATES A WOMAN

Tuesday morning, before breakfast, Rosemount House

Alexander woke with the same image in his mind as the one that had lulled him to sleep earlier that morning. The image of serenity on Margaret Ewen's face when he had assured her he did not hold her accountable for the cracked ruby—the one he had ruined when he had over-heated the setting for the earring. That she was in possession of a replacement was not only fortuitous but an excuse for him to see her again one more time before that night's ball.

She had given him not only that look, but one that might have been adoration.

He remembered catching her staring at him on at least two occasions as they arranged the gemstones for the neck-lace and bracelet by color and size. Both times, she quickly averted her eyes, pretending her attention was on the stones at her fingertips.

He had certainly stared at those fingertips, marveling at the perfect ovals, tipped in white crescents. The thought of one of them trailing down the front of his body, through his dark curlies and onto his hardened manhood had his body reacting as if she was doing it this very moment. Doing that while her lips took hold of his and kissed him until he was breathless with desire.

Alexander was about to imagine what might come next when a hand waved in front of his face.

"You and your father share that particular trait," Stella remarked as she settled her hands on her hips. "A penny for your thoughts?"

Embarrassed at being caught whilst thinking of the delectable Miss Ewen as he waited for his mother in her salon, Alexander gave his head a shake. Then he thought he may as well ask her opinion on the matter that had been plaguing him ever since he had met Margaret Ewen. "Tell me, if I wish to spend time in the company of a young woman, but I don't necessarily wish to court her—'"

"Because you want to tumble her, but not marry her?" Stella asked, managing to keep her voice even. Despite her attempt to hide a note of censure, she couldn't.

"No," he quickly replied, rather stunned by her brusk response. "I merely wish to... to *befriend* her."

Stella blinked. "You wish to be friends with a young woman?" she clarified.

"Yes. As a... a colleague. As someone who shares my interests in... gemology and metallurgy," he stammered.

Her brows arching, Stella stared at her son. "Are you speaking of Margaret Ewen?"

It was Alexander's turn to look as if he'd been slapped. "How... how did you know?"

Stella rolled her eyes and settled in the chair at her writing desk. "You could have been speaking about any woman in the world if you had mentioned the word 'jewelry,'" she replied. "But you said 'gemology.' She's the only woman I know of who specializes in such a field. Mr. Ewen has seen to it she's mentioned as such in his advertisements in *The Tattler*."

"How do *you* know her?"

Allowing a slight shrug, Stella leaned toward him and said in a quiet voice, "She's the one we go to see when we've lost a gem from a piece of jewelry."

Alexander chortled. "Surely that can't happen all that often," he remarked. From his mother's expression, he sobered. "Oh, dear," he murmured. "Are there... particular goldsmiths whose jewelry is most likely to lose a gem?" He feared for a moment that she might be referring to one of *his* creations. Either a gold chain necklace with a three-stone pendant or the two earbobs he had made from fresh water pearls.

"I've never lost a stone from either of the three pieces you've made for me," Stella assured him. "But I lost a pearl once. From a ring. I've no idea who made it, but my father gave it to me for my come-out."

"*You* had a come-out?" Alexander blurted.

Stella gave him a quelling glance. "Of course I did. Need I remind you my father is a duke?" she asked rhetorically as she slapped a hand against his. "That ball was the first time I ever met your father. He danced with me, and until this past Saturday, I was quite sure he didn't remember." She paused to take a breath. "Anyway, I took the ring to Ewen and Ewen a few months back, and Miss Ewen had the perfect pearl. Her father did the setting, and the ring looks as good as it did when Father gave it to me."

"Hmm," Alexander murmured. "And you know of others who have gone to her for this service?"

Stella nodded, deciding she could tell her son what else she knew about Caroline, Marchioness of Framingham. "Just a fortnight ago, a certain marchioness went to have a missing emerald added onto her coronet." She leaned forward and whispered. "Turns out, almost all of the stones in the coronet were *paste*. The ones that were real were common stones."

Alexander boggled. "Are you speaking of *Framingham's* marchioness?"

Stella nodded. "Caroline spoke of it over tea at Carlington House last week. She was spitting mad. And hurt."

"I can imagine," Alexander murmured.

"Poor Miss Ewen was the one who told her, but she was apparently very gentle with her. She said the coronet she brought in for repair was the one to be worn in public and the real one was no doubt kept under lock and key for safe keeping."

"Which is a possibility," Alexander hedged. "Morganfield has said his marchioness never wears her real one in public."

Stella boggled. "Well, then where does she wear it?" From the way Alexander suddenly reddened, Stella rolled her eyes. "Never mind," she added. "Those two have to be the lustiest couple in all the *ton*."

"Mother!" Alexander scolded. Then his eyes narrowed. "I'm quite sure a different couple has taken on that mantle of late," he added in a teasing voice.

"Alex!" Stella hissed.

"Back to the matter at hand," Alexander said as he quickly sobered. "The Framingham coronet," he reminded her.

Stella sighed, her shoulders sagging at the reminder of what they had been talking about. "Caroline says the coronet is the only one. So when your father mentioned that she had lost three-hundred pounds playing cards, I'm quite sure it was because of the coronet and not any... *affaire* her husband might be having. Or not." She winced. "I cannot think of a single woman who would want to have an *affaire* with that man. Including Caroline." She inhaled softly and then regarded her son with a grin, remembering his mention of befriending Margaret Ewen. "If you are so inclined to establish a friendship with Miss Ewen, then I think you must tell her so. As for where you can continue your friendship outside of the jewelry shop..." She paused.

"What is it?"

Stella shrugged. "I'm not sure what to advise. There are the obvious places where you could take a woman who you were courting—"

"Such as?"

Stella considered destinations for a moment. "Gunther's Tea Shoppe for an ice. That would have been my favorite. Hyde Park for a ride on horseback, or on a phaeton, or even a walk. Or you could go on one of those boats on the Serpentine. There's the theatre. The museum. Pleasure gardens. Regent Park." She paused a moment, an impish grin appearing. "You do realize I'm suggesting places *I* like to go to since I'll be chaperoning."

"Mother," he replied on a sigh, deciding not to mention that he had already secured the promise of a ride in the park on Thursday.

"I don't see why you couldn't escort Miss Ewen to any of those places, as long as she knew you were doing so as a *friend*. If that *is* all you want. Friendship, I mean."

"It is," he assured her. When he noted her questioning glance, he sighed. "I'm only one-and-twenty," he reminded her. "Even after listening to Hexham and Gabe Wellingham extoll the virtues of marriage over drinks last Friday, I cannot yet imagine myself with a wife."

Stella stood and moved to stand before her son. He'd grown far taller than her these past few years, so she had to stand on tiptoe to kiss him on the cheek. "Miss Ewen would be very lucky to have you as a friend," she murmured.

"Thank you," he replied. He was about to take his leave of the salon, but Stella held up a finger.

"*You* may not be of a mind to marry, but your sister's come-out is but a fortnight away."

Alexander's eyes widened. "What?"

"She's eighteen," Stella replied. "Your Aunt Evangeline has been helping me with arrangements. The ball is to be at Sommers House. Invitations have already been sent. As unlikely as it seems, your sister could end up married before you," she added with an arched brow. "I expect you to help vet anyone who shows the least bit of interest in her."

"You can be assured I will," he replied, his manner most serious. "But I cannot imagine Helen as a young matron," he commented. She was three years younger than him. "Not yet, anyway."

"Nevertheless, if you know of anyone who has put voice to an interest in her—"

"There hasn't been anyone," he assured her.

"You will let me or your father know."

"I will," he replied.

"Now, as much I have enjoyed this conversation—or rather most of it—I am *starving*." She didn't add it was because Harold had been especially attentive that morning. Again.

"As am I," Alexander replied. He offered his arm. "Shall we?"

Stella took the proffered arm, and Alexander led her as far as the first floor landing. "I've forgotten my pocket watch," he said. "I'll be down in a moment."

Furrowing a brow, Stella watched as he made his way back up the stairs. Deciding not to wait, she made her way to the breakfast parlor.

And a most unexpected commotion.

CHAPTER 26
A DUKE PAYS A CALL

A second later, in the Rosemount House breakfast parlor
"Father?"

"There you are," Stewart Jones, Duke of Westhaven, boomed when his daughter appeared on the threshold of the breakfast parlor. He was standing behind Helen's chair and was shaking hands with Harold. "I was about to come up there and wrest you from your bed."

"I haven't been in my bed for..." She paused, not about to tell him it had been more than four days since she had slept in her own bed. She'd been spending the past few nights in the master suite. "A couple of hours," she said, her gaze going to the clock on the sideboard. "I was in my salon," she added as she hurried to kiss her father on his cheek.

She stepped back and allowed her gaze to travel over her father's body, expecting to find him old and frail. Instead, he appeared in good health, his face bronzed from the sun and his paunch only slightly larger than it had been before he had left for Greece a few months prior. His hair was white, but it had been for over twenty years. "Are you on your way to the House of Lords?"

He nodded. "I am, but I wished to stop here and let you know I have returned from my latest adventure."

"Well, do join us for breakfast," she encouraged, indicating her regular chair. She motioned for a footman to bring another. "I have a letter for you," she added. "I was going to have it delivered to your townhouse later today."

"Just came from there. I've a stack of correspondence a foot high," he claimed as he mimed with a hand held over the table. He took the proffered chair at the same time the footman seated Stella. "But I wish to give your daughter my RSVP in person for her ball." He turned to regard Helen. "I will be at your ball, of course."

Helen beamed from where she sat with her father at the table. "Does that mean you'll afford me a dance?"

"Two, if I am so allowed," Westhaven replied.

Stella remembered how she had felt at the same moment in her life and was relieved Helen was looking forward to her ball.

Stella certainly hadn't looked forward to her own.

Despite having an English duke for a father, her Greek mother may as well have been a whore given how poorly Stella's come-out had been attended. How the *ton* gave Astria Zabat Jones the cut direct despite her status as a duchess. If her father hadn't spent most of his time digging up bits of pottery and mosaics in Greece and had instead spent his time in London, Stella was sure her mother would have been afforded the respect she deserved.

"Evangeline has been most helpful," Stella said, referring to her sister-in-law. "She claims it's all in preparation for her own daughter's come-out in two year's time."

"Eva's will be more subdued, I should think, given she's such a bluestocking," Harold said, referring to his eldest niece.

"Darling, it's quite all right for girls to be bluestockings these days," Stella said as she motioned for the footman to bring a plate for her father. He had already seen to the man's coffee and a cup of tea for her.

Westhaven furrowed a brow as he regarded his daughter. "You look in good health."

Stella gave a start. "That's because I am."

"There's color in your cheeks, and you've put on some weight."

"Father!" For a moment, Stella knew there would be even more color in her cheeks if her father guessed just why it was she looked so healthy. She was about to change the subject when Alexander entered and greeted everyone.

Stella would have kissed him if he hadn't leaned over and done it first. "Apologies for my tardiness," he murmured. "Grandfather!" he said in surprise. "It's good to see you again. Been ever so long."

"Not even four months," Westhaven remarked as he stood and pulled his only grandson into a hug.

"Up late at your club, no doubt?"

Alexander gave a shake of his head. "I was out in the foundry last night. I've been experimenting with gold-smithing."

His grandfather's bushy brows arched up in surprise. "Gold?" He allowed a smirk. "Well, you certainly look as if you could be a young Hephaestus," he added, referring to the Greek god of metallurgy. "And I swear you're a foot taller than when I last saw you. Either that, or I've shrunk."

"He's grown at least that much," Harold remarked.

"You must have all the young ladies worshipping you when you're not sweating over the forge," Westhaven teased. "I suppose they have an exhibit with your name on it over at the British Museum."

Alexander tried hard not to remember Margaret's comments about his pedestal at the museum. "Turns out, gold is far easier to form into collets than silver, I think. Once I got started, I just kept going until I was nearly out of gold." He had kept aside enough to complete the signet ring he had started the month before.

"Does that mean you made a lot of collets?" Harold asked, managing to avoid a glance in his wife's direction. He didn't want her to guess what their son was creating.

"Enough for now," Alexander hedged. He turned his attention to his grandfather. "Are you off to Parliament this morning?"

"In a while," Westhaven replied. "Thought I'd learn what I've missed this past session and do some reading on this Chartist issue."

"You know of it?"

"Of course. I may have spent most of the last four months in the Mediterranean, but I did read the news sheets," he claimed.

"The idea is very popular with the masses," Harold remarked. "And yet I rather doubt the lords will adopt their proposal."

"That's because most of them are idiots," Westhaven remarked. "They only look out for themselves and their fellow landowners."

"You think the general populace should have more say in their government?" Alexander asked. He thought of George Grandby, Viscount Hexham, and wondered how he might vote on such an issue in his first stint in Parliament. Given his father, the Earl of Torrington, had decided to remain in Northumberland this Season, George had been granted a writ of acceleration and would be taking his father's place in the House of Lords.

Hexham's recent wedding trip to the Kingdom of the Two Sicilies had opened his eyes to what happened when a country had been claimed by a string of monarchies, none of which had been embraced by the masses. At some point, Italy would gain its independence, but it wouldn't be because aristocrats willed it. The poor and working class would be the ones expected to fight for their country, whether or not they had representation in their government.

"I do," Westhaven replied in response to Alexander's query. "We'll have nothing but civil unrest until we give the common man what he wants. Right now, the Chartists have funding from those in the middle class. And they'll continue to gain popular opinion as long as they don't do something stupid."

"Stupid?" Alexander repeated, curious as to what his grandfather might consider stupid.

"If they resort to violence—if they cause damage or resort to killing—their cause will be lost. There will be no sympathy for them and therefore no support from the lords."

"Or very little," Harold murmured. Although he hadn't been alive for the French Revolution, he had certainly grown up knowing about its after effects. Should the Chartist movement increase in popularity, England might be due for its own revolution. As an aristocrat, he might suffer the same fate as his counterparts in France had. He shuddered at the thought of losing his head.

"You're speaking of politics over breakfast," Helen whined.

"Yes, we are, but we shall stop now," Harold agreed, aiming an apologetic look in his father-in-law's direction. "We'll save it for dinner. You *will* join us for dinner? Tomorrow evening?" he asked the duke. "We'll be attending the Weatherstone ball tonight."

Westhaven seemed to think on the query a moment before he directed his gaze on his daughter.

"You're not going to get a better offer from anyone else," Stella said with a teasing grin.

"I won't tell my mistress you said that," he countered, his eyes glittering with mischief.

"You won't because you don't *have* a mistress," Stella argued, anxious to see how he would react. Perhaps he wouldn't refer to his lover as such, though. Then she wondered if the Marchioness of Framingham was still his lover.

Westhaven rolled his eyes. "Touché!" he said with a good deal of mirth, all the while Alexander and Helen stared at their mother and then her father with looks of shock. The duke returned their gaze. "The lesson here, you two, is never argue with your mother," he stated. "You will lose."

"Yes, sir," they replied in unison.

Meanwhile, Harold did his best to hide his amusement. "Tell me, Westhaven. Do they play billiards in Italy?"

Westhaven frowned. "Not that I know of—I was only in Sicily a week to see my brother—but I have a table in my townhouse."

"We have one upstairs," Alexander said, his eyes bright. "Care for a game after dinner tomorrow?"

Suspicion appeared in the duke's expression. "A player of some talent, are you?" His gaze darted to Harold, who gave a slight nod. "Perhaps a wager—"

"Father," Stella said in hoarse whisper.

"A small wager—"

"Done," Alexander replied, a grin spreading over his face.

Westhaven stared at him a moment, his expression sobering. "My god, boy, you looked so much like Stella's grandfather just then." He turned his attention to his daughter. "It's a wonder the museum hasn't made you an offer to put him on display. He'd make an excellent addition to the Greek and Roman Hall," he said in a most serious voice.

"Oh, they did," Stella deadpanned. "They had the pedestals all prepared. One for him and one for a similarly blessed young woman, but they didn't offer enough blunt, so I turned them down."

Alexander blinked at hearing the exchange and then blinked again when he remembered Miss Ewen's comment the first day he had paid a call on her at the jewelry store.

Did you escape your pedestal at the British Museum?

"Such a shame," Westhaven replied, managing to keep a straight face despite his daughter's comment.

"Yes, well, he's worth more to me here," Harold chimed in, rather enjoying the interplay between his wife and her father. He turned to Alexander and added, "Don't let all this talk of your god-like appearance go to your head, son."

"Yes, sir," Alexander replied, his face more red than it had been the night before when he was melting gold in the foundry.

"Well, on that note, I think I shall be on my way," West-haven said.

Everyone at the table got to their feet, and Stella stood on tiptoe to kiss her father's cheek. "Come at seven. Dinner will be at eight," she said.

"I'll be along shortly," Harold said when Westhaven appeared about to offer him a ride to Westminster.

"Very good. Thank you for breakfast, daughter." West-haven allowed his granddaughter to kiss him on the cheek, and he shook Alexander's hand. "I'm not sure how to address a Greek god," he teased.

Alexander laughed. "Alex will do, sir."

They watched as the duke took his leave, and then all eyes turned to Stella.

"A bit cheeky with your father, were you not?" Harold commented as they settled back into their chairs.

"Perhaps," she replied. "But I cannot help it."

Harold's brows furrowed, realizing immediately she was

thinking of something other than their teasing comments about Alexander's good looks. "Are you... angry with him?"

Stella inhaled slowly. "I wouldn't call it anger."

"Peevish," Alexander offered, thinking he was included in the conversation. He quickly turned his attention to his breakfast when his father gave him a pointed glance.

"He's too old to still be tromping about Italy and Greece," she said as she stabbed a roasted tomato. "Climbing mountains and digging in the dirt. Bed..." She swallowed and stared into her teacup, stunned she was about to mention his *affaire*.

Harold flinched, glad he wasn't the subject of her ire. "Well, he's here now, and I rather doubt he's set to make another trip to Greece this year," he said, his voice pitched in a manner he hoped would calm her.

"You'll speak with him tonight?" she asked.

About to remind her Westhaven was a duke, Harold nodded. "I'll discover his plans and let you know."

"Dissuade him if you must," Stella encouraged.

If he'd been ambivalent about sharing a bed with her that night, Harold might have laughed at her request. If Westhaven had a mind to begin another archaeological expedition, he would not be talked out of it no matter who did the talking.

Instead, Harold remained sober and gave her a nod.

CHAPTER 27
RECOLLECTIONS

id-day Tuesday, Chamber of Lords, Parliament
Despite his attempts to keep his attentions on the man who was speaking—the first session of Parliament had been convened only the hour before—Harold found his thoughts straying to that morning's breakfast. To the odd exchange between Stella and her father.

She was obviously displeased with him, but Harold was fairly sure it had nothing to do with his archaeological expeditions.

What had she said?

He's too old to still be tromping about Italy and Greece, climbing mountains and digging in the dirt. Bed...

Bed. She had clamped down the rest of what she had been about to say so quickly, he had nearly missed the word.

Bed.

Tromping. Climbing. Digging. Bed... ding.

Bedding.

Harold blinked.

Ah! So Stella wasn't happy that her father was bedding

someone. But who could it be? Harold had never known the Duke of Westhaven to employ a mistress or engage in illicit *affaires*. Perhaps he had a lover in Italy or in Greece.

Or both.

Or he was having an *affaire* in London and was very discreet about it.

He dared a glance in the direction of his father-in-law. Westhaven's attention was entirely on the speaker. He didn't look the least bit bored with the proceedings.

He also didn't look a day older than when Harold had been sent to the Cyclades to find him, and that had been more than twenty years ago.

If he hadn't been asked to search for the duke—Westhaven had been gone from London far longer than expected and was considered missing—Harold never would have ended up meeting Stella for a second time.

If he hadn't have met her that second time, he never would have married her.

The thought had him momentarily stunned. What would his life have been like without her? Without their children? He would have ended up with someone else, no doubt, but he couldn't reason who that might be. There hadn't been anyone else he was remotely interested in to take to wife.

Unable to imagine life without Stella, he instead allowed his thoughts to drift back to his time on Mykonos.

Since he was already scheduled to embark on an exploratory trip to discover if Cretan plane trees existed on islands other than Crete, Harold had agreed to include the duke in his search. By making Mykonos the center of his research, the best place to start a search for an archaeologist was on nearby Delos. The island was considered the birthplace of Apollo and Artemis, and archaeological surveys suggested it was ripe for study.

. . .

*H*arold regarded the rubble littering the area around the ancient temple, frowning when he realized he was seeing more than just some stones scattered about. Pieces of statuary—arms, legs, and all manner of body parts—were strewn about as if they'd been tossed there by some giant.

Glancing up at what was left standing, he realized the pieces had at one time made up the pediment of the temple. *Earthquake*, he thought with a shake of his head. Such a loss considering the craft that had gone into the carvings.

He redirected his attention to the land below. From this vantage near the top of the island's only mountain, he could gaze out over the ruins of Delos and determine exactly where the main town had been located.

The foundations of houses and colonnades seemed more evident, more distinct, the closer they were to the water. Although he had taken in this same view only six years before, he had the impression pieces were missing, as if the stone blocks and statuary that had made up the town had been carted off the island.

Probably, he reasoned, remembering how the Parthenon and Temple of Poseidon had been cannibalized from the Acropolis in Athens. Their blocks had been used to build the city around the base of the hill on which it stood.

The gods were probably not very happy about that, Harold thought absently.

Probably the reason for the earthquake.

He thought of Stewart Jones. The Duke of Westhaven would have reveled in discovering such a find as what lay at his feet. Harold rolled his eyes when he realized Westhaven had probably done so before Harold was even born. The duke had no doubt stood in this very same spot and come to the same conclusions as he had—probably when he was Harold's age.

The thought of age had Harold jerking back to the present. What was it that had him so concerned about his mortality?

Was he worried for Stella? That he would be leaving her alone? With a newborn? The Everly coffers were full. She wouldn't want for anything during her widowhood. If she wished to return to Greece—to Mykonos, her mother's birthplace—she could do so and live comfortably for the rest of her days.

She was still beautiful, and she was young enough she might even attract another husband.

The thought had Harold emitting an unpleasant sound from his throat, and the lord who sat next to him shifted away an inch or two.

Would Stella remarry after his death?

Envy the likes of which he hadn't felt since he was last on Mykonos consumed him. The memory of that jealously was as clear as the day it had first occurred.

Her attention on her uncle's fishing boat, Stella raised a hand to her forehead to shield her eyes from the glare of the midday sun. "If you wish for a ride to Delos, then you must be aboard soon," she said, her gaze turning to Harold.

He regarded her with an expression of worry. "Do you always work for your uncle?"

She shrugged. "I am expected to help. Spiros is family," she replied.

"On the boat?"

Stella gave him a quelling glance. "If I'm not having to prepare the island's only inn for a guest. And even then, there are times Spiros will wait until I am finished before he heads out. The more of us there are diving, the more likely we'll find something of value."

"Does that include Leonidis?" he asked, trying but failing to keep his anger toward her uncle Spiros from sounding in his voice. Given Westhaven's disappearance, Spiros Xabat should be acting as Stella's protector, not putting her in danger by requiring her to dive for treasures. Worse were the other divers on her uncle's boat—young men who saw her dressed in very little. Her limbs were bare!

"Leonidis dives with us, of course," Stella said with a shrug. "Or he stays topside to help with bringing the heavier items on board."

Harold frowned. "I saw that brute watching you from the boat," he started to argue.

Stella let out a sound of disbelief. "Leonidis would never try anything untoward with me," she claimed. "He is like a brother to me. He was an orphan. Father saw to it he was raised right," she added when she noted Harold's skeptical glance. "He would give his life for mine."

Harold finally nodded, deciding not to ask about the other male who had been on the boat. He had realized right away the man spoke no English, but he had to wonder if he could understand some of the language.

He had given Harold a look that suggested he could easily kill him, should he deem it necessary.

Harold had decided he would make sure it was never necessary.

"Will you go back to the inn tonight?" she asked. "It will be dark soon," she added, her gaze going to the west. Already the long, wispy clouds near the horizon were beginning to take on the kaleidoscope of colors the sunsets featured in this part of the world, as if the ash from the volcanic eruptions of the past hadn't yet settled into the sea.

"I won't be going back to town. I'll sleep here on the beach tonight," Harold replied, secretly pleased to hear the concern in her voice.

Stella's eyes widened. "You will not sleep on the *beach*," she stated firmly. "There are sea creatures, and the tide will be coming in," she added when she noted his grin. "You'll drown."

Harold had to admit to feeling a hint of satisfaction at hearing her words, especially since he knew the tide wasn't as noticeable in the Aegean Sea as it was on Atlantic shores. "Where would you suggest I spend the night, my lady?" he countered, one eyebrow arching in query.

Stella regarded Harold for a moment with an expression of uncertainty. She couldn't exactly invite him to stay with her. What harm would come of it, though? They weren't in England. No one in the sleepy village cared if a man shared a woman's hovel. Leonidis wouldn't be the wiser. "On the floor in there," she replied, pointing to her house.

Never in his life had Harry been dared to do something. Never had someone looked him in the eye and challenged him to do something he shouldn't do. But right then, he felt as if he was being dared to spend the night on Lady Estelle's floor.

He could argue with himself. Present both sides of the case and work out the pros and cons and decide then. But at that moment, he decided he didn't want to be any place but on Stella's floor.

Her bed would be preferable, but he wasn't about to test his luck.

"All right, my lady," he replied. "I shall accept your offer of hospitality." *And curse myself for the rest of the night*, he nearly added.

$\mathcal{H}$arold shook himself from his reverie, rather glad he hadn't allowed his thoughts to continue. Although he had been the perfect gentleman that night on Mykonos, far from the island's only inn where he had left his trunk and his samples and drawings, his thoughts had been on Stella.

She had been in a room directly above where he was supposed to be sleeping. He had wondered if she had lain awake as he had done, his cock straining against the fall of his breeches as he imagined what it would be like to remove the strips of cloth that covered her breasts, the short skirt that hung low on her hips. What it would be like to kiss her breasts, trail his tongue over her heated body, bring her to ecstasy before taking his own pleasure whilst his engorged manhood was buried deep in her most secret haven.

He had learned soon enough what it was like. And he had continued to do so for several years, discovering the pleasures of lovemaking with the half-Greek beauty that was now his wife.

He had also learned those pleasures were not always the same as long as one took the time to create new ways to make love.

Once more, he felt regret at allowing their brief times together to become routine. Whatever had happened to cause his indifference was now past, but he couldn't help but feel as if he still had some making up to do.

A daunting task to some, he supposed. Given the uncomfortable bulge in his pantaloons, he had half a mind to take his leave that very moment and return home.

He might have, but a quick glance in the direction of his

father-in-law, who was scowling at him, and Harold's attention was back on the speaker.

His woody would have to wait.

CHAPTER 28
A GEMOLOGIST PREPARES
FOR A BALL

Tuesday evening, Margaret's bedchamber above Ewen & Ewen

"Don't feel guilty about buying the gown," Adam Ewen said as he regarded his daughter.

Margaret turned from her dressing table and gave her father a quelling glance. "I would not have bought it if you didn't have the promise from Lord Everly to purchase the shop," she replied, hoping he didn't see through her white lie.

She had actually spotted the gown in Suzanne's the day she had gone for the fabric swatches. The modiste noted her interest and then confided that the dress had been made for someone else.

"She's with child, and the dress cannot be remade to fit her," Suzanne had said with a shrug. "You can buy it, though. I'll sell it to you for a song."

About to mention she didn't sing, Margaret was stunned to learn she could afford the sapphire confection. Suzanne folded the gown into tissue, placed it in a pasteboard box, and had it ready with the fabric swatches before Margaret could change her mind.

Now she noticed how her father was dressed—his waistcoat and top coat were more formal than usual—and she asked, "Are you going out, too?"

Adam nodded. "I've decided to join the lads for our usual game of cards," he said.

"You won't gamble too much?"

"I have coins totaling about one pound," he countered. "And I promise I shan't go into further debt."

"But you'll be home late, I imagine."

"I plan to be home long before you," he countered with a smirk.

"Well, that will all depend on Lady Everly," Margaret replied as she turned her attention back to her reflection in the mirror. Blackened around the edges, the silvered glass still provided a clear image in its middle. "Since she's acting as my chaperone, I shall do whatever she tells me."

Having spent the last hour attempting to put up her hair in a more elaborate style than usual, Margaret was relieved to see the pins were holding fast.

"Well, if she asks if you want to stay for the midnight supper, do so. I hear Lord Weatherstone's balls are the best. Apparently he puts on a feast of a buffet."

Margaret allowed an impish grin. She had heard Lord Weatherstone balls were the best because amorous couples took advantage of his gardens—and his library. She had no intention of ending up in either. "I shall do so," she promised.

"Do help yourself to a necklace and some earbobs," he encouraged. "I shouldn't want a daughter of mine to appear at a *ton* ball not dressed in our finest jewelry."

Her eyes rounding with his offer, Margaret nodded. "Thank you, Father." Her sapphire blue satin gown featured only a single ruffle at the bottom and sleeves that helped hide her withered arm. Other than a silver ribbon at her waist, it was void of furbelows. Jewelry would be necessary.

She thought of the diamond necklace Alexander had pulled from its display, remembering how impressed he'd been by their fire. There were matching pendeloque earrings in a glass display case at the other end of the shop.

"Should I wait until the Everlys arrive before I take my leave?" Adam asked.

"No need, Father. I'm not expecting them until half-past-eight o'clock."

His hesitancy evident in how he hovered at her door, Adam finally said, "If you're sure. Do try to have a good time. It's so rare we close early, and I should like it if we both have memorable evenings."

Margaret once again turned from her dressing table. "I have a promise of at least two dances, so I won't be a wallflower the entire night."

Her father gave her a wink and finally took his leave.

Margaret listened until she heard him finish descending the stairs that led to the corner of the shop. A moment after that, the front door closed, and she allowed a sigh of relief.

She was gladdened to know her father had decided to take a night off. He hadn't played cards since the incident with the rubies and Mr. Baumeister.

If only she had been in the shop that day, instead of shopping for that week's foodstuffs. The cook had been ill for two days, and Margaret hadn't wanted Mrs. Crookshanks near the shop until she was feeling better.

Perhaps Mr. Baumeister knew she wasn't in at the time of his visit. Perhaps he knew her father would be easily tricked into buying low-quality gems at a high-quality price—they were equally matched in color and size. He knew her father would agree to ridiculous terms that would leave them vulnerable should something go wrong.

Perhaps Baumeister even knew that Lady Framingham was in the market for a ruby parure.

So when her father had begun placing the gems into his carefully prepared collets and they began cracking one after the other, Adam Ewen's fate was sealed.

"If only," Margaret murmured aloud. She sighed and finally stood from her dressing table. She shook out the satin gown, stood back, and gave one last look at her reflection in the mirror. Satisfied, she made her way out of her small bedchamber and down the steps.

Only a single gas light was lit in the shop, but it was enough for her to find the diamond necklace. She secured the clasp at the back of her neck and took a quick look in a small looking glass before heading for the earring display. She pulled the diamonds from their black velvet bed and was in the middle of threading the wires through her ears when the front door opened and the bell above it tinkled.

"I'm almost ready," she called out, sure it was either Alexander or Lord Everly. When she turned, she gasped in shock.

CHAPTER 29
THREATS AND DEMANDS

*M*eanwhile Samuel Baumeister stood just inside the entry of Ewen & Ewen, his gaze darting about as he struggled to determine from where Margaret Ewen's words had been said. When he finally discovered her at the far end of the shop, he pushed the door shut behind him, which had the bell above tinkling louder than upon his arrival.

"Well, well, what have we here?" he asked as he slowly made his way in her direction. "Shop closed on a Tuesday night? But the door not locked?"

"Oh, I was just about to take my leave," Margaret replied, straightening.

"For a fancy party, no doubt," Baumeister replied, his brows waggling when he noted how she was dressed.

"Not... not exactly," Margaret replied. She had a thought that the gem merchant might be foxed. The way he gazed at her had a shiver running down her spine, though, and she glanced around in an attempt to discover the best escape route.

Even if she made it to the stairs, there was really no place on the first floor where she would find safety. None of the doors had locks, and leaving by way of the windows would mean an impossible drop to the alley below. Sprained ankles at the very least, broken bones most likely. Her new gown would be ruined. "Was there something you needed?" she asked lightly, trying hard to hide her fear.

Baumeister gave his usual oily grin. "Why, yes, Miss Ewen. Payment in full for the invoice for those rubies your father bought from me. Plus interest," he stated. The faint odor of stale ale wafted around him as he leaned in her direction.

"I'm quite sure that will be paid within the next fortnight," Margaret replied, glad she had a reasonable timeline to provide. Lord Everly's purchase of the shop could not come soon enough.

Baumeister's brows furrowed into a single furry caterpillar across his brow. "The next fortnight?" he repeated.

"Why, yes." A coach light flared in one of the windows, and she dared a glance in its direction, hoping it was the Everly coach. "Perhaps within the week."

"How?" he asked, oblivious to the traffic outside the jewelry shop.

Margaret considered how much to admit. She had a mind to crow about the deal her father had struck with Lord Everly, but she didn't want to anger the toad of a man. "My father has made some... financial arrangements. To see to it there will be funds to cover the invoice... plus the interest, of course," she stammered. Whatever coach had passed by hadn't stopped, and her heartbeat increased to a hammering in her chest. "You'll be paid in full, I assure you."

He continued to approach, his steps slow and measured. "Will I now?" he asked, his tone menacing. "Do these payment terms include... *you?*"

Margaret was suddenly aware of how tight she'd managed to tie her corset. Of how hard it was to breathe. Of how her pulse pounded in her ears. "I... I don't really know, sir," she lied. "I was not privy..."

"Privy?" he repeated with a feral grin. "Of course you were *privy*," he accused at the same moment he stopped to stand directly in front of her.

She shook her head, which only sent stars darting about in front of her eyes. Darkness was beginning to surround her vision, no doubt because she was holding her breath. "I'm quite sure you'll be happy to receive your money, sir," she managed to get out.

"Money?" he repeated with a snarl. He reached out, his fingers wrapping around the diamond necklace at her throat. He tried to use it to pull her toward him, but Margaret jerked back. The clasp at the back of the necklace gave way, sending Baumeister stumbling backward and leaving Margaret with a scratch along the side of her neck.

Baumeister had to take several steps until he could regain his footing, and he stared at the necklace with suspicion. "Paste, huh?" he said with derision.

Margaret's eyes widened. "No," she replied in alarm. "It's quite real." If she hadn't been so frightened, she would have been appalled at seeing one of her father's very best creations hanging from the gem merchant's chubby fingers.

A knock sounded at the front door, and they both turned their attention in that direction. Margaret used the distraction to step to the side, and she called out, "Help!" as loud as she could manage.

Baumeister was just as quick, though, sliding sideways to stand in front of her. "Who is there?" he asked in a hoarse whisper.

"My transport," she replied, swallowing bile.

"Tell them to go," he hissed. "Tell them… tell them you've changed your mind," he demanded. "Now!"

Margaret might have obliged him, but darkness engulfed her vision. The last sensation she felt was that of falling.

CHAPTER 30
AN ARRESTING RESCUE

A few moments earlier

"Should I collect her?" Alexander asked from where he sat next to Helen in the Everly town coach. Although he had attempted to act nonchalant the entire time they were on their way to Ewen & Ewen, his nerves were getting the better of him.

He had secured two dances with the gemologist, and now he was anxious. How long would he have to wait until he could dance with Margaret? And how long would his mother allow her to remain at the ball before her duties as a chaperone would have her insisting Margaret be taken home?

"*I* will do it," Stella said as the coach came to a stuttering halt in front of the jewelry shop.

"My sweet, I really should—"

"Nonsense," Stella replied, directing a coy smile in the direction of her husband. "What if she needs help with her buttons?"

Harold pushed back into the squabs, deciding his wife knew best. "Very well," he replied. "But I'm going to claim *three* dances with you this evening."

Stella arched a brow in his direction before she placed a hand on the groom's and stepped down from the coach. "Promises, promises," she murmured, barely loud enough for anyone in the coach to hear.

"I heard that," Harold called out, which had Helen giggling.

A single light was visible through the display windows at the front of the shop, and coupled with the lanterns that hung from either side of the Everly town coach, it was enough light for the countess to see by as she walked up to the door and knocked. Testing the door handle, she discovered it wasn't locked, and she was about to open it when a loud scream rent the quiet night.

Alexander was beside her and then past her in only a second, pushing the door open so it slammed against the adjacent display case and sent the overhead bell into a frenzy of tinkling.

He paused a moment to survey the interior, his gaze finally going to the overweight man who stood at the far end of the shop. He had been bent over, but now his arm was wrapped around Margaret Ewen's shoulders. The young lady's head listed to the side, making it apparent she was unconscious. "You there!" he called out. "Unhand her!"

The overweight man merely pulled Margaret against his body. "Come any closer, and I'll..."

"You'll *what*?"

The question came from Harold, who had followed his son into the shop and now walked with purpose toward the intruder.

"I'll... I'll *kill* her," Baumeister claimed, stepping back until his backside was firmly pressed against a display case.

"Will you now?" Harold asked as he raised his right fist and planted it firmly into Baumeister's left cheek.

Alexander was behind him, and he quickly moved around

his father to plant his left fist into the gem merchant's middle.

Baumeister let go of his hold on Margaret so his hands could go to his stomach. Alexander managed to catch Margaret before she fell to the marble tiled floor.

Harold followed up his first strike using his other fist, which had Baumeister's eyes rolling up and his body sinking to the floor. The necklace fell from his fingers and slid across the smooth tiles.

Pulling Margaret well away from the gem merchant, Alexander held her pressed against the front of his body, both arms around her shoulders as his mother hurried up beside him.

"Is she all right?" Stella asked in alarm.

Bending to retrieve the necklace, Harold held it up to the light. "I think we've interrupted a robbery," he said in awe.

"Of a sort," Margaret murmured, her eyes fluttering open. She inhaled, comforted by the familiar sent of Alexander Tennison. His superfine top coat lay beneath her cheek, and his arms were obviously keeping her upright.

"Are you all right?" he asked as he pulled his head from the top of hers.

She glanced up, stunned by his look of concern. "I... I think so," she whispered. "Mr. Baumeister is not, however," she added as her gaze lowered to the floor. "The *cur*." She glanced about, as if she needed to get her bearings.

"*This* is Mr. Baumeister?" Harold asked in alarm.

She nodded. "He is," she sighed. "He came to collect what he's owed. I thought he'd be happy to learn he would be paid in full within a fortnight—that he would then take his leave— but he didn't."

Alexander allowed a sound of disbelief. "He will be transported, is more likely," he said. "Did he... did he hurt you?" he asked in a whisper. "Where's Mr. Ewen?"

Margaret's gloved hand went to the side of her neck, where the necklace had left a red welt from where it scratched her as it had been pulled off. She winced. "Am I bleeding?" she asked, examining her glove. She let out a long sigh when she noted how her shawl had come loose from her shoulders and was now in a puddle at her feet. The white wool bore the evidence of having been trampled by at least three pairs of feet.

"No," Alexander replied. He lowered his lips to her neck and placed a kiss there. He felt her body shiver in his hold, and he tightened his arms before saying, "Does it hurt?"

She allowed her head to fall back so she could see him in the dim light, grimacing when she realized a lock of her hair had come loose from its pins and hung over one of her shoulders. "No," she replied before she winced again.

"What's wrong?"

"Do you have any idea how long it took me to pin up my hair?" she asked in dismay. "And that was my only good shawl," she added in a whisper as she pointed to the floor.

His brows furrowing, Alexander dared a glance at his mother and noted how she was attempting to hide her amusement behind a gloved hand. "Perhaps my mother could help in that regard," he suggested.

Lady Everly began glancing through display cases, hurrying along them until she finally stood in front of one located near the front door. "Harold. Can you pull that one from the top shelf, please?" she asked as she pointed through the glass to a jeweled hair comb.

Harold hurried to the case and moved to the back of it. He reached in and pulled out the jewel she indicated. Handing it to her along with the diamond necklace he had retrieved from the floor, he asked, "*You're* not robbing this shop, I hope?"

Encrusted with diamonds, the hair comb looked almost

like a tiara. Stella grinned. "I am not," she assured him, "but we should ensure no one else does on this night."

Harold understood her meaning. "I'll be back in a few minutes," he promised and headed out the door.

Stella hurried back to where Margaret was shaking out her ball gown as Alexander stood entirely too close. "Step aside, son," Stella said as she moved in front of Margaret. "And see if you can't do something about her necklace." She held out the string of diamonds.

"Oh, of course," Alexander replied as he took the proffered necklace. He examined the end where the clasp had broken and then made his way in the direction of Adam's workbench.

Meanwhile, Stella gave the young woman an assessing glance before she finally reached up and pushed the hair comb into the front of the young woman's coiffure.

"But, this part has come loose," Margaret complained as she reached up and gathered the lock of hair in a gloved hand and pulled it in front of her shoulder.

"And loose it shall stay," Stella replied. "It looks rather fetching this way, and it does help hide your neck where the necklace scratched it."

Margaret dared a glance at Alexander, who gave her a grin. "She is right," he said from the workbench.

Frissons darted down Margaret's spine when she saw how he gazed at her. How different he looked in the dim light! Older and more handsome. Amused and yet so protective. Not at all like a young man who might have stepped off his pedestal at the British Museum to spend a night on the town. "I suppose I should see to retrieving a different wrap," she whispered.

"I have one that will be *perfect* with your gown," Stella said. "We'll simply stop at Rosemount House on our way to Weatherstone Manor."

"Oh, but I couldn't, my lady. Won't that be out of your way?" Margaret asked in dismay.

"Not at all," Alexander said, beating his mother to the reply. "We have to drive right by it."

"We won't arrive too late?"

"We'll be right on time," Stella said as she regarded the young woman. "Perhaps there's a different necklace you could wear?" she hinted. "It must be convenient to have an entire shop rather than just a box from which to choose your jewelry," she gently teased.

Alexander cleared his throat. "Mother, really, I've got this," he said.

"Very well," Stella replied. She turned her attention back to Margaret. "I take it your father is not home this evening?"

Margaret dipped her head. "He left only moments ago. Before Mr. Baumeister arrived," she replied. "He so rarely has the chance to play cards with the other goldsmiths on Tuesday evenings," she added. "I told him to go."

"But he didn't lock the door," Stella said in a quiet voice filled with censure.

"I know that now," Margaret replied with a sigh. She pulled a key from a pocket in her gown. "I will see to it, of course." Her attention went to the workbench, where Alexander was attempting to repair the necklace clasp by what little light there was in the shop. "Pardon me," she said before she moved to stand beside him, lighting a nearby candle lamp.

With the workspace flooded with light, both she and Stella watched Alexander. He had helped himself to a couple of the tools, and within a minute, he held up the necklace and studied the repaired clasp. "May I?" he asked.

Stunned he had fixed the necklace so quickly, Margaret turned and shivered as his fingers wrapped the string of diamonds around her neck and secured the clasp at her nape.

She inhaled sharply when she felt his lips make contact with her skin. Inhaled again when she felt his nose move aside the soft curls too short to be caught in the pins that held up her hair.

"Really, Alex. There will be time for that later," Stella scolded before she made her way to the front door.

Alexander straightened and then blinked, as if he had forgotten why he was there. "Oh, of course," he murmured. His gaze went to the unconscious gem merchant, and he frowned. "What do we do about *him*?"

"Your father has gone out to find a constable," Stella replied, her grin indicating much had happened while Alexander's attention had been on Margaret. "Perhaps it would be best for us to return to the coach. Your poor sister must be wondering what's become of us."

Giving a start—he had completely forgotten about Helen —Alexander said, "Yes, Mother." He dared a glance at Margaret and was relieved to see her grinning at his expense. "Remember, you owe me two dances, my lady," he murmured.

Margaret smiled in reply. "I owe your father just as many," she said as the front door once again opened to reveal a constable followed by Lord Everly.

"Miss Ewen?" the constable asked, concern evident in his voice. "Are you all right?"

"Good evening, Mr. Peters. I'm so sorry to have ruined your night," Margaret said on a sigh. "But this... this *cur* broke into the shop and attempted to steal this necklace just as the Earl and Countess of Everly were collecting me for the ball at Lord Weatherstone's mansion," Margaret said as she indicated the jewelry she was wearing. She pointed to the scratch on her neck. "He broke it, in fact. Mr. Tennison just finished repairing it for me."

The constable's attention went to the prone gem merchant. "Well, you needn't concern yourself further, Miss

Ewen," he said. "I'll see to him," he claimed as he pulled a pair of handcuffs from a pocket. "Wagon's on its way."

"Already?" Margaret whispered in awe.

"My father knows people," Alexander said in a hoarse whisper.

"Obviously," she replied, her attention going to the earl.

"You have a key to lock the door?" Harold asked of Margaret.

"I do," she said as she once again pulled it from a pocket. "But..." She was about to mention Mr. Baumeister's presence, but the constable had roused him with a swift kick and had already cuffed him, cursing mildly when Baumeister took too long to come to his feet. Then Mr. Peters was leading the gem merchant toward the door.

"Give my regards to Mr. Ewen," Peters called out before he disappeared beyond the door, Baumeister in tow.

Margaret stared after the constable and then turned her attention first to Alexander and then to Lord Everly. "I'm so sorry this has ruined your evening," she murmured.

Harold guffawed. "Hardly," he countered with a huge grin. "I haven't had this much fun since..." He quickly sobered, remembering what he and his countess had been doing in his bedchamber earlier that afternoon. "Well, since the last ball. Come, you two. It's time we be on our way."

Margaret exchanged a quick glance with Alexander, who had visibly reddened at hearing his father's claim.

"Yes, sir," they said in unison.

CHAPTER 31
FIRST BALL JITTERS

A few minutes later, in the Everly town coach, Mayfair

"He'll spend the night in gaol," Harold remarked when he finally climbed into the Everly town coach and took a seat next to his son. "I rather doubt they can hold him much longer."

"Is that all?" Alexander asked, dismayed by his father's comment as well as by the fact that Margaret was sitting next to his mother—at his mother's insistence—while Helen sat on her other side.

What did his mother think he would attempt to do with his entire family seated around them? It wasn't as if he could rest a hand on Margaret's thigh or lean over and nibble on her ear, both activities his father had tried to do surreptitiously to his countess as the coach made its way from Park Lane to Ludgate Hill.

Alexander was quite sure Helen had pretended not to notice until she had no choice when their mother tittered and gently scolded their father. When they exchanged knowing glances, he knew she was thinking the same thing he was—what would their parents be doing during tonight's ball when they weren't in the ballroom... and where?

He tried to imagine what Margaret would do should he try such antics on her. Would she be shocked and scold him for the rakish behavior? Or would she welcome his attentions and titter in delight? Perhaps she would place a hand on his thigh when the coach took a fast turn at a corner. Or mayhap she would nibble on his ear and murmur words of what they might do later in the gardens.

Never before had he looked so forward to attending a ball!

Alexander straightened when he realized Helen was staring at him, her eyes still wide at learning what had happened in the jewelry shop. She had been forced to remain in the town coach whilst all the excitement happened, watching in shock when their father left the shop at a run toward the Metropolitan Police Station. Then she was more stunned when a constable returned with him only a few moments later.

She had paid witness to a surly looking middle-aged man being loaded into an iron-barred wagon, his complaints rather loud despite the heavy traffic due to the shoppers who descended on this part of London at night. "Won't he be transported?" she asked in dismay. "A jewel thief, wasn't he? You must have been so frightened," she said, her head bending forward so she could direct her query to Margaret.

Their guest nearly cowered in her seat when everyone turned to look at her.

"I... I wasn't at first," Margaret replied. "I thought he would leave when he learned my father wasn't there."

"He had better be transported," Alexander said, his voice filled with menace.

"The law will see to him," Harold stated. "By the by, I told

Mr. Thorton to stop at the house. I have to retrieve something from my bedchamber."

"I told him to stop as well," Stella said. "I have the perfect shawl for Miss Ewen's gown."

Alexander watched as his parents exchanged curious glances, and for a moment, he wondered if they were planning a clandestine meeting in one of their bedchambers. If so, they might never make it to the ball! He was about to suggest he could escort Margaret and Helen on foot to Weatherstone Manor when the coach stuttered to a halt in front of Rosemount House.

"I'll send a footman to find my lady's maid," Stella said as she moved to stand up.

"I'll see to it, my sweet," Harold said as he made his way out of the coach. "The blue brocade shawl?" he asked.

"Why, yes," Stella replied in surprise. For a moment, she appeared disappointed, but she soon brightened, making small talk as they waited for the earl to return.

When Harold bounded back into the coach only a few minutes later, a shawl draped over one arm and his top hat in the other, the coach pulled away from the curb and continued on its way to Weatherstone mansion. He handed the brocade shawl to Margaret.

"Oh, this is far too fine, my lady," Margaret protested when she fingered the dark silk, noting the paisley pattern woven into the fabric by the light of the coach lantern. "I worry it might suffer the same fate—"

"Nonsense," Stella interrupted. "It's perfect with your gown, and I no longer have a gown I can wear with it," she claimed.

"But, what about the sapphire ball gown?" Helen asked, her brows furrowing at hearing her mother's claim. "The one you were having made for this Season?"

"Oh, I wouldn't have been able to wear that gown," Stella

replied. "Seems I've been eating too many cakes at tea time," she added, a teasing grin aimed in her husband's direction.

"I don't mind a bit, my sweet," Harold said, a huge grin splitting his face.

Margaret inhaled softly, realizing she was probably wearing the very gown Lady Everly was talking about. Suzanne had said the woman who had ordered it could no longer wear it because she was increasing.

Due to impending motherhood.

Well, that certainly explained why the countess appeared so healthy. So happy. Why the earl seemed to dote on her so.

Meanwhile Alexander blinked, his attention turning first to his father and then to his mother. For a moment, he feared his mother would end up on his father's lap. Then he dared a glance in Margaret's direction and caught her hiding her reaction behind a gloved hand. He was about to apologize on his parents' behalf when the coach slowly and finally came to a halt.

"We're here!" Helen said with excitement.

Margaret inhaled sharply. "You weren't fibbing when you said you lived close to Weatherstone Manor," she murmured.

"Oh, we could have walked," Alexander agreed, "But we probably would have come in a coach even if we lived next door."

A groom opened the door, and Helen was the first to step down, followed by her mother and then Margaret. Next came the earl, and finally, Alexander emerged. He quickly moved to Margaret's side and offered his arm. Remembering his sister, he offered his other arm, and Helen seemed unsure of what to do.

"You would deny me the opportunity to escort two lovely ladies to the front door?" Alexander groused.

Helen immediately took his arm, shocked to see that their parents were already making their way to the front door, as if they had completely forgotten they had arrived with three other people. "Do you suppose they will even *go* to the ballroom?" she asked. "I hear some spend their evenings in the library," she added in a whisper. "Or the gardens."

"Couples must take turns using the library for their trysts," Alexander explained. "The gardens, however, are open to all."

"Alex!" Helen scolded.

"If I discover you're out there with some young buck—"

"I will not be going to the gardens with *anyone*," Helen claimed, a hint of disbelief in her voice. "Remember, this *is* my first ball."

Margaret suppressed a grin as they made their way, a mix of nerves and giddiness making for a heady combination. Lady Everly's shawl made it possible to hide her withered arm, and even if she spent the entire evening merely acting as a wallflower and watching from the wings, she knew she would enjoy herself. She had never before attended a ball in Park Lane.

Although a footman asked if he might take her shawl, she politely declined. Alexander led her and Helen to the receiving line, which was surprisingly short given the number of carriages that were parked in front of the mansion. A few minutes later, and Lady Weatherstone was pulling her into an embrace.

A countess! Hugging her!

"I cannot tell you how happy I was to learn you could attend this evening, Miss Ewen," Lady Weatherstone gushed. She turned her attention to Alexander. "Every Greek god needs someone more beautiful than him on a night like this, don't you agree, Tennison?"

Alexander couldn't hide the red that flooded his face just then. "As I'm sure Lord Weatherstone has come to appreciate," he replied, one brow rising with his compliment.

The countess tittered. "Careful, young man, or you shall be forced to dance with the likes of me," Agnes Peele said.

"Nothing would give me greater pleasure, my lady," Alexander replied.

"Now see here, Mr. Tennison," Lord Weatherstone said, his attention on Margaret. "I'll be expecting a dance with these two lovely young ladies if you insist on dancing with my wife," he claimed, a huge grin splitting his face.

"I would be honored, my lord," Margaret said as she dipped a curtsy.

"As would I," Helen said. She'd spent the afternoon afraid no one would dance with her.

"Did you hear that, my sweeting? I have willing partners for dancing this evening," Lord Weatherstone said to his wife.

"As do I," Agnes countered, giving Alexander a wink.

Alexander bowed and lifted her hand to his lips. "A Scottish reel, my lady?"

"Oh, but I don't think there's a Scottish reel on the list for this evening," Lady Weatherstone replied, giving him a moue.

Alexander feigned disappointment as they were hurried along in the line. Somewhere near the top of the stairs, he heard his parents being announced.

How had they managed to make it through the receiving line so quickly?

Helen, Alexander, and Margaret were nearly to the top of the stairs leading down to the ballroom when Margaret said, "You knew there wasn't to be a Scottish reel, didn't you?"

"Every year, for the past three years, I have offered to dance a Scottish reel with her," Alexander replied. "I am actually left feeling offended when one isn't included in the program."

Helen rolled her eyes. "Do not be surprised if she makes a special request of the musicians on this night," she warned.

"So that she might dance in the arms of a Greek god," she added in a whisper filled with humor.

"I shall honor my offer," Alexander replied as he stepped up to the announcer. "Lady Helen, Miss Margaret Ewen, and Mr. Alexander Tennison," he whispered.

The announcer repeated his words in his loud baritone, and the three made their way down the short flight of stairs.

If he had been by himself, Alexander would have hurried down the steps. In deference to the women on both his arms, he took his time, his gaze surveying the room in an attempt to learn who was taking note of their arrival.

Although his sister would have her formal come-out in a few weeks at the ball his mother and aunt were arranging for her, he knew there would be opportunists looking for a young lady tonight, someone they could marry quickly to fill their coffers or pay off gambling debts. As for Miss Ewen, he had a mind to warn her off of everyone but him.

Or Lord Weatherstone.

If she danced with their host, he wouldn't feel the least bit of jealousy. Anyone else, and he feared they might come to the same fate as Mr. Baumeister.

A fist in the face and another to their midsection.

The thought had him frowning.

What the hell was wrong with him?

Never before had he thought to harm a peer. To punch an aristocrat until he fell to his knees. But then never before had he cared so much for a young woman.

A quick glance in Margaret's direction found her gaze slowly taking in the ballroom, the crush of people, the chandeliers, their gas lights bathing the ballroom in a golden glow, the musicians, the tables of champagne and other refreshments. Despite the crush below, she displayed a pleasant expression.

To his right, Helen trembled in fear and anticipation. "What do I do?" she whispered.

"Accept the offers of dances," he replied.

"Which ones?"

"All of them," he replied with a smirk, noting how a number of young bucks were making their way to the bottom of the steps. His sister's dance card would be full on this night.

He didn't even consider that Margaret's might be as well.

Upon reaching the bottom step, Helen had a line of young aristocrats asking for dances. Recognizing several of his fellow peers, he nodded in her direction. She could decide for herself whose offers of a dance she would accept.

He turned his attention to Margaret and discovered she had a similar line of admirers, although not nearly as long as Helen's.

"Why, I would be honored to dance a Scottish reel with you, sir," he heard her say to the first man in line.

"I will find you," George Grandby, Viscount Hexham, replied, giving Alexander a nod. "Tennison," he added with an arched brow, before he disappeared into the growing crowd.

"A Scottish reel?" Alexander whispered.

"You implied Scottish reels are never done here," she said in a hoarse whisper.

"Not for the past three years, true, but that doesn't mean it won't happen this year," he countered.

"If I offer the same dance to everyone? What then?" Margaret asked as she curtsied to the next man in line. "I shall be honored to offer you the Scottish reel," she said, her eyes widening when she recognized Gabriel Wellingham. "Mr. Wellingham," she added as she dipped a curtsy. "I do hope Mrs. Wellingham liked the sapphire bracelet you bought for her."

"She did indeed. I make her wear it every day when we're

at the museum," he claimed. "And she's wearing it this evening. I will come find you," he added, giving her a bow. He directed an arched brow in Alexander's direction before he hurried off to join his wife, Frances, for the first dance.

"I have no idea what would happen should you offer the same dance to everyone and they actually came to collect," Alexander murmured, finally answering Margaret's query.

Tom Grandby stepped forward and held out a hand to Alexander. "Since my wife has already abandoned me for the horse enthusiasts, I thought to arrange a dance with Miss Ewen," he said. He turned his attention to Margaret. "May I request you join me for the first cotillion?"

Margaret struggled with her response, noting how Alexander grinned as he shook Tom's hand.

"The cotillion?" she repeated.

Alexander realized Tom probably knew Margaret from having purchased jewelry at the shop. "I'll allow it," he said with a grin.

"I'll find you," Tom said as he bowed over her hand and then hurried off.

Before another man could step forward, Margaret whispered, "Is it always like this?"

Alexander chuckled. "I wouldn't know. This is the first time I've escorted *two* young ladies into a ballroom," he replied.

"Shouldn't you be asking for dances with the other young ladies?"

He nodded toward the short wall to the left where several girls, most of them Helen's age, were standing in front of a row of potted palms. "I will when I discover which one of the wallflowers is without a partner," he said.

"Oh, then I should probably stand over there," Margaret remarked.

Alexander shook his head. "You underestimate my sex,"

he replied, even as his eyes widened when his father stepped up and bowed to Margaret.

"May I have this dance?" Lord Everly asked.

"Of course, my lord," Margaret replied, just before she aimed a look of shock in Alexander's direction.

"I'll have a glass of champagne waiting for you," he promised. He watched as his father led Margaret to the end of a line for a longways dance, and then he remembered the Weatherstones were old-fashioned in their choice of dances for their balls.

He was about to head in the direction of the refreshment table when he realized Helen still stood beside him. "Come. Let's join them," he said as he placed one of her hands on his arm.

She gave him a quelling glance but allowed him to lead her to the end of the long line of dancers, where women faced the men.

"What is it?" he asked before they took their places.

Rolling her eyes, she said, "I rather hoped my first dance at a *ton* ball wouldn't be with my *brother*."

"If not me, it would have been Father," Alexander claimed.

"Really, Tennison, no young lady wants to dance her first dance with her brother," Tom Grandby said, deftly moving in to take Alexander's place in line. "Trust me. I have five sisters."

Alexander blinked but stepped out of the line, his gaze immediately going to the wallflowers. There were three who at least looked interested in dancing. He hurried to one in the middle, well aware her chaperone was no where nearby. He bowed and said, "I know we haven't been formally introduced—"

"Christina Bennett-Jones, sir," she said as she dipped a curtsy.

Blinking, Alexander furrowed a brow. "Lord Bostwick is your father?"

She nodded as she displayed a brilliant grin, as if she thought him the most clever man in the world. "He is."

"Will he do me bodily harm if you dance with me, Miss Bennett-Jones?"

Giggling, she shook her head and said, "I doubt he will even know. He's with my mother, in the library, I think."

"Capital," Alexander replied, offering his arm. "I am Alexander Tennison—"

"Oh, I know who *you* are, of course," Christina interrupted. "Why, I do believe I've seen you at the British Museum."

Alexander's eyes rounded—what was it about him that had every young woman thinking he was part of the display of Greek gods in the Greek and Roman Hall?

Before he could ask, they had joined the end of the line. The English country dance had already begun. Given the dance required a change of partners every few steps, he was unable to speak with Christina again until the dance was nearly over. He was heartened to see that Margaret seemed to be enjoying herself with Tom, although she struggled to keep her withered arm beneath the shawl given the requirements of the dance. Twice Alexander was paired with her during the rounds, and both times he merely grinned at her.

"You mentioned seeing me in the museum," Alexander said when he finally offered his arm to Christina as he escorted her back to the line of potted palms. "Was it... recently?"

"Oh, last year, I think."

"Oh?" he prompted. "In the Greek and Roman Hall, no doubt?"

He was about to mention that his pedestal wasn't as high as some were led to believe, but Christina said, "It was! You were admiring a vase. One of those red pottery vases from the Hellenistic period," she gushed. "You were quite entranced."

Alexander nearly laughed out loud, relieved she wasn't referring to him standing on a pedestal. "No doubt," he said when he sobered. Having reached one of the palm trees, he bowed and said, "Thank you for the dance, Miss Christina."

"Thank *you*, Mr. Tennison." She curtsied to his bow and was soon joined by other young ladies who swept her away in a wave of giggles and quiet murmurs.

His gaze about to take in the dance floor, Alexander was stunned to discover Tom delivering Margaret to him. For a moment, he was breathless and jealous. She had her good arm on Tom's, and the two were speaking as if they were long lost friends.

"Are you enjoying yourself?" Alexander asked.

"I am, of course," Margaret said before thanking Tom and giving him a curtsy.

"Would you like a glass of champagne?"

"Would you think me fast if I said yes?"

"I would think you were as thirsty as I am," Alexander replied. "Is Mr. Grandby a client of yours?"

Margaret directed a gaze at the departing back of the investment advisor. "I am a client of his," she replied. "Or my father is, actually. We have some funds invested in one of his railroad endeavors."

Alexander stared at her for a moment. "Oh," he finally replied. "Lucrative, are they not?"

Giving him a secret smile, Margaret leaned in and said, "They are."

For a moment, the green monster of jealousy had him feeling possessive. Angry. And then he remembered that Tom Grandby had married a duke's daughter. There was no reason for him to feel any jealousy. "I promised you champagne," he said as he pulled her withered arm onto his and led her to the refreshment table.

A tower of champagne glasses were being filled by a tall footman who emptied yet another bottle of champagne into the uppermost glass. The bubbly liquid dribbled over the sides, filling the carefully arranged rows of glasses beneath. He gave them a grin before he offered the topmost glass to Margaret and one of the glasses from the next row down to Alexander.

Margaret examined the glass of bubbly before she took an experimental sip. "Oh, this is delightful," she murmured.

"Deceptively," Alexander replied, offering her a strawberry from a platter that was heaped with the red fruit. "It's quite easy to drink too much, which will have your knees feeling disconnected from the rest of your body and your head feeling quite light."

Margaret tittered. "Spoken as if you have experienced its effects first hand," she whispered. She nibbled the strawberry, its juice staining her lips a bright red.

Alexander couldn't help the frisson of excitement that coursed down his spine. The shiver of awareness that had him hoping she would be dancing with him—and only him—for the rest of the evening. "Something like that," he admitted, before he felt the telltale warmth of the crush beneath his top coat. "Would you join me for a walk in the gardens? I find it's entirely too warm in here," he added.

"The gardens it is, Mr. Tennison," Margaret replied, finishing off her glass of champagne.

Given her arm was already on his, Alexander left their glasses with a passing footman and led them toward the French doors at the back of the ballroom.

With any luck, there would be a kiss in his immediate future.

And another before the evening was over.

CHAPTER 32
A STROLL IN THE GARDENS

few minutes later, in the back gardens of Weatherstone Manor

"Although I thought it rather chilly only an hour ago, I'm rather glad to be back outside," Margaret said as they traversed the series of travertine flagstones that led from the French doors to the back gardens of Weatherstone Manor.

"It is a relief to be able to breathe," Alexander admitted as he inhaled deeply.

"I hated to leave the ballroom, but I was having trouble with all the scents. All the perfume and cologne and the sheer number of people," Margaret explained. "Lady Weatherstone must be thrilled by the crush, though."

"I suppose," Alexander agreed. He covered her small hand with his own, glad she didn't pull her hand away or otherwise give a start at his hold on her.

"I must admit to shock at seeing all the jewels," she commented. "All the gems on display. Especially the designs I don't recognize. It reminds me that my father's shop is not the only jewelry shop in Ludgate Hill," she added on a sigh.

"Did you see anything you especially liked?" he asked,

thinking he might one day make her something special. Something her father wouldn't be able to create. Something she might keep and treasure for the rest of her days, or pass down to her oldest daughter.

The thought of Margaret with a daughter had the oddest sensation gripping his chest. Margaret with a daughter implied Margaret with a husband. Margaret living with a man. Eating dinner with him. Sharing his bed. Making love with him.

Alexander found he couldn't abide such an idea, and he turned his attention back to the topic of jewelry. "Did you see anything you thought you might like in your own jewel box?" he asked, attempting to keep his voice from sounding as if he hadn't just been considering murdering her non-existent husband.

"You will think me daft if I tell you about it," Margaret replied, her gaze taking in the plantings visible beneath the Japanese lanterns.

"I won't," Alexander countered. He would only think her daft if she ended up married to the non-existent husband.

"I saw Lady Bostwick wearing a pendant featuring a brown diamond on a gold necklace," she said as her other hand went to the diamond necklace she wore. "It was very simple and yet so elegant. It was perfect with her hair and with her gown."

Alexander furrowed a brow. "Just a single diamond?"

"Indeed," she affirmed. "I remember when my father made it to Lord Bostwick's specification."

"So the viscount designed it?" Alexander half-asked.

"Somewhat," she agreed with a shrug. "I remember thinking he probably couldn't afford something more ornate, but then father had him sit with me to choose the stone."

When she didn't continue, Alexander prompted her with an, "And?"

"Well, he surprised me by saying that he wanted a large diamond, but only one. And not the usual white diamond because he didn't want his wife wearing what every other aristocrat's wife might be wearing."

"So, a brown diamond because it was unique?" Alexander guessed. Brown diamonds weren't especially valuable—at least they hadn't been when he last checked.

"And because he intended to have a different colored stone added to the necklace every Season thereafter," she explained.

"Replacing the brown diamond with something else?"

"Oh, no. *Adding* another gemstone. That necklace now features seven pendants, and it works with any gown," she claimed. "Yet it's still elegant and it's still simple. He always buys a matching bracelet for whatever stone he adds, as well as earbobs, so he still gives her the equivalent of a new parure every season."

Alexander considered her words. He was sure Lord Bostwick was doing the same with his daughter Christina, for the young woman was wearing a single pendant this evening. He had spent part of the dance attempting to guess the identity of the pear-shaped gemstone featured in the necklace, and then had given up when its color appeared merely gray.

"I was dancing with Miss Bennett-Jones, Lord Bostwick's daughter," he commented. "Might you know what gem was in her simple pendant necklace?"

Margaret angled her head, surprised he hadn't recognized the type of stone that would feature in the parure he was making for his mother. "A ruby, of course. An expensive one. I thought he might order earbobs to go with it. I even had a couple set aside in the event that he would add them to the order, but he did not." She didn't add that those rubies were the ones she had sold him for his mother's earrings.

"Perhaps he'll have your father make them for her birthday or for Christmas," Alexander mused.

After a pause, Margaret said, "I really shouldn't have told you about Lord Bostwick's purchases. You won't tell anyone?"

He shook his head. "Of course not." After a time, he said, "I shall have to be sworn to secrecy when I begin making jewelry for the shop. When I'm taking orders for commissions."

Margaret inhaled softly, wondering if he intended to do his work in the jewelry store once his father owned it. "I don't know that you have to keep too many secrets," she replied. "But won't you be giving up time you would rather spend with your family?"

He furrowed a brow. "In favor of spending it with you? Hardly."

Staring at him, Margaret felt the heat of a blush and was glad for the relative darkness. "That's not what I meant, exactly," she hedged. "You're young. You could be racing coach-and-fours, or playing cards, or spending time at your club."

"I am born to privilege, but that does not mean I must take advantage of it all the time. I have often thought I should temper what I can do with what I should do." When he noted her look of confusion, he gave his head a shake. "I suppose one must give up something when they have too much of anything else," he murmured. "A price to be paid, so to speak."

Margaret frowned at hearing his comment. She hadn't expected such a response from the son of an earl. Her gaze went to her withered arm. Had she benefitted in other ways as a result of having to accept a less than perfect arm? If so, she wasn't sure how. "And what did you have to give up, Mr. Tennison? To be bestowed with your handsome features?"

Alexander dipped his head. Would his complaint seem

petty compared to what hers must be? To be born with a withered arm surely relegated her to a much lower place in Society than she would have otherwise enjoyed.

He thought of his grandfather's description of the ancient Romans. Of how they lived. What they valued and what they didn't. About how babies born with defects would be taken to the edge of town and left for the wild dogs to discover.

He shuddered at the thought that had Margaret been born in a different era, she, too, could have been disposed of in a manner no better than that of garbage.

Before he knew what he was doing—before he could even think about the repercussions of his actions—Alexander pulled her into his arms, hugged her so close, she was forced to take a stutter-step forward lest she fall against him. She let out a sound of surprise, but was unable to say anything when his lips came crushing down onto hers.

He immediately softened the kiss. He had to—her mouth had been slightly open as she tried to speak, and his had been far too hungry for her. The moment he did, her rigid body seemed less so, the hand trapped between them gripping his lapel for support.

A slight moan emanated from her throat, and he took it as permission to continue the kiss, to continue to slide his lips over hers, to suckle her lower lip before once again claiming both lips.

Once he knew she wasn't pushing him away, he slipped his tongue inside her mouth. He felt her jerk in his arms, although she still didn't attempt to pull from his hold. His tongue traced the edge of her teeth, tasted the champagne and the strawberry she had so delighted in eating before their foray into the gardens.

The experience was far headier than he expected, but then, he hadn't truly kissed a woman before. Not like this. Not open-mouthed, with her body fully pressed against his.

This was a kiss that could lead to so much more. To thoughts of what his tongue could be doing on the rest of her body. Trailing down the side of her neck to the hollow of her throat, where the central diamond in her necklace rested. Down past her collarbones to the top swell of her breasts and around her nipples.

This was a kiss that had him imagining making love to her in a soft bed. Oh, what his lips and tongue could do to her then. The sensations he could incite in her so that she might beg for him. Beg for his manhood to fill her over and over again until her ecstasy crested and he allowed his own pleasure to take him.

He couldn't help how his cock hardened. Couldn't hide how it strained against the front of his pantaloons, especially with her lower belly pressed against it. He didn't try, hoping she would understand *she* was the reason for his arousal. She was the reason they were in the gardens, consumed in a kiss that he didn't wish to end.

End it he did, though. Slowly, reluctantly. He didn't pull away or step backward. Instead, he rested a hand against the back of her head and pulled it until her cheek rested in the small of his shoulder.

Although he expected she might fight the move, she once again relaxed in his hold and allowed a sigh.

A sigh that sounded like frustration.

"Please don't ask me to apologize," he murmured, his voice nearly a whisper. "I could not help myself."

He felt her head tilt, felt her gaze bore into him despite the darkness. "Mr. Tennison, I am not some young girl fresh from the schoolroom—"

"Thank the gods," Alexander whispered.

"—But that *is* the first time I've been kissed. Properly. Like that," she added, as if to ensure he remembered the brief peck they had shared in her office. There was no censure in her tone. No hint she was offended by the liberties he had taken.

"Mine as well," he replied, knowing almost immediately she wouldn't believe him.

She didn't believe him, and the throaty sound she made was proof.

"I've been... practicing. On the base of my thumb," Alexander said as he moved the hand that was resting against the back of her neck to show her what he meant. "For several years, in fact. And I've seen how my parents kiss when they don't think anyone is watching."

"Surely not like that," she said with some surprise.

"Oh, very much like that. Just recently, too. They've, uh, seem to have fallen in love. Again."

Margaret regarded him for a long time before she said, "You never did tell me what you had to give up to gain your handsome good looks."

A wince momentarily marred those good looks before he said, "Color."

Her brows furrowing, Margaret leaned away from him. "Color?"

Alexander had a thought to simply kiss her again in the hopes she would forget the query. Instead he decided he owed her an explanation. "*Colors*, I should say," he amended. "Reds and greens, mostly, but I may as well be unable to see any of them," he replied on a sigh.

A week ago, he had felt sorry for himself at learning he was color blind. Now his reaction to the words describing his color blindness had dulled. As if he could no longer muster the passion to protest or question why he had to be the one to suffer. Perhaps his color blindness was the cost of his good looks.

"You're color blind," she whispered in awe. "Color blind," she repeated again, well aware he had taken one of her hands in his and gripped it, as if he thought she might pull away. Escape his hold.

Alexander jerked at hearing how she said the simple proclamation. "You needn't make it sound like I've been *blessed*," he scolded.

She gave her head a shake. "I apologize. It just... it explains so much," she murmured. At seeing his furrowed brows, she added, "Why you asked about the rubies and the garnets and the color of my gown and... and my eyes."

"Are they really gray?" he asked.

"Gray, yes, with very dark gray rims around the irises."

He stared into her eyes for a long time before he sighed "Then at least I see them correctly," he murmured, despite the dim light from the lanterns barely lighting her face.

Her eyes suddenly rounded. "The garnets. You... if you can't see the red, then... then what *do* you see?"

"Just gray," he replied. "Same with the rubies. Emeralds. Apparently anything you see as red or green, I see in shades of gray."

Although Margaret knew she should pull away from his hold—what if someone saw them out here in the gardens?—she rather liked how he held her. How he gazed at her. The moment passed quickly, though, for Alexander seemed to remember where they were and who might be watching.

"Come, let's take a walk through the rest of the gardens. See if we can't find the reason why we ended up out here in the first place."

"Whatever do you mean?" Margaret asked. She glanced around, realizing if he intended to escort them anywhere, it would be a short walk—despite the beauty of Lord Weatherstone's gardens, they weren't *that* large.

"Lord Weatherstone was in wont of a particular flower for his garden," Alexander replied. "My father happened to have at least a dozen in his conservatory. When he brought one here for the earl, he learned Lord Weatherstone was considering buying the jewelry shop." He paused when Margaret inhaled sharply. "Meanwhile, my mother had joined my father on the walk here and then prevailed upon Lady Weatherstone to send you the invitation."

"Because you asked her to," Margaret said, not making it a question.

"True," he admitted. "Mothers are good like that. Especially when all they can think about is the possibility of grandchildren," he remarked with a grin.

The thought of Margaret with a daughter once again entered his thoughts. A beautiful daughter with a halo of dark curls and eyes like Margaret's. With a dimple to match his at the base of her right cheek.

"Or more children of their own," Margaret murmured. She giggled again. "She probably just wants you out of the house to make room for the new one."

Alexander paused on the crushed granite path and then turned to stare at her. "Whatever are you talking about?"

Margaret sobered. "Well, the baby she's going to have, of course."

After a moment, Alexander gave a quick shake of his head. "Oh, my mother isn't breeding," he claimed. "She's merely been eating too many cakes at tea time."

When Margaret broke out into a fit of giggles, Alexander glanced around, sure there were other couples turning to look in their direction.

He gave a start when he noticed his parents were one of them.

CHAPTER 33
CAUGHT IN THE ACT OF A KISS

A second later

Standing at the edge of a hedgerow, locked in an embrace, the Earl and Countess of Everly had apparently been kissing while Alexander and Margaret had been doing the same thing.

For a moment, Alexander feared they had paid witness to his momentary lapse of judgement. His momentary imaginings of what life might be like with a daughter who looked like Margaret.

For another moment, a flash of what their son would look like appeared in his mind's eye, and he was awestruck by the idea that Harold Tennison II, with his jet black hair and Greek god features, would be the handsomest man in all of Parliament. As such, he would have more power than even the oldest duke at seeing to it his legislation was passed without argument. At seeing to it all the people of England were treated as citizens. That none were marginalized due to their financial status or the origins of their forebears. Due to their ownership—or not—of land.

A Chartist, he thought with some surprise. Perhaps his son wouldn't be the first in the family, though. He thought he could adopt such ideals before he had to take his place in Parliament.

Not sure what to do now that his parents were staring at him—was that surprise they were exhibiting? Or shock?—Alexander simply waved at them and then hurried Margaret along on the path toward the west end of the house.

Well away from the Japanese lanterns and the gaslights of the ballroom, the west gardens were barely lit from the glow of the quarter moon. Still, it was easy for Alexander to make out the *Fritillaria meleagris*. The drooped flower had bloomed, its tulip-like shape made up of checkered petals that appeared as if they were studying the ground below.

Margaret bent down to regard the flower for a moment. She used the hand at the end of her withered arm to lift the flower, and she stared at it a moment before she carefully lowered the bloom. She straightened. "What do you see?" she asked.

"It's just dark gray," he whispered. "With small darker specs of gray on the petals."

"Well, it appears exactly the same way to me," she said. "But—"

"Without light, there is no color," Margaret remarked.

Alexander furrowed a brow, thinking at first she meant the comment as a metaphor. "Are you saying I need more light in my life?"

Margaret dipped her head. "I merely wished for you to know that there are times when we all see colors the same way. Before sunrise, after sunset, in a room where no candles or lights have been lit. When everyone merely sees shades of gray."

Alexander considered her comment for a moment. "And in the middle of the night?" he asked, his voice barely a whisper.

"You might think it black, but if it is a clear night like tonight, there are stars shining like the most brilliant cut diamonds, and the moon is the color of a pearl."

Alexander raised his gaze to the stars above, immediately understanding her meaning. "And when it's cloudy?"

"Then everything is a dark gray here in town. Like a smudge of soot, from the street cobbles, up the sides of the buildings, and to the sky overhead." She sighed.

"What is it?" he asked, rather liking how easy it was to talk with her. He wondered if it was because they were alone in the dark or if it would always be like this for them.

"I've never been outside of London," Margaret replied as her gaze continued to take in the sky above them, "but I hear in the country it can be completely black in the middle of the night. So dark you cannot even see a hand in front of your face." She turned her attention back to him. "Is it true?"

Allowing a chuckle, and remembering his times at the Everly country house, Alexander nodded. "It's true," he whispered. "Even candlelight seems to be swallowed up by the night."

They stood in the darkness for a long time, watching the stars and listening to the faint sounds of the orchestra from the ballroom.

"Would you think ill of me if I offered to see for you?" Margaret asked in a whisper.

Alexander gave a start. "How do you mean?"

"You could simply ask me," she replied. "Show me what you cannot be sure of. I promise I would not lead you astray when I tell you what color it is."

"Are you referring to a time when I might make jewelry in the shop? If my father does decide to buy it?"

She winced. She had thought the decision to purchase the shop was already made.

"When my father buys the shop," Alexander amended, as

if he could read her mind.

Margaret winced again at the reminder of what her father was being forced to do, all because he had trusted an unscrupulous gem merchant and a client who had no business buying jewelry given her financial situation.

That Margaret had been able to sell one of those rubies to the man who now stood next to her was a small consolation. At least Mr. Goldman had taken some of the other rubies in exchange for the garnets and citrines she needed for Alexander's parure. Lord Everly's immediate payment for those gems had allowed her to pay most of the shop's outstanding bills, but the debt owed to Mr. Baumeister for the original collection of rubies increased with each passing day due to the interest.

A kiss on her forehead had Margaret inhaling. Pulled from her reverie, she remembered his query and said, "You can ask me to help you whenever you are of a mind to do so."

Alexander's eyes narrowed. "Not just about colors? Not just about gemstones?"

Margaret gave a slight shake of her head. "I would welcome the opportunity to share whatever help I can."

"Does that mean you would... marry me?" Before he allowed her a moment to answer, he added, "I know I am too young to marry, but... I shouldn't want to discover you've gone off and married someone else and had three children by the time..."

One of her fingers had lifted to touch his lips, effectively silencing him. "I can wait for you, if that is what you are suggesting I do," Margaret murmured. "But not too long."

"How long?"

Margaret gave a start. For a moment, she had thought their discussion was merely speculation. A "what if" scenario.

Torn, because she thought he might use a long betrothal to spend time with Cyprians, Margaret considered the most logical reason why she couldn't wait for him longer than a few years. "I am older than you." When she noted his look of confusion, she added, "By four years, at least."

"Oh, I don't think it will be *that* long," Alexander whispered. "And it's only fair I warn you that I have this obligation I must take on when my father dies, and any wife of mine will be forced to take on the one that goes with it."

"You mean the Everly earldom?" she asked. Giddiness had her feeling light. The champagne had gone straight to her knees. None of this was real. An earl's son was speaking of marriage.

To her.

"Indeed. Which means you'll be my countess."

Margaret began giggling. "You'll be an earl."

"Hard to believe, I know," Alexander said, joining her merriment before he suddenly grew serious. "Does that mean you will? Marry me? I... I will give you a ring, of course, but I have to make it first, and you'll have to choose the right gemstones, of course. Perfect stones with no occlusions. In your favorite color." After a pause, he asked, "What is your favorite color?"

Margaret inhaled softly. "Uh, sapphire blue, I suppose," she replied, thinking of the gown she wore.

"Thank the gods." When she furrowed a brow, he added, "That's a color I apparently see correctly."

"Oh," she murmured.

He felt her hold on his arm tighten, and all at once she seemed to sober. "What will you be doing while I wait?"

Alexander lowered his head to hers. "I have some things I must learn from my father. About the earldom. My sister's come-out means I'll probably have some vetting to do. Of her prospects. I shouldn't wish for her to end up married to a scoundrel. Or a rake."

"Surely your father will help with that."

"My father's social circle is the Royal Society. Hardly a bastion of rogues and rakes," he replied.

Margaret turned her head at the sound of a bird. "I suppose you'll have to sow your wild oats," she murmured on a sigh.

Alexander struggled to clear his throat when the oddest moan sounded. "About that. I..." He paused and dipped his head.

"What is it?" she asked, sure he was going to admit to keeping a mistress despite his claim that he didn't employ one.

"I haven't yet been with a woman," he blurted.

Margaret stared at him a moment before she gave her head a shake. "Despite all those women who must come to worship you on your pedestal at the museum?" she half-teased. Then her eyes widened. "Men, then?" she guessed.

His eyes rounded. "Oh, god, no," he countered as he shook his head. "It's just that, my father warned me about the danger of brothels before I left for university, and I've never had a mistress. Before I wed, I should probably learn how—"

"Don't," she said with a shake of her head. At seeing his look of uncertainty, she whispered, "We can... we can learn together." When she noted his hesitancy, she added, "There are books. With color plates. Although, in the dark, everything will appear gray."

"You're saying we'll see everything the same way?"

She nodded.

"Minx," he accused in a whisper that had her shivering. "You deserve a man who knows exactly what to do. Knows exactly how to pleasure you."

"I prefer a diamond in the rough. One I can polish as I see fit," she countered playfully.

"As opposed to a stone that's been on someone else's finger," he half-asked. When she nodded, an impish grin lightened his face. He scoffed. "You just don't want to wait so long for me," he accused, his grin widening into a huge smile.

"If I give you too much time, you could change your mind, and then I'll be left ruined," she countered.

She knew all too well about young women who agreed to wed and then were bedded long before the wedding was to take place.

Betrothals allowed a couple as much freedom to engage in lovemaking as the state of matrimony.

Long betrothals meant a young woman's virtue would be forfeit.

Broken betrothals meant ruination.

"You're just worried that I might have a wandering eye," he accused.

"You might," she replied.

"I don't, and I won't change my mind," he murmured, his head shaking. "Besides, there is the matter of Mr. Baumeister. I want to be sure he's brought to justice for what he's done to—"

"Mr. Tennison—"

"Call me Alex, won't you?"

Margaret gave a start. "Alex," she said, as if attempting to say the word for the first time. "Mr. Baumeister will go away when the debt is paid."

Alexander shook his head. "Mayhap. But something tells me he will not. That he will believe something belonging to him has been taken from him."

"But the shop never belonged to him," she argued.

"I was referring to you," Alexander remarked.

Margaret gasped. "Never, sir."

"What would you have done? If your father had to give him the shop to pay the debt? You were part of Baumeister's deal, were you not?"

She shook her head. "I told my father I could not be.

That I would not—*could not*—be compelled to marry that despicable man."

"What would you have done? Run away?" When she barely nodded, he added, "How? Where would you go?"

"I have some money hidden away," she quickly replied. "A valise packed with some things. I know the steam bus schedule to Bath—"

"Bath?" he repeated in alarm.

"There are jewelry shops there. Gem merchants. A position for me." Now that her secret was out, she looked uncertain, as if she might have shared too much information.

"Promise me you will not leave London," Alexander demanded as he gripped her shoulders. "Should anything ever happen, *I* will be you protector. I *am* your protector now," he insisted. "Do you understand?"

Margaret stared at him for a long time before she finally nodded. "Yes, sir."

"Call me Alex."

"Alexander," she murmured quietly.

"That's... better," he said on a sigh. "May I call you Margaret?"

She nodded. "I suppose. But never Peggy. I will not answer to it."

"Understood. Margaret," he whispered, as if trying out the word and deciding he liked it. He leaned over and kissed her forehead.

The sound of a clearing throat had the two of them turning in alarm to discover the Earl and Countess of Everly regarding them from the crushed granite path. "Good evening, Mother. Father," Alexander said, trying to sound nonchalant. He pointed toward the flower near their feet. "The *F. meleagris* bloomed," he added lamely.

"We saw it earlier this evening," Harold replied. "Is there something else that's... bloomed as well?"

Alexander straightened and pulled Margaret's arm onto his. "Miss Ewen has agreed to marry me. Not right away, but—"

"But in less than four years," she interrupted, still not convinced such a union might ever happen.

"Probably less than two years," Alexander amended. Then he remembered what Margaret had said about his mother being with child. "I wouldn't want our first child to be born so close in time to my new sibling."

Stella gasped. "Who told you?" she asked, her gaze immediately going to Harold.

He had a hand held up, though, as if to stave off her accusation. "I haven't told a soul," he claimed.

"Oh, dear. I might have... mentioned it to him," Margaret murmured. "I thought Mr. Tennison already knew."

"Well, no harm done, my dear," Stella murmured. "But I insist I be allowed extra cakes at teatime until this one is born," she added with a quick look in her husband's direction.

"You'll hear no argument from me," Harold replied.

"Nor me," Alexander agreed.

"Nor me, either," Helen announced from where she stood well behind her parents. "That is, if I knew what we were all agreeing to," she added as she came abreast of her mother.

"We're allowing Mother to have as many cakes as she desires at teatime," Alexander stated. "Or anytime, really."

"Oh, I do prefer that option," Stella said, a brilliant grin aimed in her son's direction.

Helen made a sound of disbelief even as her attention stayed on Alexander—or rather on his arm, where Margaret's was firmly held in place by his other hand. "Very well," she said, obviously suspicious. "I've had an offer of a dance from Lord Cougham, but I couldn't find you to ask if I could accept or not," she complained, aiming her words at both her mother and her brother.

"You may dance with him," Stella replied.

"Don't let him get within ten feet of you," Alexander said at the same time.

Stella and Alexander exchanged quick glances.

"He's a rake of the worst kind, Mother."

"He's the only son of our hosts," Stella reminded him. "The only heir to the Weatherstone earldom."

"And old enough to be her father," Alexander countered. He dared a glance at Margaret, as if he hoped she might chime in with an opinion.

"He's a client. I dare not say a word," she murmured.

Harold dipped his head in an attempt to stifle a chuckle. "*I'll* make the decision on this one," he said with a good deal of authority. "Accept the dance, Helen, but if he tries anything untoward, stomp on his foot and head for the potted palms."

"Harry!" Stella hissed.

"Thank you, Father," Helen replied happily before she dipped a curtsy and skipped off. She disappeared through the French doors leading back into the ballroom.

Turning his attention to his son, Harold said, "You'd best return to the ballroom."

"Yes, sir." Alexander aimed an apologetic glance in Margaret's direction before leading her towards the French doors.

Stella and Harold watched them go before they regarded one another. "Shouldn't we return as well?" Stella asked.

Harold shook his head. "Not yet. I wasn't finished kissing you," he claimed.

"Well, make it quick, darling. I do wish to dance tonight," Stella replied before she stepped into his hold.

Any other protests were soon quieted as Harold captured her lips with his.

CHAPTER 34
A CHALLENGE

ednesday, House of Lords, Westminster

Yawns prevailed during the next session of Parliament, and the speakers seemed to realize their points would be best made quickly lest anyone fall asleep during their time in possession of the floor.

Last night's ball had been another success for Lord and Lady Weatherstone. Rumors abounded that there were still couples in the gardens as late as three o'clock in the morning, and early bets suggested there would be a number of newborns in nine month's time.

The talk of impending heirs and spares had Harold admitting to Lord Weatherstone that Stella was breeding, which had the elderly man beaming in delight.

"I wagered Agnes on the topic not ten minutes after you took your leave last week," Weatherstone claimed. "She can spot a lady with child even if she's wearing a sack," he added in delight. "I, of course, was of the opinion it was possible but not probable."

Harold frowned. "Why not?"

Weatherstone gave him a quelling glance. "At your age?"

Not prepared for the comment, Harold felt as if a fist had been driven into his middle.

Did everyone think he was on his deathbed? Or that he could no longer make love to his wife?

Well, he could, damn it. And he had been. Frequently. With determination and fervor. So much so, he felt as if he had youthened ten years. He was also sleeping far more, but it was probably better he do so than spend that time in the conservatory communing with his plants.

Not about to tell the aged man he had been bedding his wife both day and night for the past week, Harold merely arched a brow and asked, "What do you owe Lady Weatherstone for your egregious error in judgement?"

Wincing, Weatherstone rolled his eyes and said, "Two nights at the theatre next week instead of the usual one," he groused. "And a ring."

Harold's brows shot up. "Which you will purchase at Ewen and Ewen," he stated.

"Are you buying the shop?"

"I am. Ewen has accepted my offer." Harold didn't mention his son's intent to marry Miss Ewen. Although he didn't expect Alexander to change his mind, there was always the possibility Margaret wouldn't wait for him.

"Well, I shall look for another business in which to invest," Weatherstone replied. His nose suddenly narrowed, and Harold knew why when he turned to discover Lord Framingham hovering nearby.

"Framingham," Harold acknowledged with a deep nod.

"Everly," the marquess replied.

Harold gave Weatherstone an apologetic glance and then turned his full attention on Lord Framingham. "My lord, I should warn you that if you ever again approach my countess with the intention of proposing an *affaire*, I shall employ my skills with a sword and relieve you of the reason you think you need a woman in your bed."

Framingham's immediate response was to move his hands to the vicinity of his crotch. "Now see here, Everly. There's no need for threats," he replied, managing to seem reasonable despite the fact that his voice sounded an octave higher than usual.

"Good. Then I'll inform my second he won't need to appear in Wimbledon Common at daybreak tomorrow," Harold responded.

Weatherstone lifted a hand to cover his smirk, but a chuckle erupted despite his best effort to hold it in. He quickly sobered when the marquess aimed an especially vile look in his direction.

"Hard to believe *you* would keep company with such a bombastic earl," Framingham said, ignoring Harold.

"I don't know why," Weatherstone replied. "I thought I'd be in need of a brisk walk at dawn tomorrow morning. I've never been anyone's second before, and I was so looking forward to a spirited fencing match."

Glowering, Framingham said, "It's a good thing your wife is an old crone, or you might discover she's been in my bed."

Harold's eyes widened in horror, sure the two elder aristocrats were about to come to blows. Despite the awful odor of the Marquess of Framingham, he was about to step between them when the two burst into laughter.

"Ha!" Weatherstone said as he lifted a finger in the marquess' direction. "If only you could have seen your face just then," he chortled.

"Me?" Framingham countered. "For a moment, I thought *you* were going to punch me."

"For a moment, I was," Weatherstone claimed, his humor having dissipated. "In fact..."

Harold watched as Lord Weatherstone balled up a fist and drove it up and into Framingham's midsection.

The marquess let out an '*oomph*' that was probably heard all the way down to the House of Commons. Then, bent nearly in half, he would have ended up crashing head first onto the marble floor if not for a pair of footmen who rushed up and grabbed the marquess' arms to steady him.

Both nearly let go of Framingham when his body odor made its way to their nostrils.

"Let go of me," Framingham boomed, jerking his arms from the servants.

"Yes, my lord," they said in unison. They returned to their stations, exchanging looks of disgust as they did so.

"Now what did you do that for?" Framingham asked, his attention entirely on Weatherstone.

"My countess is *not* an old crone," Weatherstone replied cooly. "Nor is your marchioness." He stepped closer and lowered his voice, although it was apparent he was attempting not to breathe too deeply. "If you would have the good sense to take a bath on occasion, you might find she no longer requires the attentions of a lover."

Framingham dipped his head. "I rather doubt a bath is the reason she—"

"Trust me, it's the reason," Weatherstone said with a bushy brow arched so high it nearly disappeared into his powdered wig.

When Framingham's gaze went to Harold, the earl allowed a nod. "Lord Weatherstone speaks the truth, sir."

For a moment, the marquess looked rather unsteady on his feet, and Harold wondered if the footmen would attempt to come to his rescue a second time or allow him to fall to the floor.

Instead, Framingham steadied himself and then straightened. "Everly, I shan't approach your countess ever again."

"Very good, my lord."

"And Weatherstone, I apologize for having referred to Agnes as I did." He huffed.

"Apology accepted." When Framingham didn't say anything more, Weatherstone asked, "What about Caroline?"

Framingham grimaced. "I'll speak with my valet about having a shower bath installed," he groused. "I refuse to take a bath in a... in a *tub*," he added.

A huff sounded from the older earl. "Such a shame," Weatherstone said with a shake of his head.

"What are you about?"

"Well, if you have a big enough tub, you can take the bath *with* your marchioness," Weatherstone whispered, his brows waggling suggestively. "Bubbles make for such wonderful foreplay, don't you agree, Everly?"

Both Harold and Framingham stared at the old earl before they blinked several times.

"Well?" Framingham asked as he turned his attention to Harold.

Harold cleared his throat. "The earl is right, my lord." He had an idea and every intention to see to its execution as soon as possible. "If you'll excuse me." He gave a bow, turned, and quickly made his way to the exit.

He had to locate a large bathtub.

CHAPTER 35
A RIDE IN THE PARK
IT'S NOT

Thursday afternoon, Ludgate Hill

Alexander aimed the horse hitched to his father's phaeton toward the curb in front of Ewen & Ewen and was met by a street urchin.

"See to your hors', guv'nor?"

Tossing him a coin, Alexander told the boy he would be but a moment—"Mayhap two, but no more,"—before he entered the jewelry shop. He tucked his riding crop beneath one arm as he opened the door, the gold bell above tinkling softly upon his entry.

Glancing around, Alexander was stunned to find no one in the shop—not even Margaret nor her father.

"Hello?" he called out before a sense of unease settled over him. When he glanced back at the door, he noted the oval sign with the word 'Open' had been turned so it displayed 'Closed' to those outside.

How had he not noticed?

Well, he was anxious to see Margaret, he supposed. Why he was so nervous, he couldn't say. The night at the ball had gone better than he expected. He had secured a promise of her hand when he was ready to take her to wife. His mother had said there was no need for her to chaperone if the two of them were to marry.

His gaze went back to the door. Why was it unlocked if the shop was closed?

The thump of footfalls above had him heading toward the stairs in the far corner of the shop. Listening intently, he was about to call out again when a loud *thump* and a groan had him freezing in place. A scuffle ensued, which had Alexander climbing the carpeted stairs two at a time.

A few doors lined the corridor at the top of the stairs, and moving shadows on the worn carpet in front of one open door had Alexander pausing. He crept to the edge, glanced into the room. He blinked.

Adam Ewen was on the floor, his hands and feet bound with strips of linen. Another strip had been wrapped around his head and across his mouth, making it impossible for him to speak. The makeshift ropes had obviously been torn from linens that were now left in a rumpled heap on the bed.

Given Adam's position on the floor, he had apparently fallen from the bed, either during a struggle or because he was attempting to escape his assailant.

When the older man spotted Alexander, he gave a quick shake of his head before his gaze seemed to deliberately avoid Alexander.

About to head into the room to help the jeweler, Alexander paused. He remembered the sound of the scuffle and realized whoever had tied up Adam was probably still upstairs—perhaps in the same bedchamber.

But where was Margaret?

A sick sensation developed in Alexander's gut as his gaze darted down the hall. He listened intently, hoping to determine if she was in another room or merely gone from the premises.

Please be gone. Please be gone, Alexander thought as he tried to decide what to do.

But she had known he was going to fetch her for the ride in the park. He had confirmed it with her after the ball Tuesday night.

A quick glance back at Adam showed the man's attention was on something—or someone—to the left of the open door. Perhaps he could rush in and surprise the intruder, but without a weapon...

His gaze dropped to the riding crop tucked beneath his arm. Although it wouldn't do much damage to someone at close range, it would certainly sting someone if wielded from a few feet away, perhaps enough to give him time to use his fists.

He winced at the thought of ruining his hands. His middle knuckle still hurt from when he had punched Baumeister the night before last, making it difficult to hold the tool he used to secure gems into their collets.

If Margaret was in danger, though, as her father obviously already was, then he would have to use whatever he could to fight.

"Where is she?"

Alexander froze, sure the voice had come from inside the room. He watched as Adam shook his head.

"Which room is she in? Nod for as many doors as I must pass. Get it wrong, and you'll regret it."

Relief settled over Alexander. Margaret wasn't in the same room as Adam, but whoever was looking for her would be out in the corridor in a moment in search of her.

There were four other doors along the corridor. Only one at the very end was closed. Making his way slowly toward it, he prayed the wood floor beneath the carpet runner wouldn't creak or otherwise give away his presence.

Once he was in the front of it, he lifted a finger to the

handle and slowly depressed it. "Margaret?" he said in a whisper, barely pushing on the door when the latch came free of its mooring.

When it was wide enough, he nudged a boot into the opening and was about to slide into the room when an umbrella came down on his knee—hard.

Struggling to keep from crying out in pain, Alexander whispered, "Margaret," once more before he entered completely—just as she was about to wallop him across the head with her makeshift weapon.

Her eyes wide with fright and then with relief, the umbrella held above them by the hand at the end of her good arm, Margaret gasped. She fell into his arms as he carefully shut the door.

"Did he kill Father?" she asked in a hoarse whisper.

Alexander's eyes rounded. The poor woman had thought there was someone capable of murder in the house! "No, he's merely bound and gagged," Alexander replied quietly, pushing her away from him so he could be sure she hadn't suffered any damage. "You?"

"I'm frightened near to death," she replied. "I was about to come down to meet you at the door when I heard him bellowing—"

"Who?"

"Mr. Baumeister."

Alexander stared at her in shock. "He's out of gaol?" he asked in dismay.

"Out and angry as a hornet," Margaret whispered.

The two stilled themselves when the floorboards along the corridor creaked. From the way the footfalls paused, Alexander knew Baumeister was looking into each open-doored room before advancing to the next.

"Hide," Alexander ordered.

Margaret's eyes rounded. "Where?" she mouthed. The

bedchamber was small. The single wardrobe wasn't very large, and there didn't appear to be a door to a dressing room.

Alexander indicated the bed. "Under it," he mouthed before he readied the riding crop. As Margaret scrambled to the floor and struggled to pull herself beneath the bedstead, the skirts of her carriage gown impeded her progress. Alexander stepped back from the door and held the crop poised above his head.

"Ah ha!" Baumeister said as he flung open the door. "I've got you!"

His words were cut off when the crop hit Baumeister's cheek, the button at the end of it doing as much damage as the cut leather. Before Baumeister could react, Alexander struck from the other side, which had the gem merchant howling in pain, one arm lashing out in an attempt to catch Alexander's coat.

Alexander lifted a foot and shoved it into Baumeister's midsection, sending the man backwards into the hall and onto his backside. The *thump* of his hard fall seemed to shake the building. With the wind knocked out of him, his gasps for air made it appear as if he was being strangled. Scrambling backwards, crablike, his escape was impeded by Adam, who, despite his bindings, had somehow managed to sit up and scoot into the corridor.

Readying the crop to bring it down on the intruder once more, Alexander was prevented from doing so when Margaret grabbed his arm. Just beyond her Father, Constable Peters stood with his hands on his hips.

"Well, what do we have here?" the constable asked in a loud voice.

"He assaulted me!" Baumeister cried out, pointing to Alexander as he held one hand to his bloodied cheek.

"He was defending me. And my father," Margaret countered. She was about to step around Alexander to get to her father, but Alexander held out a hand to stop her.

Staring at the constable, Alexander recognized him as the same one who his father had found Tuesday night. "How did you know to come?" he asked, suspicious. Baumeister was already out of gaol. Had he even been arrested?

Rolling his eyes, the constable reached down and removed the linen from around Adam's mouth. "The boy seeing to your horse complained that you'd been gone more than two moments," he replied. He stepped over Adam and stared down at Baumeister. "You again?"

"This is *my* shop now," Baumeister claimed. "On account of his owing me more money than he can pay," he added as he tried to point back to Adam.

"Oh, shut it," the constable said as he kicked the merchant in the shoulder, which disabled Baumeister's only support on that side of his body. He tumbled over onto his side and howled in pain when his crop-stung face hit the carpet.

Kneeling, the constable used the linen he had removed from Adam's head to tie the gem merchant's hands.

"You again as well," Peters said as he straightened and stood before Alexander. He turned his attention to Margaret, giving her a quick look up and down. "Afternoon, miss. I take it your father's assailant didn't get to you?"

"I was hiding in my bedchamber," she admitted in a voice filled with uncertainty.

"Miss Ewen agreed to ride with me in the park this afternoon," Alexander explained. "When I arrived and discovered she wasn't in the shop, I heard the commotion up here." He indicated Baumeister. "Why isn't he in gaol?"

The constable shook his head. "Something to do with a solicitor and not enough evidence to hold him," he groused. "Didn't have any stolen jewels on him."

"I'm pressing charges," Adam said from where he was still sitting, his knees bent nearly up to his chest.

"Oh, Father," Margaret said as she managed to step around Baumeister. She knelt down and began undoing the knots that held his bindings. "Are you all right?"

"I will be when I can straighten out and stand up," he murmured. He stared down at Baumeister. "First, you assault my daughter before a ball and now this? You cannot have the shop."

"You *owe* me, Ewen," Baumeister countered, managing to roll onto his side so he faced the jeweler.

"No, I don't," Adam argued as he allowed Margaret to help him to his feet. "I sold the shop—and the debt—to the Earl of Everly. He knows exactly how much you're owed, and you'll get no more," he warned.

This bit of news had Baumeister's eyes rounding. "We had an agreement—"

"You gave me an invoice, and I agreed to see it paid—"

"Which included your daughter—"

"My daughter was never part of the deal," Adam argued, his voice growing louder.

The two men stared at one another, their faces' both red with rage. Meanwhile, the constable rolled his eyes and shook his head. "Shut it, the both of ye." He turned to regard Alexander, who had moved to stand next to Margaret. The heir's attention was entirely on the young woman, his expression suggesting he was deaf to anything being said. "I don't think either one of ye has a claim to her."

Adam and Baumeister both gasped at the sight of Margaret kissing Alexander, the two behaving as if the rest of the world didn't exist.

"You could have just told me she was ruin't," Baumeister complained. "You allow her to kiss young men like that?"

"She's not ruined," Adam argued before he noticed the

ring on his daughter's finger. "She's... she's betrothed," he murmured in awe.

"She's betrothed, but she's kissing *him*?" Baumeister asked in dismay.

Adam furrowed a brow. "They're betrothed to each *other*, you idiot."

"Shut it, you two," the constable yelled, his gaze on the kissing couple.

"You know, for a man who sells gems, you really are thick in the head when it comes to the reason for jewelry," Adam said, his attention still on Baumeister.

"Am not. It's just for show. The wealthy have to prove they have blunt, is all," the merchant argued.

"I'm warning you," Peters said, his gaze still on the kissing couple.

"For show, yes, but not just for the wealthy," Adam countered, his attention still on Baumeister. "It's proof of love and affection, adoration, and regard for another," he explained. "And sometimes it's a show of wealth," he finally admitted.

"Well, aren't you going to do anything about it?" Baumeister asked, his attention turning to the constable.

Peters gave him a quelling glance. "Course not. I'm learning something here. Me wife never lets me kiss her, but somethin' tells me she would if I kissed her like that."

A sound of disgust emanated from the gem merchant just before Margaret had to break off the kiss, a fit of giggles sounding before tears began falling.

"It's all right, my pearl," Alexander said as he pulled her against him, a grin splitting his face as he understood the range of emotions she had to be feeling at the moment.

"Oh, that's good," Peters murmured. "*My pearl*. I'll have to remember that one," he added as he watched Alexander fish a handkerchief from his pocket and offer it to Margaret.

Adam loudly cleared his throat, which had Alexander

turning around and Margaret sniffling. "I thought you two were going for a ride in park?"

Reminded of why he had come to Ewen & Ewen, Alexander nodded. "Right away, sir. I'll have Miss Ewen back here in two hours." He offered Margaret his arm.

"Two hours?" Baumeister howled. "Do you have any idea what he can do to—?"

"Shut it!" both Peters and Adam yelled as Alexander escorted Margaret down the stairs and through the shop.

The constable hauled Baumeister to his feet, examining his face as he did so. "You're lucky, you know."

"Lucky?" Baumeister countered in disbelief.

"If someone threatened me woman like what you just done, you'd be dead."

Sobering at hearing the constable's claim, Baumeister allowed Peters to lead him out of the shop.

Out on the pavement in front, a small boy stood beaming in delight as the phaeton carrying Alexander and Margaret pulled away from the curb.

"What are you grinning at?" Baumeister asked gruffly.

Holding up a coin, the urchin said, "Most I've ever been paid to hold a hors', sir."

Spotting the denomination, Baumeister's eyes rounded. "Would you be interested in parting with that in exchange for a gem, now? Why, I've got an emerald on me—"

"Shut it," Peters said as he hit Baumeister on the back of the head and led him toward the Ludgate Hill Metropolitan Police Station.

CHAPTER 36

A DEAL OFFERED, A DEAL
ALMOST REFUSED

The following morning, Ludgate Hill Metropolitan Police Station

Knowing he had little time before Parliament resumed that day, Harold Tennison entered a tiny police station in the jewelry quarter of London. Although Robert Peeler's Metropolitan Police had been formed some eighteen years prior, there were few daytime constables on the streets of London. The force at night was tenfold in numbers, though.

Dressed in the familiar blue uniform of a constable, the only officer in the station acknowledged Harold with a nod. "Sir?" he asked, noting the earl's fine clothing.

"Are you still holding Samuel Baumeister here? Or has he been—?"

"He's here," the man said as he rolled his eyes. "Charged with assault. Can't release him until he's gone before a judge."

"Oh, I don't want him released," Harold assured the constable. "But I do need to see him if I might?"

The constable motioned toward the back of the station. A single iron-barred cell, the length of a man's height, took up nearly a quarter of the space. Sprawled on the cell's only cot was Baumeister. Disheveled, his balding pate shining with perspiration and his top coat unbuttoned and wrinkled, Baumeister looked as if he'd had a restless night.

"Baumeister," Harold said as he stood before the cell. He winced when he caught site of a scar across one of the gem merchant's cheeks.

Baumeister slowly turned his gaze toward Harold before he gave a start and stood up. From the way he wavered, it was evident he did so too quickly. He gave a slight bow. "Sir?"

"I take it you remember me from Tuesday past? At Ewen and Ewen?"

"I do," Baumeister admitted as he attempted to adjust his top coat. A hand smoothed over his head in order to put what little hair he had left to rights. "What do you want?"

"I wish to pay an invoice, with interest," Harold replied as he pulled a parchment from his waistcoat pocket. Unfolding it, he held it out. "According to the terms, interest in the amount of ten percent per month is to be included at the time of payment."

Baumeister moved to examine the paper. "This is Adam Ewen's debt," he said as he waved a chubby finger in the direction of the parchment.

"Debt which I have purchased and which I would see paid now." Harold turned and motioned for the constable to join them. "Would you be so kind as to witness this transaction? I wish it to be known I have cleared this debt with your prisoner."

"I ain't no prisoner," Baumeister argued.

"Shut it," the constable said in a tired voice, sounding as if he had used the term far too many times since his shift began. "I'll make him sign that he's received the funds, sir."

"Much appreciated." Pulling a purse from inside his top coat, Harold extracted a wad of bank notes. "You will count with me," he said to the constable as he rifled the twenty-pound notes in front of Baumeister. The gem merchant's eyes widened as the earl and the constable counted out the notes. Once they reached the amount on the invoice, Harold handed the notes to Baumeister. "And now for the interest." He started to count out more bills, but the constable put up a staying hand.

"Ten percent per *month*?" he said in disbelief.

"Those were the terms," Baumeister claimed, a beefy finger pointing to the words written at the bottom of the invoice.

"That's criminal."

"Nonetheless, those were the terms that were agreed upon by the original party from whom I purchased the debt," Harold explained. He started to hand over the additional bills, but pulled them back just before Baumeister could take them. "You will sign that you have been paid in full?"

The gem merchant's attention went from the bank notes he held to the additional notes in the earl's hand. "If I don't?"

The constable made a rude noise, one hand snaking through the bars to the hand that held the notes. He gripped Baumeister's wrist—hard—until Baumeister said, "All right, I'll sign."

"You will never again step inside of the Ewen and Ewen jewelry shop, nor will you go anywhere near Adam or Miss Margaret Ewen," Harold stated, still holding the last of the notes.

"What? How am I supposed to sell gems—?"

"You will not," Harold stated. "At least not to Ewen and Ewen. An unfortunate but necessary condition given your past behavior. And your *criminal* interest rates," he added, rather liking how the constable had put it. "Agreed?" Harold pressed.

Baumeister sighed. "Oh, agreed," he finally said. He took the pencil Harold offered. As the earl held the parchment against the bars with his palm behind it as a sort of support, Baumeister wrote his signature. He cursed when the charcoal threatened to poke a hole in the invoice. He allowed another sigh when he wrote 'paid in full' at the bottom.

Harold handed him the rest of the bank notes and took back the pencil.

"How do I know these are even real?" Baumeister asked, suddenly suspicious of the bank notes.

"You can take them to the Bank of England," Harold stated. He turned to regard the constable. "Thank you for your help, sir."

"My pleasure. Never seen so much blunt in all my life," the constable replied.

"Well, whatever you do, don't buy gems from him. But if you're in need of a bauble for your wife, do consider a trip to Ewen and Ewen," Harold said, hardly believing he was so shamelessly promoting the jewelry shop he now owned.

"Can't say I have the funds for it, sir, but should I come into an unexpected windfall, I'll certainly pay a call," he replied, his brows waggling as he turned his attention back to Baumeister.

Not about to pay witness to whatever the constable was about to do, Harold took his leave of the small station and hurried back to Westminster.

He had no idea what his countess was doing in the meantime.

CHAPTER 37
A CLANDESTINE SEARCH IN
THE FOUNDRY

*M*eanwhile, in the breakfast parlor at Rosemount *House*

"You were out late again last night," Stella remarked when Alexander settled himself at the breakfast table. Helen had long since finished her meal and was off with her cousins for an exhibit of early spring flowers in Regent Park. "Whites?" she guessed.

"Only for a short time," Alexander replied. "The novelty of marriage hasn't yet worn off the newlyweds, and once they left, there was no reason for me to stay," he groused, referring to Gabe Wellingham, George Torrington, Viscount Hexham, and Christopher Carlington, Earl of Haddon.

The latter might have been old enough to be their father, but he seemed determined to socialize with a younger crowd, probably because he had married a lady younger than even Alexander. Sure the earl sported a slight bruise at the top of his forehead, poorly covered by a forelock of hair, Alexander had asked if he'd suffered an accident.

"Oh, I keep banging it into the damned headboard,"

Haddon had replied, waggling his brows in a teasing manner. "But it's always well worth it."

The other two in their party struggled to maintain impassive expressions, well aware of the earl's recent penchant for bumping his head. At least it seemed to keep him feeling young, and he was always quick to remark on how besotted he was with his new wife, Juliet.

"So I started a present for Helen," Alexander added, deciding he could tell his mother that truth about why he was out so late.

Although working with pearls and diamonds for a necklace was proving easier than the patterns he was following for his mother's parure, he feared he might not have time to complete so many pieces before his sister's come-out ball.

His father hadn't seemed too concerned when he had warned him over a game of billiards the afternoon before. "Just means I can spread out my gifts to her over the course of the Season," the earl had said before he sank a series of balls. He had won that match and the next, which had Alexander wondering when he'd had time to practice. They would have played another, but the dinner bell sounded.

"That's terribly generous of you," Stella said as she gave him a brilliant smile. "A string of pearls, I suppose?" she asked, referring to his gift for Helen.

"And diamonds," Alexander said before he began eating.

"Diamonds?" Stella repeated in surprise.

Alexander nodded. "Small ones in between each pearl."

"Threaded like a bead?" Although she didn't have many necklaces strung on silk, she had never heard of diamonds drilled with holes.

Shaking his head, Alexander said, "No. Each diamond is

mounted in a double-sided collet," he explained. "To add brilliance."

"*Two* diamonds for every pearl?"

He acknowledged her query with a nod. When he saw how she frowned, he asked, "What is it?"

Stella sighed. "I merely had a string of pearls for my come-out, is all," she murmured.

"Are you jealous of your daughter?" Alexander teased. His grin disappeared when he noted her expression.

Lifting her teacup to her lips, Stella angled her head to one side. "I am," she admitted.

"Well, you needn't be," Alexander said. "I'm quite sure Father has something planned for you."

"Does he?"

Not wanting to give away his Father's secret—nor his own—Alexander dipped his head. "What would make you happy?"

The query was entirely unexpected, and Stella stared at her son for a long time before she said, "Well, I would be thrilled if he remembered the occasion of our wedding anniversary, even if he only brought me flowers."

Remembering the flower designs he was working into the earrings and the pendant for her necklace, Alexander said, "Oh, there will be flowers, I'm sure."

Stella stared at him a moment. "You're going to remind him of the occasion, aren't you?" she accused.

He shook his head. "He doesn't need reminding, Mother."

Surprised by his comment, Stella furrowed her brows as she watched him finish his breakfast. "Where are you off to now?"

"Ewen and Ewen," he replied. "I wish to see Margaret. Make sure all is well at the shop."

"He told me last night about that awful Mr. Baumeister,"

Stella said in disgust. "That he attacked Mr. Ewen and was goin to kidnap Margaret."

"He was prevented from hurting Margaret," Alexander replied, glad she had learned about what had happened. He was fairly sure his father hadn't yet told her he had purchased the shop, though.

Alexander was near to bursting with excitement at remembering what Margaret had proposed during the ball—that she would be his eyes for seeing colors—and the fact that there would be the means for him to sell his jewelry designs at the shop. "I am as happy as I am relieved," he admitted. "Working with Margaret gives me the confidence to continue my avocation."

Stella watched him take his leave, a combination of happy curiosity and excitement settling over her.

Her son had proposed marriage. Soon, she would have another daughter. One that worked in a jewelry shop.

She could hardly wait to go shopping, and she thought she might do just that once she finished her correspondence. But curiosity about the necklace Alexander was making for Helen got the best of her.

Once she thought he was gone from the house, Stella made her way out the kitchen door at the back of the house and into the small brick building that housed the foundry.

In the dim light from the open door, she couldn't make out anything until her eyes adjusted to the dark. Once they did, she frowned when no jewels were apparent on the work table. She opened one drawer but found only small tools. Another drawer revealed fusees. A series of small black boxes were lined up at the back of the table, though, nearly invisible given it was so dark.

She helped herself to the first one, opening the lid as if something might pop out. Aiming it toward the light, she frowned when she discovered it was empty.

The next box held a few red and yellow stones, all rather small and unremarkable. She put it back and opened the next. This one contained a couple of gems mounted in gold. "Oh," she murmured, although her discovery was tempered with disappointment at seeing their small size. Then she remembered what Alexander had said about a signet ring. She supposed these were the stones that would surround the seal.

Sighing, she was about to open the next box when a shadow fell across the open door.

"Mother?"

Stella jumped in shock. "Oh! You nearly frightened me to death," she accused, her hands going to her hips as she regarded Alexander.

"As did you me! I thought someone was trying to steal what little I had left in here," he claimed. "What are you doing in here?"

She inhaled. "I wanted to see the necklace you're making for your sister." It wasn't the entire truth, but he didn't need to know that.

Alexander rolled his eyes. "Oh, Mother. If it bothers you that much, I'll make one for you, too," he offered.

"I don't want one," she replied stubbornly. "I was just... *curious* about hers is all."

"Well, you're not going to find it in there," he replied. "Father locked it up. In the safe, I think."

"Oh, all right," Stella said as she made her way out of the brick building. "Why are *you* here?"

"I've got some gems I need to have Margaret take a look at. I'm thinking about using them on Father's signet ring, but I might need more."

"Oh," Stella said, sounding even more disappointed.

"Mother. I'm about to leave for Ewen and Ewen. Would you like to come with me? Shop for a bauble, perhaps?" he offered.

Stella's face brightened. "You wouldn't mind me tagging along?"

"No, Mother. As long as you don't mind waiting while I work with Margaret?"

"Oh, I won't," she promised. "I'll change clothes and be ready shortly."

Alexander watched her hurry back into the house before he examined the interior of the foundry. From the position of the first three boxes, he knew she had peeked into them. He sighed in relief at seeing the others hadn't been disturbed, for they held the components of her parure.

Helping himself to the box containing the pieces for the signet ring, Alexander shut the door. This time, he locked it, deciding he would need to do so every night until his mother's parure was finished.

Returning to the phaeton, he delayed his departure while he waited for his mother. A half hour later, they were on their way to Ewen & Ewen.

CHAPTER 38
PLANNING A WEDDING
WITH A JEWEL

wo hours later, Ewen & Ewen
Despite his Mother's presence in the jewelry shop—Alexander had left Stella to peruse the displays while he joined Margaret in the office—he spent a good deal of time kissing his betrothed in between conversations about gems and where they might live once they were wed.

After an especially long kiss, one which left Margaret breathless and him hard with need, Alexander broached the subject of their wedding. "Perhaps we shouldn't wait to marry," he said, settling a thigh on the edge of the desk.

Margaret stared at him. She had felt his arousal when it was pressed into her belly and wondered if it was the reason for his comment. "We're betrothed. According to what I've learned about betrothals, we're... expected to consummate—"

"It's not that," Alexander whispered.

Her gaze darted to the bulge in his pantaloons. "It's not?" she countered in a hoarse whisper. "I thought those were supposed to be..." She paused, her face taking on a reddish cast.

"What?" he asked, curious as to what she was about to say. He was sure the color of her complexion had darkened.

"My father once referred to them as 'wiggly bits,' but on you, they don't seem wiggly at all."

Alexander struggled to keep a chuckle from sounding. "They are when I'm not around you," he murmured, leaning closer. "Unless I'm thinking of you."

She inhaled softly. "Do you think of me... often?"

He nodded.

"I think of you, as well," she admitted, dipping her head.

"Not in a vexing manner, I hope?"

Margaret shook her head. "More tingly, really. I grow warm and..." She swallowed. "Sensitive in certain places."

"So... thoughts of me arouse you?" he asked in a whisper, his forehead touching hers.

"They do," she admitted. "Do you think me wanton?"

Alexander shook his head, his breaths coming quickly at the thought of what it would be like to make love to her. "I wish to be close to you," he murmured. "With you. All the time," he added quickly. "I worry about you. I think about you all night. I wake up thinking of you."

"As do I. About you," she admitted.

"I know I said I wanted to wait to marry, but... I have several friends who are happily wed."

"Are you feeling left out?" she teased.

"It's not a club, exactly," he countered. When she didn't respond, he said, "Tell me your thoughts on the matter."

Margaret sighed. "I want to marry. I do. Sooner rather than later," she finally admitted.

"Marry *me?*"

She chuckled before she sobered. "Yes, you. But I worry that you'll come to your senses and decide you require a more suitable lady to be your future countess. Perhaps you should."

"I won't. You're perfectly suitable."

"You're blind to my arm, but others are not—"

"I am not. It's just not..." He inhaled and let out a sigh of frustration. "It's not important," he finished. "It's part of you, Margaret. I love you, which means I love your arm, too." He reached for it, pulling on it when she didn't immediately allow him to hold it. He kissed the palm of her hand and inside the elbow, which had her gasping.

Margaret stared at him, swallowing at hearing his declaration. "If we marry, and you change your mind—"

"I won't."

"Promise me you won't send me to the country to live."

Alexander blinked. "What?" He stared at her, shocked by her comment.

"I couldn't bear it," she said. "I've never been out of London. I think I'd go mad living outside of the city. Where it's black at night? No one nearby? You can send me to Bath—"

"I'm not sending you to the country—or to Bath—unless I'm going with you," he countered.

She swallowed. "Would you take me there someday, do you think?"

"To Bath?" Alexander shrugged. "Of course. Would you like to go next week? We can marry and go there for our wedding trip," he suggested. "Go in the traveling coach or take the steam bus. I hear it's quite an interesting way to travel."

Margaret blinked. "We could? But... what about the... what about the reading of the banns?"

He gave her a quelling glance. "Despite what I'm about to pay you for pearls and diamonds for my sister's necklace, I'm sure I can afford a special license," he said. "We'll marry in a few days and be off. Stay for—"

"You have a parure to complete," she reminded him, her gaze darting toward the office door window. "And a necklace for your sister, apparently." Out in the shop, the Countess of Everly was studying every jewel in every display case as if seeing them for the first time.

"True," he replied on a sigh. "How about we marry just before Helen's come-out?" he suggested. "Leave for Bath the day after the ball?"

"We could do that? *You* would do that?"

Not bothering to answer, Alexander merely pulled her into his arms and kissed her quite thoroughly. When they finally came up for air, he sighed and said, "Now that we have our wedding settled, will you help me with the design for my father's signet ring?"

She blinked. "What about your sister's necklace?"

"Oh, that's easy. Two colleted diamonds in between each pearl. It will take me two or three days to complete," he claimed. "I'm more worried about my father's ring."

Margaret stared at him in disbelief before she grinned. "Of course. Tell me all about it."

CHAPTER 39
SECRETS AND SURPRISES ABOUND

A half-hour later, Ewen & Ewen Alexander and Margaret emerged from the office, murmuring excitedly about the design for the earl's signet ring and their plans to wed before Helen's come-out.

Anxious to tell Margaret's father, they found him at work on a necklace behind his workbench. Having expected the news for several days, he wished them well and assured them he would cover the shop while Margaret and Alexander were on their wedding trip.

When the bell above the front door of the shop tinkled, they looked up to see the Earl of Evenly entering.

"Father?" Alexander said as he joined the man near the door. "Or should I say 'proprietor'?"

"Father is fine," Harold replied, his gaze darting around the shop. "I was told I could find your mother here. Did you tell her I was the owner now?"

Alexander shook his head. "I did not," he replied. "I thought... I suppose I thought you had."

Reminded he had brought Stella with him to the shop, Alexander glanced around. "Where is my mother?" he asked of his future father-in-law, thinking perhaps she had left and was shopping elsewhere.

Adam pointed to an upholstered chair in the far corner of the shop. Nestled into the wingback chair, Stella was sound asleep. "She said shopping for jewels was exhausting and asked if she might have a seat," he said with a grin. "Never had a countess do that before," he added. "Good of you to come, my lord," he added, directing his attention to the new owner of the shop.

Harold acknowledged his welcome. "You'll be relieved to know that Samuel Baumeister has been paid in full, and he has agreed never to darken this door again," he said as he motioned to the front of the shop. "The constable at the police station paid witness to the signing."

"I am glad to hear it, sir," Adam replied.

"I told him he cannot sell his gems here," Harold went on, including Margaret in his edict as he addressed the three of them.

"I hadn't planned to buy any more from him," Margaret said. "I can get what we need from Mr. Goldman. And there are others, of course."

"Very well," Harold replied before he glanced around. "So, did my wife already run up a huge bill?"

Adam grinned and held up a hinged box. "Just asked that I set aside this for her, sir," he replied. "Although I don't think she intends it for herself."

Harold frowned as he opened the small box. Inside was a pearl bracelet. In between each pearl was a small diamond. When Alexander leaned over his shoulder, he said, "I told her what I was making for Helen. For her come-out. This will be a perfect companion to it."

"I thought that necklace was supposed to be a surprise," Harold whispered, hoping Stella was still asleep. He had kept her awake far too late the night before, his need for her nearly insatiable. The conversation he'd had with Weatherstone and Framingham and then Weatherstone's comment about his age when he admitted he was once again to be a father had him determined to prove he was not an old man.

Although he'd had trouble stepping off the bed this morning, he had once again felt as young as the day he had met Stella. As vital as the man he'd been when they were on Mykonos. As loved as the day he had married her.

Piss on Weatherstone. Piss on anyone who thought him too old to father another child. He was going to live to be older than Weatherstone. Live long enough to see this new babe married with babes of their own.

He might spend the time feeling stiff and sore, but damn it, he wasn't going to let thoughts of mortality ruin it for him.

"She was in the foundry this morning," Alexander whispered. "Thought I'd already left to come here. I think she's suspicious. Or mayhap just curious."

Harold blinked away his reverie. "Did she discover what you were making for her?" he asked in alarm.

Alexander shook his head. "I caught her before she opened those boxes," he assured him. "Your surprise will still be a surprise, but I did infer there would be flowers for your wedding anniversary. So... you might want to order some from a hot house," he suggested.

Chuckling, Harold nodded. "Oh, there will be flowers," he murmured. "I've ordered red roses."

"Is this to be a special wedding anniversary?" Margaret asked. "Five-and-twenty years, perhaps?"

Harold furrowed a brow. "No. Just... two-and-twenty, actually," he replied, giving Alexander a quick glance.

When Margaret's gaze darted to Alexander, obviously curious as to his age, he said, "You needn't worry, my sweeting. I was a honeymoon baby," he added, his brows waggling in delight.

"And an adorable one at that," Stella said, joining the conclave that stood around Adam's workbench.

"Mother," Alexander said, giving her a slight bow.

"Did you have a good nap, my sweet?" Harold asked as he lifted one of her gloved hands to his lips. The tinkling of the gold bell above the door signaled an arrival, and he turned to see several couples entering.

"I did," Stella replied. "It was quite refreshing, Harry, but now I'd like to pay for my purchase and be on my way. It's nearly time for tea, and I'm hungry for a slice of cake."

"The pearl bracelet has already been paid for, my lady," Adam said as he handed her the box. "Do come again."

Stella noted how the store was filling up with shoppers. "Oh, I will," she assured him.

Threading her arm around Harold's elbow, she gave him an impish grin as the two took their leave.

Alexander watched them go before he kissed Margaret on the forehead. "I should go. Let you see to your clients," he murmured. Turning to Adam, he was about to say more, but a customer stepped up to ask a question. Margaret was already seeing to one couple, while another waited for help at one of the display cases.

Deciding to make himself useful, Alexander offered his assistance to the older couple and was soon showing them pieces from a tray of brooches.

For the next four hours, no one seemed to recognize him as he answered questions and offered his expertise.

"You seem to be quite at home doing this," Margaret whispered when she was between clients.

"I am rather enjoying myself," Alexander responded. "I'm quite surprised at hearing what some people like and don't like. It's giving me ideas," he added before turning his attention to the next customer. "Lord Framingham," he said in surprise. "Welcome to Ewen and Ewen. How may I be of assistance?"

The marquess held a large, velvet-clad box beneath one arm. "I need to speak to someone about jewels," he said.

"You've come to the right place, sir," Alexander said.

The box landed on the counter in front of Alexander. "It seems this coronet is missing its jewels."

Frowning, Alexander peeked into the box, noting that there seemed to be jewels in all the mountings around the front of the filigreed gold band. On closer inspection, he understood what the marquess meant. "Are they all paste now, sir?"

"That's what I've been told," Framingham murmured. "Or my marchioness, rather. Since I didn't have the originals replaced, it's possible... well, let's just say I must have inherited this as it is."

Alexander pulled the gold coronet from the box and peered at the various gemstones. To his eyes, most appeared gray, which is how he knew they were probably emeralds or rubies. "For paste, they're very good, which leads me to suspect this is not the real coronet, but rather the one that's to be worn to balls and such," he explained.

"You don't understand," Framingham said. "It's the *only* one I have. I've no idea what became of the real one."

"Was it stolen, sir?" Alexander asked.

The air seemed to go out of Framingham all at once, leaving him looking far older than his true age. "Truth be told, I don't know. But when my marchioness discovered the truth of this one, well, let's just say it's made some trouble, so I want this one made right. With real gems. As soon as possible."

Nodding his understanding, Alexander placed the coronet back in the box. "We can see to its delivery—"

"I'll come for it when it's ready," Framingham said. "Just

send word to my house when it's done."

"Of course, sir," Alexander replied. Remembering the emerald ring that had been recovered from the marchioness' nephew—Alexander had arrived at Ewen & Ewen shortly after the thief had been removed from the shop—Alexander's eyes widened. "Sir, I believe there is an emerald ring here that belongs to your wife."

Framingham frowned. "What?"

"A thief stole it and brought it here, intending to pawn it. He had separated the emerald from the ring, but Mr. Ewen was able to repair it."

"And the thief?" Framingham moved closer, intending for their next words to be private.

Having overhead part of their conversation, Margaret stepped up and whispered, "He was arrested, sir. He claimed to be a nephew of the Marchioness of Framingham."

The marquess' eyes widened. "What happened to him?"

"He was arrested, sir. A Runner took him."

"A Runner? Not a peeler?" Framingham questioned.

"He was a Runner, sir," Margaret affirmed. "He'd been on the case for some time and had followed the man as he made his way into jewelry shops looking to sell either the emerald or the gold." Her eyes suddenly widened as her gaze went to the coronet. "Sir, is there a chance this nephew might have absconded with the real coronet?"

Framingham regarded Margaret with an expression of shock. "You've a good head on your shoulders, miss," he murmured. His gaze went to his mind's eye for a moment. "He stayed with us, you see. For about a fortnight. Left in quite a hurry, though. Said he had to return to Kent."

Alexander and Margaret exchanged quick glances. "Someone at Bow Street should be able to tell you where you can find the nephew," Alexander said.

"I'll fetch the ring from the safe," Margaret offered, not

mentioning that the marchioness had denied owning the ring.

"I'll go to Bow Street now," Framingham said, his eyes narrowing.

"Do you still wish to have us replace the paste jewels with real gemstones?" Alexander asked.

Framingham seemed uncertain for a moment. "Do," he finally replied. "I'd like it ready for the marchioness to wear to a ball this Season."

"Very good, sir," Margaret said as she passed the ring box to him.

Framingham opened the box and then shook his head. "This isn't mine," he murmured. "I've never seen this ring before."

Alexander and Margaret exchanged quick glances.

"Then please pardon me for the misunderstanding, my lord," Margaret said.

His expression softening, Framingham nodded. "No harm done," he replied. After a moment of reflection, he closed the box and gave it back to her. "It seems I'm off to Bow Street."

Margaret dipped a curtsy while Alexander bowed.

After the marquess left the shop, Alexander turned his attention on Margaret. "What do you suppose just happened?"

She shook her head. "Lady Framingham denied it was hers. Since Lord Framingham has never been a client of my father's, I've come to suspect someone else had it made for her ladyship. A long time ago. Father made it back when he was still cutting gems," she explained.

"Ah, a lover, perhaps?" Alexander guessed.

Margaret nodded. "I think Father knows who, too, although he hasn't shared what he knows."

Although he was curious, Alexander's thoughts turned to the marquess. "Did you notice something different about him?"

Margaret shook her head. "I've never met him before," she said. "Only his wife. Why do you ask?"

Alexander scoffed. "He... he smelled good," he stammered.

Her eyes widening, Margaret gave her head a shake. "I take it that's not normal?"

"It's not for him," Alexander replied. "He is famous for not bathing. His odor is usually so bad, no one can stand to be around him. Even his cologne cannot hide the atrocious odor."

Her nose wrinkling in disgust, Margaret said, "Promise me you'll not adopt that particular habit."

"Oh, I promise. I take shower baths on a regular basis," he assured her. "Although I could be convinced to take a bath in a tub if..." He stopped speaking, his face reddening.

Margaret stared at him. "In a tub if... you're blushing," she accused. "If *what?*"

"If *you* were in the tub with me," he whispered, rather enjoying how the color of her face seemed to change. Although he couldn't see reds, he knew she must be embarrassed. "Now who's blushing?" he teased.

"Mr. Tennison," she scolded. "I thought you couldn't see the color red." Before she could say anything more to him, another customer stepped up to the counter.

*W*hen Alexander finally took his leave of the shop and of Margaret, he felt ever so satisfied at having sold several pieces of jewelry and taken orders for a few custom creations—not the least of which was that of the Framingham coronet.

He also had plenty of ideas of what he would make once he finished the parure for his mother.

Margaret would need a ring, after all.

CHAPTER 40
BESTOWING JEWELS ON A COUNTESS

An hour before Helen's come-out ball, Stella's bedchamber, Rosemount House

"Darling, what were all those workmen doing here this afternoon?" Stella asked when Harold appeared at her door. She turned from her cheval mirror, the bell skirt of her red watered silk gown following suit a moment later before reversing its movement and finally coming to a halt. The red slippers Harold had purchased for her peeked out from beneath the hem.

Her lady's maid had done her hair in an especially elaborate style, a red-jeweled comb tucked onto her crown making it appear as if it were a tiara.

All that was left to be done was to choose the jewels she would wear.

"Installing a larger bathtub in my bathing chamber," he replied before he stepped into her bedchamber. In his right hand, he carried a flat, black velvet box. In his left hand was a huge bouquet of red roses. "Happy anniversary."

Stella's eyes rounded before one hand smoothed over her belly. "A larger tub? Whatever for?" she asked as she accepted the roses, burying her nose into one of the blooms. She inhaled slowly, a grin appearing before she moved to drop them into a vase on her dressing table. "They're gorgeous. Thank you."

"It's for us," he replied as he held out the black box. "So we might take baths together," he said as he waggled his brows.

"Have you been speaking with Agnes?" she asked in alarm.

Harold blinked. "No," he said before allowing a chuckle. "Actually, her husband made the recommendation. Was I... wrong to act on it?"

Stella's gaze went to the black box. "Probably not," she hedged, an impish grin appearing. "I'll need assistance getting in and out of it, though," she murmured, her hand once again moving to her middle. Despite her growing waistline, her pregnancy wasn't yet evident.

"This is for you," he said as he held out the box. "Alexander made it."

Gingerly removing the lid, Stella inhaled softly. "Oh, Harry," she breathed. "The gemstones are the perfect color," she added as she pulled the bracelet from the box. She held it out for him to wrap it around her wrist and secure the clasp. "The colors..." She paused and looked up. "You must have—"

"My only participation was commissioning it and paying for it," Harry interrupted. "Miss Ewen chose the garnets."

"They're beautiful," she replied as she waved her wrist in front of her skirt to show that the reds were a perfect match.

"Well, that's a relief, since there's a necklace," Harry said as he pulled the jewelry from his pocket.

"Harry!" Her eyes rounded. She gasped. "Is that a ruby in the pendant? In a flower!"

"Indeed," he replied proudly, as he moved behind her and wrapped it around her neck. Her gloved hand moved to the ruby, holding it against the hollow of her throat as he closed the clasp. "The pendeloque can also be worn as a brooch."

As soon as he finished, Stella hurried to the cheval mirror. "Oh, it's perfect," she said, nearly weeping in delight. "A ruby and garnets and citrines," she whispered. "I can even wear this with the other gown Miss Suzanne made for me."

"Which is the reason for the citrines, at least according to our son," Harold said as he moved to stand behind her. He placed his hands on her arms.

The two stared at their reflections a moment. "I suppose Miss Ewen helped choose them, too," Stella whispered.

"Alex can see yellow, so I think he had some say in the matter. And speaking of our son, he's out in the corridor. He has something for you."

"He does?"

"You can come in, Alex," Harold called out.

"Good evening, Mother," Alexander said as he joined them. He was about to ask about the necklace and bracelet, but Stella collided with him, her arms wrapping around his shoulders. She kissed him on the cheek, and tears brightened her eyes.

"All this time, I thought you were making a signet ring," she said in a scold.

Alexander extracted an arm from her hold and reached into a pocket. "Actually, I was," he said as he pulled out the gold ring. A raised number "3" surrounded by the shape of the Everly earldom insignia protruded from the flat top of the ring, and a circle of garnets were set around the seal. He held it out to his father. "Thought you might want to leave your initial in wax as well as the cheeks of offending marquesses," he teased.

Harold stared at the ring a moment before he finally reached for it. "It's magnificent," he whispered. He slipped it onto a finger and held out his hand as Stella let go her hold on her son.

"Oh, now. You'll have to be careful to guard that or you'll discover I have borrowed it on occasion," she teased, tears streaming down her face.

"Mother," Alexander said as he held out a hand in her direction. "I believe you are in need of these to complete your parure."

Stella tore her gaze from the signet ring and stared at the earrings that rested in the palm of her son's hand. "Earrings, too?" she whispered. "Pendeloques!"

"I can help you..." Alexander started to offer, but Stella scooped the jewels from his hand and immediately returned to the cheval mirror. She threaded the delicate wires through the holes in her plump earlobes and sighed in delight. "Pendeloques," she breathed. "Rubies! Oh, I shall be the envy of every woman in the ballroom," she claimed as she turned to the men in her life. "Thank you. Thank you, both," she said before she embraced her husband.

Harold let out an "*oomph*" and steadied them both as he wrapped his arms around her shoulders.

"Here you all are," Helen said from the threshold. "I was beginning to wonder if I was going to be the only person in the coach going to Sommers House," she complained.

Dressed in a white muslin gown with an overdress of nearly transparent muslin embroidered with white flowers, Helen was the epitome of a pretty young English miss about to make her formal come-out.

Her appearance before Queen Victoria had been nerve wracking but otherwise uneventful. Her gown—and this one —fit to perfection. Her hair was styled the same as it had been for the queen, a riot of curls interlaced with white rose-tipped pins and ribbons. Pearls decorated her earlobes.

The only things missing were a necklace and a bracelet.

"Oh, my dear daughter," Stella said as she took a steadying breath. "Let me give you some pearls," she said as she moved to the flat jewel box on her dressing table.

At the same time, Alexander pulled a string of pearls and diamonds from his waistcoat pocket.

He held it out to his sister. "Don't say I never gave you anything," he said as he watched her mouth drop open.

"Are those... *diamonds?*" she asked in alarm.

Alexander blinked, his attention going to the strand that hung from his fingers. He had strung a pair of diamonds mounted in collets and backed with silver foil between each pearl. In the gaslight of his mother's bedchamber, the diamonds were more noticeable than the pearls.

"Why, yes, yes they are," he replied as he moved behind her. "Double mine cut," he added as he secured the clasp. "Backed with silver foil to enhance their fire."

Her attention went to the box her mother had opened and was now holding out to her. "A bracelet, too? With pearls *and* diamonds," she breathed.

"Oh, I might be borrowing that from you," Stella said as she hurried over to finger the strand that hung around her daughter's neck.

"Only if I can borrow yours," Helen countered, her eyes wide. She turned around and hugged her brother. "Thank you, Alex," she said into his waistcoat. "I get pearls and diamonds *and* a sister for my come-out."

"You're welcome," he replied before extricating himself from her hold. "If you'll excuse me, I promised to pick up Mrs. Tennison at eight o'clock," he said with a grin. He didn't wait for anyone to reply, and took his leave of Stella's bedchamber.

His sister, mother and father watched him go before Harold turned to Stella. "I suppose a chaperone isn't necessary any longer, is it?" he asked in a quiet voice.

Stella gave him a quelling glance. "Now that they're married, I should hope not. Besides, I'm hosting a ball that's due to start within an hour. I cannot be two places at once."

"Where do you suppose they're spending the night?" he asked.

"Harry! Here, of course, I should think."

"There's a townhouse down the street I was considering buying," he said. "We can have him moved out of the house before his sibling arrives."

"Harry!" Stella scolded. But her expression suddenly softened. "It's not a bad idea," she murmured. "Keep them close but not underfoot."

"I wholeheartedly agree," Helen piped up. "Although I do like having a sister."

"Good," Stella replied. "Now, you must assure me you won't accept the first marriage proposal you receive tonight."

Helen blinked. "I rather doubt there will be any tonight," she replied. "Wait. How many did *you* have before Father proposed?"

Harold and Stella exchanged quick glances. When Stella didn't say anything right away, Harold crossed his arms and regarded her with an arched brow. "Well?"

Stella shook her head. "That's none of your concern."

"Sweeting..."

"It's time we go downstairs," Stella said.

Helen gave a huff and took her leave. Stella was about to follow, but Harold hooked an arm around hers and held her back.

"How many?" he asked in a whisper, his lips moving to hover just above hers.

Stella seemed to melt against him, her gloved arms wrapping around him as he moved to hold her in his. "*You* were the only one who proposed, and you know it," she whispered in dismay.

"Oh, thank the gods," he replied on an exaggerated sigh.

"What?" Stella said as she pulled away from him.

"Well, I was about to plant my fist into a few faces if I discovered someone else was competing for your affections," he claimed. He held out the signet ring. "Leave my new mark."

Stella rolled her eyes. One of her gloved hands went to the necklace. "You paid for all the gold, didn't you?" she asked in a whisper.

"The gold and the garnets, and the citrines, and the rubies," he replied. "And the pearls, and the diamonds." He held up his fist, his signet ring more than evident on his fourth finger. "It's a good thing I've purchased a jewelry store."

"You did *what?*" Stella exclaimed.

Harold's eyes rolled upward before he said, "I'll tell you all about it on the way to Sommers House," he promised.

Grinning in delight, Stella accepted his proffered arm and they took their leave.

CHAPTER 41
AFTER A COME-OUT BALL

*L*ater that night

"I thought the ceremony went quite well this morning," Alexander said as he walked with Margaret in the gardens behind Sommers House. Although not nearly as impressive as those behind Weatherstone Manor, they were perfect for a ten o'clock stroll beneath a new moon. A series of round Japanese lanterns above them gave off a golden light.

"It was perfect," Margaret murmured, glad they had opted for a small gathering in the Weatherstone gardens for the wedding. The civil ceremony had been quicker than one would have been in a church, but it allowed for the vows to be exchanged outdoors, in a garden. "I do hope your parents weren't disappointed we didn't do it in St. George's."

"Oh, not at all," Alexander said. "Besides, Helen will probably have her wedding there," he added with a grin.

"Has she already had an offer?" Margaret asked in surprise.

"Not that I know of, but then, I haven't really been paying attention these past few weeks," he admitted, still grinning.

"Why are you grinning so?"

"Because... I'm married, I suppose. Because I can hardly wait to make love to you. Because we're leaving for Bath tomorrow, and we won't be back for a fortnight," he murmured. "I'll have you all to myself."

Wearing the same pale pink gown she had worn for the wedding ceremony, Margaret looked as if she could have been one of the young ladies lined up before the potted palms in his aunt and uncle's ballroom. She was no wallflower, though. Her dance card had the names of a half-dozen gentlemen scrawled on it.

Alexander had been her first partner, though, leading her in a waltz. Only moments after the music for that had ended, his father had announced their marriage to the crowd. When the well-wishing had threatened to eclipse Helen's come-out, Alexander insisted he and Margaret take their leave by way of the French doors.

Now he was thinking of taking her back to Rosemount House.

With everyone else at the ball, they would have some privacy for at least a few hours.

"Would you think me horrid if I told you I'd like to take you home right now?"

Margaret's eyes rounded. "Would you think me fast if I told you I'd like that?" she countered.

Alexander's grin widened into a smile, his white teeth gleaming in the dim light. "You minx," he said happily.

"Is this why we didn't go in the same carriage as the rest of your family?" she asked, suddenly suspicious.

"Well, that, and there wouldn't have been room for your valise and trunk," he replied as he led them around the side of the house and out to the coach.

After Alexander had arrived at Ewen & Ewen and helped the driver load her luggage into the town coach, he had the driver take them back to Rosemount House. Footmen saw to it her trunk was taken to a guest bedchamber. His sister's lady's maid would see to her needs until they left for Bath.

"Shouldn't we tell someone we're leaving the ball?" Margaret asked as he helped her into the coach.

"My father knows," Alexander replied as he sat next to her. He cleared his throat. "He might have... suggested it, in fact."

"Oh, dear," Margaret replied, her face burning with embarrassment.

"Don't worry, my pearl. It's better that we not take the attention away from Helen and her come-out, and it's not as if we're the first to do this," he murmured. He leaned over and kissed her. "I will admit that I am nervous."

"*You're* nervous?" she countered in dismay.

"I've never done this before."

"Well, neither have I."

"You're the one who didn't want me to have any—"

"I'll be fine," she whispered, "*we'll* be fine." She kissed him, holding on tight as the coach rumbled the short distance to Rosemount House.

"Can we go straight to my bedchamber?" he asked. "I can help you with your buttons," he offered.

"Well, I was going to take down my hair—"

"I can do that."

"And brush it."

"I can do that, too."

"Take a bath."

"You did that this morning."

"Put on a new nightrail—"

"Oh, you're killing me," he groaned.

Margaret tittered. "Do you expect me to sleep in my chemise?"

"I was hoping you wouldn't be wearing anything at all," he

admitted. When he saw her look of shock, he added, "Well, except for the bed linens." Even in the dim light from the exterior lantern, Alexander could see her eyes rounding.

"Well, what will *you* be wearing?" she asked, her voice pitched low.

"Uh, bed linens?" he guessed. He chuckled before he sobered. "You're not frightened of me, I hope."

She glanced down. "Not of you, exactly, but I have felt *that*... against me. Although it didn't appear overly large when you were on your pedestal at the museum, it certainly seems as if it is now."

"That's because as a good Greek knows to do, I am in control of my urges," he replied. "Just not around you. When we're alone like this." He kissed her, hoping to take her mind off what they might be doing, hopefully in less than an hour or so, because he felt as if he was about to explode.

The coach slowed and came to a halt. "We're home," he said with relief.

"Already?" Despite her nervousness, Margaret tittered again. "Can you even walk?" she teased.

"I'll manage," he said, kissing her once more before he struggled to step out of the coach. He acknowledged the driver with a nod. "We're home for the night," he said as he turned to help Margaret down.

"Very good, sir. See you in the morning for the trip to Bath."

The front door opened before they reached it, the butler bowing as they entered.

"Is all in readiness?" Alexander asked in a low voice.

The butler nodded. "The champagne has been in a bucket of shaved ice since your departure."

Margaret inhaled softly. "Champagne?" she asked as Alexander led her to the stairs.

"So much for my secret," he said, tempted to take the stairs two at a time.

"I am thirsty," she murmured, her steps as quick as his as they made their way to the second floor. Alexander had his top coat off his shoulders before they made it to his bedchamber door.

"I can see you're not a bit anxious," Margaret teased.

"That's because my wiggly bits are by no means wiggly," he said with a grin as they burst through the door.

Margaret inhaled sharply, the sound of the closing door nearly drowning out her murmur of appreciation for the bedchamber. "What a beautiful room you have," she whispered.

"I'm so glad you like it since... well, it's *our* bedchamber," he said as he moved to pour them champagne. He handed her a glass and then touched the rim of his to hers. About to say something, he suddenly sobered. "I can't exactly toast *us*," he murmured. "It wouldn't be proper."

Margaret allowed a grin. "To wiggly bits," she said as she once again touched her glass to his.

"And not just any wiggly bits," Alexander agreed. "Although, I have to warn you, they haven't been wiggly for a while." He drained his glass before moving to stand behind Margaret. While she sipped her champagne, he undid the row of jet buttons down her back.

"Will you allow me to keep my arm covered?" she asked, turning her head so her chin rested on a shoulder.

Alexander kissed the back of her neck. "How am I supposed to kiss it if it's covered? You must know I intend to kiss every inch of you tonight."

Shivering beneath his touch, Margaret swallowed. "You do?" With all the buttons undone, the front of her gown fell forward, exposing her stays and petticoat.

"We can sleep in the coach tomorrow, so we have all night

tonight," he reasoned. He speared the fingers of one hand into her coiffure and then plucked out all the pins he could easily find.

Margaret was about to scold him, but the sensation of his fingernails against her scalp had her inhaling sharply. "Well, then I suppose I'll let you," she whispered. "Do you think we can turn off the lights?"

Alexander paused in the pin removal. "All of them?" he asked, disappointment sounding in his voice. He plucked a few more pins from her hair, delighting in how a series of dark locks tumbled down well past her shoulders. "I didn't know your hair was so long," he breathed. His fingers smoothed over the black silk, one of them hooking the strands near the front of her face to push them past a shoulder. He lowered his lips to her exposed neck.

"Won't the light from the fire be enough?" she asked, ignoring his comment about her hair. At least she felt as if she'd have some coverage. She hissed when his lips nibbled the top of her shoulder and then suddenly gave up their hold on her.

Moving to the gas control on the wall, Alexander turned it until the flames disappeared from the overhead chandelier. The room was left in a golden glow from the fireplace. "Ah, that's better," he murmured. "Now you'll be a color I can see correctly."

Margaret inhaled softly. She hadn't even considered that he might not see the color of her skin properly. "And you'll look like a golden god," she teased, her nervousness increasing.

Alexander refilled her champagne glass. "I'm afraid I cannot allow you to do the worshipping tonight, my love."

"Why ever not?" she asked, not sure she knew what she was expected to do. Worshipping him from the base of a pedestal was so much easier when she merely had to gaze at him. Besides, the color plates in the book she had read might have been well done, but they lacked a good deal of detail.

His lips hovered close to hers as he undid the buttons of his waistcoat. "I'm afraid if you merely touch me, I'll... well, I'll..."

"*Cum?*" she guessed, her eyes rounding with excitement.

"Yes," he breathed. "How do you know that word?"

"It was in the book."

"Oh." He glanced at the bed and then at her as he attempted to undo the knot at his neck. His gaze fell on her stays. The edge of her chemise peeked out from behind them, barely hiding the swells of her breasts. His fingers stopped working as he stared.

"Allow me," Margaret said as she pushed aside his hand and pulled apart the ends of the silk fabric. She unwound it from around his neck as he absently struggled with the fastening of his pantaloons, all the while staring at the tops of her breasts.

Thinking she would be embarrassed at being seen uncovered, Margaret found she rather liked how he stared at her. How his gaze seemed to caress her as effectively as if his fingers were touching her.

She pushed down the sleeves of her gown and shimmied out of the pink satin, rather enjoying the way Alexander's throat seemed to have trouble swallowing.

"Could you undo the tie?" she asked. When he continued to stare, she lifted one of his hands to the bow that held her stays and petticoat, a single garment, closed. "Just tug on it," she murmured, heartened when he seemed to finally come alive.

All at once, the tie was undone, the laces loosened, and his hand slipped beneath one of the white silk cups, gently pushing it aside as she pulled the corresponding strap of the stays off her shoulder.

She was about to pull down the strap from the other side, but Alexander understood what to do. Understood how to rid her of the undergarment. Even before the white silk fell to join the satin puddle at her feet, Alexander had his lips on hers, had his hands sliding down her arms and around to the globes of her bottom.

The fine muslin that separated his flesh from hers seemed to chafe Margaret, as did his linen shirt, which she struggled to pull from his pantaloons.

Their lips were forced to part as the shirt was removed from his body, but they once again joined as her body pressed against his. Another moment of tasting one another, and Alexander lifted her into his arms.

She let out a squeak before he placed her on the bed, well aware his gaze had returned to what he could see behind the translucent fabric of her chemise. Despite the darkened room, she knew he could see how her nipples had puckered with her excitement, how they left their silhouette in the chemise. Knew he could see the dark triangle at the top of her thighs. Could he also see how something in between her thighs was throbbing with need?

He could also see her withered arm, but his attention wasn't on it. Perhaps her breasts would keep him occupied. Keep his attention away from her arm.

About to hide her withered arm beneath a pillow, Margaret froze when he said, "I'm going to start with that arm, you must know."

Scoffing, she said, "Not my breasts?"

Alexander sat on the edge of the bed and removed his stockings. "I'll get to them next," he said with a grin he hoped might have her relaxing.

"You needn't make it sound like a threat," she replied.

Kicking off his shoes, he quickly doffed the pantaloons, wincing when he caught her rounded eyes.

"Oh, my," she breathed.

"Don't worry. My father told me what to do."

Margaret scoffed, sure he could see her blush even if he couldn't see the color red.

"You needn't blush," he whispered, "but I do love how the color of your skin changes in this light. All warm and golden and bright." He climbed onto the end of the bed.

"What are you doing all the way down there?" she asked, her breathing far too fast. "My arm is up here."

But Alexander's attention was on something else.

Reflexively, Margaret pulled her knees together. She inhaled sharply when his hands smoothed up her thighs, the chemise bunching up around her hips as his thumbs brushed the inside tender flesh of her thighs.

Without thought to what might happen next, Margaret relaxed her legs. Allowed him to lift her knees and then part them with gentle nudges. Her chest arched when she felt his fingers parting the dark curls. Wet and throbbing with need, she whimpered and spread her knees wider.

She knew he was touching her *there*. Swirling a finger around the very spot that had her wishing he would simply impale her with the not-so-wiggly bit—or bat, rather—she had seen bobbing about before he had made his way to the end of the bed.

Certainly his manhood would provide a modicum of relief from the need she felt growing deep inside.

When he replaced his questing fingertip with his tongue, Margaret cried out.

She didn't even realize it was his tongue that had her insides turning to molten lava, setting off an eruption of pure pleasure until he murmured a sound of appreciation. "To think, I might not have known about this until after we'd made love a few times," he whispered as he moved up her body, occasionally kissing her skin as he did so.

"It was in the book," she managed between gasps for air. When he was nearly over her, she lifted her knees to the side of his thighs, heartened when his bat—she could no longer think of it as a bit—slid along her damp folds.

He glanced back at how she had trapped him and arched a brow. "I suppose that was in the book, too?"

Her gaze darted to the side. "Mayhap," she said with a nervous grin.

"Will you help me into you?" he begged. "Please?"

She smoothed her right hand down the side of his chest and to where their two bodies were about to meet and meld. When her fingers touched him, when they felt the velvet softness coupled with his hardness, she inhaled softly. Guiding him to her opening, she held her breath.

Alexander's head dropped so his mouth could cover one breast. When she gasped, her chest rising from the bed, he pushed into her, but only an inch or so. "Does it hurt?" he whispered, his own breath held.

She shook her head. "No," she whispered, sounding surprised. "But I don't think..." She gasped again when he pulled out and pushed into her again, this time further.

"Breathe, my pearl," he whispered. He closed his eyes in an effort not to see her engorged nipples. In an effort to suppress the excitement of the moment.

How he managed to maintain control, he knew not. But he was determined to be all the way inside of her warm, wet haven before he allowed his release. Determined that she feel more pleasure than the little he had already managed to impart with his tongue.

When he pushed into her again, he did so slowly, reveling in how her body seemed to finally welcome him, opening to his entire length. Reveled in how her muscles clamped onto him, making it nearly impossible for him to pull out of her again.

"Are you all right?" he asked, his lips coming down onto one of her chemise-covered breasts. His tongue pressed onto an engorged nipple as he suckled.

"I am," she whispered before she inhaled sharply.

"I want *you* to... to *cum* before I take my pleasure," he murmured.

Her eyes rounded. "How...?" Her chest once again rose from the bed when he moved a hand to where their two bodies met. His thumb made contact with her womanhood, caressing the throbbing nubbin so it set off her ecstasy.

Once he knew she was lost to pleasure—he knew, because his manhood was suddenly gripped from all around—Alexander thrust into her again and again. His own ecstasy came fast and hard, causing him to throw back his head as his body arched and seized above hers.

He couldn't breathe. He couldn't see. And the spasms of pleasure that coursed through his body were entirely unexpected. They were far more intense than he had imagined. Far more satisfying than when he had taken himself in hand on the nights he desired a release. Far more pleasurable than anything he had ever experienced in his life.

Well, this certainly explained why some of his friends employed mistresses. Why others paid prostitutes. But even as his reasoning abilities quickly waned, he knew he would never have had such a satisfying experience with a Cyprian.

It would have felt empty. Hollow. Pleasurable, perhaps, but not nearly as much given the one he was making love to held him in the same regard.

At some point, Alexander had no strength. No means of holding himself up. So he slowly collapsed atop Margaret. Before he lost consciousness, he murmured, "I love you," and kissed her.

· · ·

argaret watched in wonder as Alexander's ecstasy had him poised above her, a god caught in the throes of a powerful force.

A force she had apparently wielded rather well.

When he kissed her, it was all consuming despite how quickly it ended, for his head settled onto her shoulder and his body seemed to collapse in a heap atop her.

"I love you," he had whispered. Although he had said the words before—several times over the course of the past fortnight—he had done so just then as if his very life depended on him saying them.

She lifted a hand to the back of his head, her fingers spearing the silken black hair. He might have stirred, but only for a moment. After a few minutes, his breathing finally slowed.

Sure he was asleep, Margaret carefully lowered her legs, and she relaxed beneath him. Her other hand smoothed down the side of his body, up his arm, her fingertips caressing him until she felt his body quiver.

She grinned as she felt his entire body quake. How easy this was, to bring pleasure to him. How quickly he had done the same to her.

Thinking of how his parents behaved with one another, she understood their eagerness to be alone. Understood why they seemed so happy with one another.

Deep in thought, her breathing having returned to normal, Margaret sighed and then gave a start when she felt one of his fingers caress the length of her withered arm. "That tickles," she whispered.

"So it feels?" Alexander asked.

"Oh, yes. For as long as I can remember," she murmured. Her eyes rounded when she was sure his eyes darkened. "What are you—?"

"I was distracted earlier," he said as a hand guided her arm to rest on his right arm. His lips settled onto the tender flesh on the inside of her wrist and slowly worked their way down to the inside of her elbow.

Inhaling sharply, she closed her eyes and whimpered softly.

Somewhere down below, where their two bodies were still joined, Margaret felt him harden. Before she could ask what was happening, his lips came down onto the inside of her wrist, nibbling on the skin over her pulse.

"Oh," she breathed.

He gently took her hand in his and moved it so it rested in the pillow above her head. Margaret understood why when his hand then pushed the hem of her chemise up and over her breasts, exposing them to his questing tongue and lips.

Without even thinking—how could she, after all?—Margaret lifted her thighs to trap his. She reveled in the groan that erupted from his throat. Reveled in how he moved inside her, slow at first and then faster and deeper. His mouth gave up its hold on her breast when he was forced to breathe harder.

"I shall never tire of this," he whispered, one of his hands moving to smooth over one of the globes of her bottom. Her soft gasp and the way her chest rose to meet his had him cursing softly. He would not last long, but he wanted—nay, needed—to see to her pleasure before he took his own.

Moving his thumb over her womanhood, he delighted in how her eyes rounded, in how her chest rose, in how her entire body seemed to glow in the golden light.

He knew the moment her pleasure crested and broke, for his own followed suit only a few seconds later. The groan that erupted from his throat sounded as if it had come from the other side of the room, given how his pulse pounded in his ears.

Holding his body as still as he could manage above Margaret's, Alexander stared down at her. He took one long breath at seeing her look of delight. Her look of adoration. Her look of appreciation. He made sure his own expression held all those thoughts and more before he slowly lowered himself onto her soft body.

"Good night, my love," Margaret whispered.

"An understatement for the ages, my sweet pearl," Alexander murmured before sleep took him.

EPILOGUE

A year later, Rosemount House parlor

"I'm so glad you two could join us for dinner tonight," Stella said as she stood with Margaret on the threshold of the Rosemount House parlor.

"I am as well. Alexander has hardly allowed me or the babe out of his sight since little Harold was born," Margaret murmured as she fingered the sapphire necklace her husband had given her when Harold Tennison II was born. It was a perfect match to the sapphire ring he had bestowed on one of her fingers the day they had married. "Father is happy to oversee the shop when we come over here." Ever since the queen let it be known she had purchased a ring from the shop, Ewen & Ewen had enjoyed a resurgence in shoppers.

Although Margaret and Alexander lived close to Rosemount House—they had moved into a townhouse the Everly earldom owned in South Audley Street—they came for dinner only a few times a month. "I took Harry into the shop yesterday so Father could see him," Margaret said. "Alexander has been crafting the most beautiful parure for Lady Framingham. One that matches her coronet."

"Oh?" Stella's eyes widened with interest. "Pray tell, who ordered it for her?"

"Well Lord Framingham, of course," Margaret replied. "He's been ever so... *generous* of late." Her attention went to the Duke of Westhaven, who had fallen asleep in a wing-back chair near the fireplace. Recognizing the emerald ring he wore on his pinky finger as the one that had been recovered from the jewel thief, Margaret had come to realize that it was the duke who had at one time been Caroline Framingham's lover. Given the marquess' attentions towards his wife for the past year, though, it was apparent the *affaire* had ended—probably well before the theft had occurred.

"No wonder Caroline has been so happy," Stella said in wonder. "And here I thought it was only because the marquess had begun taking baths." She didn't add that she and Harold had been enjoying the especially large bathtub he'd had installed in his bathing chamber. She found playing mermaid again after so many years rather enjoyable.

Margaret's gaze next settled on her father-in-law.

Harold Tennison, Earl of Everly, with one booted foot resting on the opposite knee, was sound asleep and snoring softly. He was also holding his three-month-old grandson against his shoulder with only one hand as a glass of port managed to stay upright in his other.

Meanwhile, Stella's attention was on her oldest son, who at the moment was passed out in one of the upholstered chairs next to the fireplace, oblivious to what his seven-month old brother was doing to his cravat as he bounced on his lap.

"How long before the port spills, do you suppose?" Margaret whispered.

"Oh, it won't," Stella assured her. She moved into the parlor and extracted the glass from her husband's tenuous hold before drinking the remaining contents. Just as deftly, she put the glass back into his hand.

Margaret tittered. "Was he this involved when Alexander and Helen were born?" she asked. She had always thought aristocrats left their children with nurses and tutors, never so much as seeing them again until the boys were breeched.

"Oh, yes," Stella whispered. "I was so tired those first few weeks after the Greek god over there was born," she said as she motioned toward Alexander. At that moment, he looked nothing like a god, with his chin on his chest, his dark hair disheveled, and his white cravat no longer perfectly pleated. "I was happy he had a nurse. Everly insisted on spending at least an hour in the nursery every night and in the mornings, too. Claimed his own parents had done that with him and with Evangeline when they were young," she explained, a wistful expression crossing her face.

"It sounds as if you weren't afforded the same?" Margaret asked carefully.

"Oh, well not exactly. After my poor mother gave birth to me, and before I was even two weeks old, we were off on a ship bound for Mykonos for my father's next archaeological dig," Stella explained. "I slept in an ancient creche my father had discovered somewhere on the island of Naxos."

Margaret's mouth dropped open. "But, your father is a *duke*," she whispered, her gaze going back to the older gentleman who was still snoring softly. Surely the man was wealthy!

"He is, but he never let that stop him from playing in the dirt," Stella explained. "I was right beside him, though, my little shovel in hand, unearthing pottery shards and mosaics. Dipping my head beneath the water in search of shells and such." She rolled her eyes. "That's how I found *him*," she added as she indicated Harold. "Let's just say I appreciate being married to a civilized man, even if he does still play in the dirt now and then."

"I heard that," Harold murmured, his eyes still closed.

Margaret tittered again, which had her brother-in-law giggling—loudly. Alexander woke up so suddenly, the babe nearly lost his balance. His grip on his brother's cravat ensured he stayed upright while the neckcloth nearly strangled Alexander.

"My leg has gone to sleep," Alexander complained, struggling to put the cravat to rights with one hand while he supported his brother with the other. "By the way, what have you been feeding Bradley? He's far too heavy to be a babe."

Stella audibly sighed, crossed the room, and easily lifted Bradley from his lap. Happy to be in his mother's arms, the babe settled his head onto her shoulder and gurgled noisily.

"Was it hard to remember what to do? How to do everything after so many years?" Margaret asked as she took her own son from Harold's hold, her withered arm supporting one side as her longer arm lifted the babe to her shoulder. Despite the move, the boy continued to sleep.

"Not hard at all," Stella assured her. "Besides, we know more now, and Helen is always willing to help. She can hardly wait to have one of her own."

"Has she accepted an offer of marriage?" Margaret asked in surprise. Helen's second season had only just begun the month prior.

"Oh, no. She's only had two suitors so far. But if she was allowed to have a baby before she was married, she would do so," Stella murmured, one brow arching in worry.

"Not going to happen," Harold mumbled from where he still dozed on the settee.

As if the mention of her name had conjured her into existence, Helen appeared on the threshold. Dressed in a jonquil gown, she appeared as fresh as the day of her come-out. "Oh, can I please hold Harry? At least until you have to go?" she asked as she hurried up to Margaret.

"Of course," Margaret replied as she relinquished her son to his aunt. "I'm surprised at how long he's slept. He'll be hungry soon."

Having stood up in order to shake out his leg, Alexander moved to stand next to Margaret. "That's probably my fault," he said before kissing the side of her head.

"What makes you say that?"

"I may have kept him awake when he was supposed to be napping this afternoon."

"Oh?"

"We were having a long conversation about chartism in the nursery."

"Rather one-sided, wasn't it?" Margaret teased.

"Perhaps, but he's a very good listener."

"You were once like that," Stella said, an eyebrow arching as she regarded her oldest son. "Your father would tell you stories about plants and birds, and you would lay in his arms just staring at him."

"Lot of good it did," Harold murmured. "He chose metallurgy over botany, but I suppose it is a more lucrative avocation." The most recent sales numbers from the shop, recorded in the ledger Margaret had brought with her that evening, showed that Ewen & Ewen was once again profitable.

Stella ignored her husband as she continued to gaze at Alexander. "You looked just like your son does now, too, what with that shock of black hair and handsome good looks."

Alexander chuckled. "Well, good, because someone has to replace me on that pedestal at the British Museum. I am only available to be worshipped by this beautiful goddess," he said as he wrapped an arm around Margaret's waist and pulled her closer. He grinned. "You're blushing," he accused.

"How would you know? You can't see red," Margaret countered playfully.

He glanced over to where Helen stood holding little Harold. "As for the pedestal, it may as well go to these boys," he suggested with a grin.

Harold straightened on the settee and stared at his son. "Pedestal?" he repeated. "What pedestal?"

Margaret hid a grin behind a hand, thoughts of Bradley and Harold in their twenties and on display in the Greek and Roman Hall at the museum.

The young women of London who would worship them probably hadn't even been born yet.

"The pedestal you gave up when I married you," Stella said, lowering herself onto the settee next to her husband. A quick glance at her youngest son showed he was sound asleep on her shoulder.

"Oh, *that* pedestal," he replied, his smirk of satisfaction forcing his dimple to appear.

"The one at the museum, yes," Stella affirmed with an impish grin.

"Yes, well, I thought the trade for the alternative option was more than fair. It's certainly more comfortable. More enjoyable. And I'm still worshipped as much as I was before."

"Trade for the alternative option?" Stella repeated. "Whatever are you talking about?"

Harold bent close and whispered, "The bed, my sweeting. Our bed."

Stella's eyes rounded. "Oh, of course." It was her turn to blush before she suddenly scoffed. "Worship you?" she said in a hoarse whisper. "Is that what you think I've been doing?"

Harold gave a one-shouldered shrug. "Well even if I'm not Greek, I do feel like a god—as if I'm immortal—when I'm with you."

Stella gave him another impish grin as her fingers speared his wavy dark hair. "My very own Adonis."

Grinning broadly, Harold chuckled. "My very own Aphrodite. Which reminds me that I haven't yet worshipped you today." He stood and turned to offer her a hand after he lifted Bradley from her hold.

"I wasn't going let you forget," she replied in a whisper, accepting his help to stand. The two took their leave of the parlor, oblivious to their older children paying witness to their departure.

Alexander watched them go, an eyebrow arching before he chuckled. He turned to his sister. "So, I take it the situation hasn't exactly returned to normal?" he asked. He had thought his parents would have returned to their old sleeping arrangements once Bradley was born.

Helen's eyes widened. "Not in the very least," she complained. "Their behavior at breakfast is entirely improper, and Mother practically sits on Father's lap during dinner."

Alexander exchanged a quick glance with his wife. "Oh?" Margaret dipped her head, her blush apparent under the gas lights.

Scoffing, Helen said, "Surely you noticed?"

Leaning in Helen's direction, Alexander said, "I'm not *completely* blind, Sister." Now that he had his very own gemologist—his very own jewel—to see colors for him, he had long ago accepted his lot in life. "But I will turn a blind eye to anyone who publicly shows their affection for one another. Our parents especially."

From somewhere outside the parlor, they heard their father call out, "I heard that." After a pause, he added. "Much appreciated."

Helen sighed but finally displayed an impish grin.

AUTHOR NOTES

*Harold and Stella's story can be found in **The Epiphany of an Explorer**, available for sale at all major retailers. Although Evangeline is only mentioned in passing, her story is part of **The Tale of Two Barons**, also available at all major retailers.*

Gold Standards

Prior to 1854, the two gold standards allowed for hall-marking by the crown were 18 karat and 22 karat. Hallmarks were the small impressions struck in jewelry by official, government-controlled assay offices which guaranteed the fineness of the material. If the impression was struck by the jewelry maker, it was called a maker's mark.

The main metals used to make jewelry were high karat gold, tri-color gold (made up of a combination of yellow, white and either green or rose gold), and silver.

Cameos

Since Queen Victoria loved cameos, they enjoyed a resurgence in popularity during her reign. Originally carved from large sea shells (the pink background is the inside of the shell and the white is from the wall of the shell), high-relief cameos were possible when carved from onyx, amethyst and other gems.

Jet

Jet, most commonly used to make buttons, could be found on the Yorkshire coast at Whitby. Due to its elasticity, it was stronger than jet from other parts of the world and could hold a polish and be more finely carved.

Ferronieres

Although Lady Framingham was upset about the lack of real jewels in her coronet (most coronets did have a matching version with the real jewels for wear at court), most women were wearing ferronieres during the early Victorian era. A tribute to the Middle Ages, they were simple chains or cords worn around the head from which a simple gem was suspended on the forehead. They could be worn with or without hats, day and night.

Jewels and Clothing Colors

To accommodate the interesting colors of Regency and Victorian fashions, a number of gemstones were used by goldsmiths in the creation of their jewelry.

Stella's red watered silk gown was a saturated red with hints of pink and orange. Her matching jewelry could have been made of red coral, but Alexander insisted on gemstones, so rubies and garnets were chosen.

Like the blooms for which they are named, jonquil, primrose and evening primrose were all varying shades of yellow. These colors added warm and optimistic hues to the gown palette, and they were frequently paired with amber and citrine or sapphires or emeralds for contrast.

Named for the Greek goddess of fruiting orchards, Pomona, a dark shade of apple green, paired well with emeralds. Paris green was the first colorfast green available, so it was quite popular and worn with chrysoprase and jade. Unfortunately, and much like the verde paints popular for

Victorian parlor walls, it was produced by mixing copper arsenic powders and other toxic chemicals. Your gown—and your parlor—could literally make you sick!

Puce, the French word for flea, was similar to the brownish purple-red of old blood that could be found in the pests. Despite its name, puce was one of the top fashion colors and was worn with jewelry that included garnet, pearls, and rubies.

The everyday wardrobe colors of the time—white, Spanish brown, dove grey, powder blue, pale lilac, peach blossom and wild rose—were incorporated in great abundance. Both freshwater and saltwater pearls, amethysts, sapphires, emeralds, black onyx, jet, aquamarines, "Persian blue" turquoise, peridot, topaz, rubies and citrine were the gems of choice for the everyday wardrobe.

ABOUT THE AUTHOR

A self-described nerd and student of history, Linda Rae spent many years as a published technical writer specializing in 3D graphics workstations, software and 3D animation (her movie credits include SHREK and SHREK 2). Getting lost in the rabbit holes of research has resulted in historical romances set in the Regency-era as well as Ancient Greece.

A fan of action-adventure movies, she can frequently be found at the local cinema. Although she no longer has any tropical fish, she follows the San Jose Sharks and makes her home in Cody, Wyoming.

For more information:
www.lindaraesande.com
Sign up for Linda Rae's newsletter:
Regency Romance with a Twist
Follow Linda Rae's blog:
Regency Romance with a Twist